Lights, Camera, Bones

ALSO BY CAROLYN HAINES

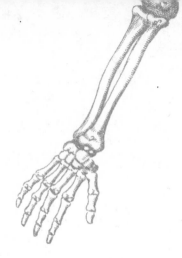

Lights, Camera, Bones

A Sarah Booth Delaney Mystery

CAROLYN HAINES

MINOTAUR BOOKS
NEW YORK

First published in the United States by Minotaur Books, an imprint of St. Martin's Publishing Group

LIGHTS, CAMERA, BONES. Copyright © 2024 by Carolyn Haines. All rights reserved. Printed in the United States of America. For information, address St. Martin's Publishing Group, 120 Broadway, New York, NY 10271.

www.minotaurbooks.com

Library of Congress Cataloging-in-Publication Data

Names: Haines, Carolyn, author.
Title: Lights, camera, bones / Carolyn Haines.
Description: First edition. | New York: Minotaur Books, 2024. | Series: A Sarah Booth Delaney mystery; 27
Identifiers: LCCN 2023058481 | ISBN 9781250885944 (hardcover) | ISBN 9781250885951 (e-book)
Subjects: LCGFT: Detective and mystery fiction. | Novels.
Classification: LCC PS3558.A329 L54 2024 | DDC 813/.54—dc23/eng/20240105
LC record available at https://lccn.loc.gov/2023058481

Our books may be purchased in bulk for promotional, educational, or business use. Please contact your local bookseller or the Macmillan Corporate and Premium Sales Department at 1-800-221-7945, extension 5442, or by email at MacmillanSpecialMarkets@macmillan.com.

First Edition: 2024

1 3 5 7 9 10 8 6 4 2

For Sue Walker—champion of writers

Lights, Camera, Bones

1

"Would you want to be an extra in the movie?" Tinkie Bellcase Richmond asks as we walk down Main Street in Greenville, Mississippi. We've come to the river town to scope out the new Trinity Studios production of *Hero at the Helm*, an action thriller about the 1927 Mississippi River flood.

For the first time in ages, Greenville is hopping with streets jammed and businesses going strong. The entire Mississippi Delta is abuzz with celebrity gossip and speculation. The nine-figure Hollywood production is filming right in our backyard, and Tinkie and I have been seduced by the possibility of movie magic. Our friends Millie Roberts and Cece Dee Falcon have been reporting on the movie for the past two months, and at long last the film crew is in town. Lights, camera, action! It's happening.

"I wouldn't mind being an extra in an action film." My true love is the stage, but I put that dream aside long ago. Still, a few scenes in a movie about the history of my state would be fun. Especially if I get to pretend to drown or something dramatic.

"I want to be a tavern wench," Tinkie says.

I burst into laughter. Tinkie is the Queen Bee of Delta society. She knows every rule in the Daddy's Girl handbook of conduct and etiquette. "A tavern wench?"

"I like those little corsets the wenches wore."

"The flood was in 1927, not 1827," I remind her.

"I could still be a hot tavern girl. It's Hollywood."

I can't argue that point. Films are great fictions created to entertain. "Okay. Then I want to be a female pirate."

"You could train that black raven that's taken up with you to ride on your shoulder. Like a pirate's parrot," Tinkie says. "Have you taught Poe to curse yet?"

"I am not going to teach that raven to curse. You act like I'm a bad influence."

Tinkie just laughs. "You *are* a bad influence, and you know you curse like a sailor, which is excellent since you want to be a river pirate."

I do curse. Sometimes. Very creatively. I change the subject. "Look at all the people in town." Greenville had been slowly dying. River traffic was down, and cotton was no longer king. The movie is helping the town reinvent itself. "It's good to see Greenville bustling."

"Look at the crowd sitting outside the bookstore," Tinkie points out. "Is that Marlon Brandon, the star?"

"Looks like it." The actor was even more handsome in

the flesh than on the screen. "He is . . . good-looking." His dark good looks came packaged in a manicured body. He exuded sex appeal.

"Yes, he is." Tinkie grabs my hand. "Let's go over and meet him."

I hold back. "People are all over him." That is true. Women, men, and children are three deep around the little table where he sits drinking a coffee and trying to read a newspaper. The actor handles it all with grace. He poses for selfies and lets giggling young girls kiss his cheek for their social media posts.

"It's a swarm." Tinkie is about to drag me by the hand. "Two more lookie-loos won't suffocate him. You realize he legally changed his name to Marlon when he went out to Hollywood? He liked being one letter removed from the famous Brando."

I roll my eyes at Tinkie. "You should change your name to Nosy Parker. Let's give him some space. I'd like to see some of the filming before we're banned from the set and told never to come back."

"I hear they're going to shoot some of the rescue scenes when that big storm is scheduled to come through."

I'd read the same information in Cece's and Millie's popular column *The Truth Is Out There*.

"When that front gets here, the possibility of tornadoes is seventy percent." Like any good farm girl, I am keenly attuned to the weather. The April skies so far have been remarkably calm. April is one of those months of incredible sun when the crops seem to jump out of the brown soil and grow an inch a day. Or it can be Dorothy: tornadoes and flying monkeys.

In April of 1927, the weather had turned treacherous

and deadly. The 1927 flood killed more than a thousand people and was still one of the worst natural disasters in the history of the United States. In the lead-up to the levee breach, the rain had been relentless for weeks. The Delta is a triangle of rich alluvial soil bordered on the west by the Mississippi River and the Loess Hills on the east. It stretches from south of Memphis down to Vicksburg, the perfect floodplain, totally flat, productive alluvial soil. On the day the levee north of the city broke, the Mississippi River poured into the flat Delta and rushed down to Greenville, mostly submerging the town and drowning hundreds.

The creation of Lake Ferguson, an oxbow lake, somewhat protects the city now, but in 1927, nearly 50,000 homes in the Delta region were flooded and more than 20,000 buildings were destroyed. Another 62,000 were damaged. Nearly 300,000 chickens, hogs, cattle, and work animals drowned. Human deaths from the flooding numbered more than a thousand in the Delta alone.

Tinkie swept a hand in front of her, echoing, as her words often did, my own thoughts. "I don't think I'm tough enough to have survived that flood," she said. "People clung to tree-tops for days, waiting for rescue. When the levee broke and the river flooded inland, there wasn't a chance to escape. Zinnia was lucky, upstate from the levee breach. Do you think the movie will be able to depict that?"

"CGI is an awesome thing," I told her. "They can recreate some of the worst weather with computers. I'll be curious to see how they do it. I know the movie company brought in a riverboat."

"How will they show the town being flooded? You know the floodwaters were waist high in the downtown section for weeks?"

I wasn't a film expert, but Tinkie obviously believed my unsuccessful career on Broadway had given me insight into how movies are made. I was perfectly happy to pander to that view. "Did you see they're building a rooftop set at the north end of Broadway? Maybe they'll actually flood it. That would be exciting."

"What's this movie really about?" Tinkie asked. "I know it's supposed to be an action film about the great Brandon family stepping up to help save hundreds of people stranded on the levee. But there's also some gossip that it's more than that. What have you heard?"

Millie and Cece were my primary sources of celebrity gossip. Tinkie had the same resources. "I've heard vague mentions that Marlon Brandon is going to whitewash his family. Folks have opinions but no evidence. Gossip is delicious but it's an empty feast."

"Is that another of Aunt Loulane's sayings?"

"No. It's mine. I made it up."

"No wonder." She rolled her eyes and grinned. "The Brandon family made out okay after the flood," Tinkie said. She knew local history—especially financial history—as well as social etiquette.

"Are you implying they were river pirates?" I couldn't help but tease her. The Brandon family had been a force in the Delta for well over a century. They owned a large and beautiful estate inland and farmed close to six thousand acres. In 1927, they had also owned a downtown hardware store in Greenville, until the flood destroyed it. But the real Brandon fortune seemed to come from politics. Marlon was a big-time Hollywood actor but his grandfather, Brandon Brandon—a man so proud of his name he used it twice—had served six terms as a U.S. senator. In Mississippi, one of the poorest states in the union, politics was the golden ticket to wealth. No one left the Senate poorer than when they went in, and Senator Brandon had not only feathered his own nest, he'd brought home the federal bacon for the entire state. He was beloved by his constituents, and even I could see his charm.

"The Brandons aren't river pirates, but let's just say they may have cracked a few federal piggy banks." She sighed. "Senator Brandon was very good for the state."

"Not arguing. But did the Brandon family truly play a role in saving people from the floods?"

"I think so. They owned a riverboat and I've heard that the local boat owners confronted the dangerous storm to rescue people who were stranded by the rising floodwater."

"No wonder Marlon wants to make the film."

"Exactly," Tinkie said. "Look!" She pointed. "Marlon is heading up on the levee. Let's scoot over there and get a photo before he goes back to work. And we should take some photos for Cece. The newspaper will love them."

She was right about that. "Let's hit it." I was following Tinkie when I caught a flash of something green and shimmery slithering through the river. I had a really bad feeling. "Go ahead and catch him," I told Tinkie. "I'll be right behind you."

"What's up?" she asked.

"Nature calls," I told her. She'd sympathize with that because when she'd been pregnant with Maylin, she'd had to go every ten minutes. "Catch him before he gets away and get a selfie. I can't hold it any longer."

She gave me the side-eye as she trotted after the star. I scurried toward the river. I had bad suspicions. The flash of green came again, and I saw a beautifully glistening body slicing through the water like a fish. A fish with mocha skin, black hair, dark eyes, and green scales over the lower half of her body. Her boobs were covered with decorated coconut shells. She looked like an exotic tropical phantom.

I looked around but no one else saw her.

"Jitty!" I called out to her. "What are you doing here acting like a mermaid?"

She flipped onto her back and fluttered her mermaid tail just enough to keep her head above water. "I'm following the lure of the sea," she said. "All this hubbub goin' on about the 1927 flood. Handsome actors all over the place. Film crews skinny-dippin' in the river at night. I wanted to get in on some of all this."

The disguise of a mermaid would be the perfect solution. If she wasn't a ghost. "No one can see you but me."

"That's what you think."

She had me there. The rules of the Great Beyond were complicated. And without consistency. If she appeared as a mythical creature, would she then be visible to others? Jitty would never tell me the truth, and I had to follow up on one point. "People are skinny-dipping in the river?"

"Oh, Sarah Booth, if you weren't snoring into that sheriff's armpit, you would be down here on the river at night with the rest of them. Marlon and his crew know how to have fun." She slapped the water with her tail for emphasis. "My heavens, those people take good care of their bodies. They don't eat all that sweet potato fluff, swill wine, gobble carbohydrates, and bloat up. You could learn some things."

"Watch it, Jitty. You're always saying you need to eat to keep up your strength. Maybe humans need their calories, too."

She was being especially prickly today. "Who is skinny-dipping? Cece would love to have that scoop."

"And you'd like to have a photo of that, no doubt. Forget it. Tonight, I'm going to scare them out of the water. This river is no place to frolic. Folks who don't respect the river tend to drown. That current can grab a person and pull them down to the bottom. They might not float up again for three days, or the body might wash out to the Gulf of Mexico and get eaten by sharks."

"Lovely." Jitty could sometimes be even more gruesome than I could. "Why don't you just go home?" I asked. "Leave the film crew to its own devices. And while you're at it, leave me and the armpit alone, too."

"Wouldn't you like to see that Marlon Brandon step out of his skivvies and dive in the river?"

I held up a hand. "Stop it. I can't have the picture in my brain. Coleman's feelings would be hurt." Coleman Peters was sheriff of Sunflower County and the man who'd stolen my heart.

"Coleman don't have any jurisdiction in Washington County. He's not the sheriff here." Jitty put her hands on her hips and dared me to disagree.

"True. And I'm going home to Sunflower County as soon as Tinkie gets her photos with the movie people. Baby Maylin will be waiting for her." I had a sudden clue as to what Tinkie was really up to. She was probably badgering the movie people to give Maylin a walk-on part. Oh, that would be so like her. "I have to go save the movie people from Tinkie."

"You go right on, Sarah Booth. But remember there are things in this river that folks don't see until it's too late. You stay out of the water. I'm not kiddin' you, either."

"Even if I wanted a swim, I wouldn't get in the river now. It's April. The water is still cold. I like to swim, but only on a hot, hot day and I happen to agree that the Mississippi River is no place for swimming."

"Your mama didn't raise no fool," Jitty said. She dove into the river, rose like a dolphin into the sun with a spray of foam, and disappeared into the dark depths. The last thing I saw were the fins of her tail.

2

I stopped atop the levee when I arrived near the set. Workers swarmed about, moving camera equipment, lights, and all the technical instruments of modern-day moviemaking. The person I assumed to be the cinematographer was with a camera crew, pointing out an angle to catch the sunlight dancing on the water.

The location the film crew selected was on the eastern side of Lake Ferguson, which was technically an oxbow lake with the southernmost end opening into the river. The lake protected the town and farmland behind the levee. Lake Ferguson was a beautiful location with sandbars and other recreational facilities, including a dock. An incredible riverboat from the early 1900s, in pristine condition and with fresh paint gleaming, was tied up at the dock. Beside it the rough outline of a raft was taking shape. Two men hammered on the raft. The riverboat I understood. The raft, not so much. Until I realized that in filming the 1927 flood, a raft might be a vessel that rescued folks stranded in the floodwater.

Just as I'd anticipated, Tinkie was sitting in a director's chair beside Marlon Brandon, and she had her phone out, apparently showing him photos. I'm sure they were of Maylin. Tinkie was going to be an awful backstage mother if someone didn't stop her.

I'd learned that some of the cast and crew were scattered around various bed-and-breakfasts or hotels, but travel trailers and tents had also been set up for dressing rooms and offices. In a way, the set reminded me of the hubbub of the local fair when it came to town. Lots of equipment and lots of people who craved an audience.

Another woman sat to Marlon's left. When no one was looking at her, she glared at Tinkie. Was this a paramour of Marlon's who felt Tinkie was competition? Or a crewmember impatient to get back to work? I decided to ask when the opportunity presented itself.

"Isn't Maylin adorable?" I said to the group as I walked up. "She's the smartest baby I've ever seen."

"I always figured that Sarah Booth didn't have a maternal bone in her body," Tinkie said, giving me an impish grin. "But then Maylin came along, and Sarah Booth is a servant to her smallest whim."

I couldn't deny it. I'd do anything for that baby. "Yep, she's special," I said. "Are you going to cast her in the film?"

"Yes," Marlon said. "Once the dangerous filming is over—the action scenes—we'll bring her on set and see how she does."

Marlon did seem to have a way of making everyone feel included and special. It was a gift. "That's terrific."

Marlon glanced over at Tinkie, taking in her sassy leggings and hooded pullover. The temperature was chilly near the river. "I might even find a part for Mrs. Rich—"

"Call me Tinkie," my partner interjected. "I'm just Tinkie. And that would be lovely, but Sarah Booth is the actress."

I wanted to hug her *and* knock her on the head. "Not anymore. Tinkie and I have a detective agency. Today, though, we're tourists like everyone else. Your film has added new life to Greenville. It's exciting."

"Are you investigating Jules?" Marlon asked.

"What?" Tinkie and I said together.

"The gaffer who disappeared last night. Are you searching for him?"

Tinkie shook her head. "No. We didn't know anything about it. What happened?"

Marlon sighed. "He was working on the raft last night. Most of us went to Doe's Eat Place—I gotta say that was the best steak I've ever eaten. And the tamales! Anyway, we went to have some drinks and eat, then I had some business to do. Jules stayed on the raft. He was preparing to set the mainsail."

"And?" I prompted.

"And when we got back, he was gone. His stuff was still in the hotel, but he'd vanished." Marlon pointed to three men moving lights around. "Jules was the best. I can't believe he left like he did. He seemed to love the job and he didn't even ask for his check. It was like the work was enough. It's hard to find people who love this job that much."

Marlon wasn't overly upset, but Tinkie and I exchanged

glances. This did not sound good. "Do you think he went back to Los Angeles? Have you checked?"

"He was from Memphis, and we did call his phone. Repeatedly. No one answers."

"Where could he have gone?" I asked.

"Ana McCants, our producer," he nodded at the beautiful but sour woman sitting next to him and listening intently to the conversation, "thinks he went back to Memphis. There was talk a girl showed up looking for him here."

"Talk?"

Marlon shrugged. "I don't babysit the crew. Jules is a grown man."

"You feel certain he just left?" I asked.

"Until you began to make it sound like a federal case, I did." Marlon's brow was furrowed. "Maybe I should call the local law enforcement and file a report."

"I'll do it," Ana said. "We should have done it first thing this morning. I don't believe Jules just disappeared. He isn't that kind of person, from what everyone says. He's been on time and working hard since we got here, too. He didn't seem like he'd flake out."

"You said this morning that you thought he left with that woman who came looking for him." Marlon sounded annoyed.

"I changed my mind." Ana seemed to relax as soon as she figured out we weren't competitors for Marlon's affections. Maybe she was just the jealous type. When she smiled, she was radiant.

"Did you see this woman?" I asked Ana.

"No, but some of the cinematographers said a pretty young woman was asking about Jules." She shrugged a shoulder. "It stood to reason they were involved, until you pointed out a few things. Now I'm worried."

I looked at Tinkie, trying to get a read on what she thought. Her expression was inscrutable.

"So you're private investigators," Ana said, not even bothering to pretend she hadn't been eavesdropping. "That must be interesting work."

"We're glad to be on vacation right now," Tinkie said. "We've worked solid for nearly two years. Every time we think we have a break, someone hires us. But today, we're officially unemployed." Tinkie made it clear we weren't there for business. Ana seemed to loosen up even more.

"Thanks for shaking me out of my lethargy. I'll call the sheriff right now and make that report on Jules. Good suggestion." She got to her feet and walked away.

For a long moment, silence stretched between the three of us.

"Ana and I were serious last year," Marlon said, though he owed us no explanation. "I hurt her. She's still a little prickly, but she's a good person and she fought so hard for my movie. She found the first investors. Were it not for her, *Hero at the Helm* would never be made."

"She's beautiful," Tinkie said, once again using her social skills to smooth us past a rough spot. "And now Sarah Booth and I should head back to our homes. I have my baby waiting, and Sarah Booth has a moonshine business to check on."

My jaw dropped open, but Marlon ignored me. He was tantalized by Tinkie's lie. "She's a bootlegger?"

"I am—"

"She is," Tinkie said, talking over my protest. "She'll tell you all about it when you have time to listen."

"Excellent. Maybe we could all have dinner soon."

"Absolutely. I'd love to host a party for the crew," Tinkie said. "Whenever you can take time. And I'd love to show your crew more of the Delta. With your family ties to Greenville, I'm sure you know all about the region but some of the crew might not."

3

By the time we got back to Zinnia, Tinkie had sent all our photos to Cece at the newspaper. We'd also dropped a dime with her on the missing gaffer. It was likely the young man had gone back to Memphis or was with his girl, but it never hurt to be sure. Cece would gnaw on the gossip like a dog with a soup bone.

I parked at the front door of Hilltop and raced Tinkie inside. She was short and took two steps to every one of my strides, but she managed to get to Maylin before I did. She held the baby up and spun around. Maylin giggled with joy. Even Pauline, the nanny, was smiling. Seeing Tinkie with her daughter always flooded my heart with joy. Tinkie and Maylin were surely the tonic for depression, rabies, or anthrax. I just didn't know how to bottle the cure to sell it.

"Maylin is going to get an audition for the movie," Tinkie told Pauline.

"Wonderful." Pauline was as big a supporter of Maylin as I was. "She's such a special baby, I'm sure it will come through on film. What would a baby wear in 1927?" she asked. "Maybe I can whip up a costume for her."

Maylin had a legion of people who would help her accomplish whatever goal in life she wanted. If only every child could be so lucky.

"I believe I have an old christening gown in the attic at Dahlia House," I offered. "Maylin is the right size, I think. Anyway, you're welcome to alter it however you feel is appropriate."

"Thanks." Tinkie gave me a hug. "Now I'm going to feed my child."

"And I'm going for a horseback ride. The weather is perfect. And still no mosquitoes or yellow flies."

"Call Coleman to ride with you," Tinkie suggested. "If he isn't busy, it would be good for him, too."

"Your wish is my command." I tipped a fake hat to her and ran to my car. On the way home I dialed Coleman and he agreed to join me. Crime was slow in Sunflower County for a change.

I had Reveler and Ms. Scrapiron groomed by the time he got home. Sweetie Pie was lounging in the sun, keeping a watchful eye on us. She didn't want to be left behind. Pluto had more sense than to try to keep up with us. The cat never burned an unnecessary calorie. I was pleased to see Poe sitting on the fence. He pretended to ignore me, but when I walked over, he jumped on my shoulder.

"Let's go for a ride," I whispered to him.

He gave a throaty squawk and hopped back on the fence.

When Coleman and I mounted, he took to the air. He flew circles around us as we walked down the long driveway to warm up the horses. By the time we hit the open fields, Poe was soaring and dipping and playing with us and Sweetie Pie. I couldn't be certain, but there seemed to be a real friendship between the raven, my dog, and my cat. Only two days before I'd seen Pluto sleeping in the sun on the front porch, with Poe on a rocker guarding him.

The day was sunny and growing hot. It was only April, but the brown fields would soon be an electric green. With hot weather, the Delta would be lush with soybeans, cotton, and other crops. The vast tracts of land would be crawling with combines and tractors, plowing, planting, or spraying fertilizer. Some crops were now Roundup Ready and required herbicides. The number of cancer cases was also spiking all over the region. The fields around Dahlia House that belonged to me were free of chemicals and GMOs. Billy Watson, a local farmer who managed my land, was deeply into sustainable farming, which was one reason I leased him my land.

Coleman put Reveler into an easy canter and Ms. Scrapiron and I fell in beside him. I could smell the newly turned earth. In the brakes, where wildlife hid, birdsong filtered into the air. Poe swooped into the tree line and for a moment I worried that he might attack a smaller bird, but he only circled my head, playing with me and Coleman.

When Coleman and I neared the road on the way home, Poe settled atop a vine-covered power pole. When I was directly beneath him, he croaked, "Action."

"Did that bird just say 'action'?" Coleman asked.

"That's what I heard." We stopped the horses and looked up at him. "Lights. Camera."

"Action!" the bird croaked again.

"Maybe he wants to direct a remake of *The Crow*," Coleman said.

"Or better yet, *The Birds*." I grinned. "Tinkie does remind me of Tippi Hedren. You know Ms. Hedren is a big animal activist."

"Even after being attacked by birds?" Coleman teased me.

"She didn't hold a grudge." I held up my arm and Poe flew toward me, settling gently on my forearm. "Hello, Poe."

He made a grumbling sound that might have been a salutation, but I couldn't be sure. Coleman held up his forearm and the bird hopped over to him. Sweet relief. The bird was heavier than you'd think a bundle of feathers would be.

"We should build Poe an aviary," Coleman said.

"Awwwwk!" Poe was having none of that.

"He's happy in the house," I reminded Coleman. The bird had impeccable manners. When he wanted to go outside, he flew to the door and pecked it. He preferred being free to fly and roam, but he also liked to come inside to see what we were doing. He was way more curious than Pluto.

As we untacked and groomed the horses, I gave Coleman the lowdown on the movie set. "Maylin is going to get a part, I think."

"What about you?" he asked. "Are you going to audition?"

"Nope." I had considered it, but that door was closed. "I have my own business to run. I don't want to get distracted."

"You know the film will be shot and the crew will leave soon enough. It might be fun."

"I'll do it if you do it." I put the challenge out there.

"I never wanted to be an actress."

"I would hope not," I said. "I can't visualize you in a slinky dress and heels." I walked toward him and kissed him with passion. "Now let it go. I'm happy with my life as it is. Very happy." We led the horses to the pasture and set them free. They took off with hooves pounding. It was a sight that gave me instant joy.

While Tinkie spent time with Maylin and Coleman went back to work, I decided to work on a few sections of the pasture fence that needed attention. It was a perfect day for farm work, and the horses followed me as I walked across the pasture. Poe flew around me, talking a mile a minute in the croaks and twitters that made up his language.

I turned to look back at Dahlia House, atop a slight rise. The sycamore trees that lined the driveway were budding out in electric green. I'd made some improvements on the house over the years. I thought of the many generations of my family who'd lived there. Being connected to the land was a long tradition.

Just as I set about hammering a staple into a fence post to secure the woven field fencing, my phone rang from my back pocket. I answered without checking the caller ID, figuring it was Tinkie or one of my other friends.

"Ms. Delaney, this is Marlon Brandon."

I was surprised.

"The missing gaffer, Jules Valiant, didn't go back to Memphis. And he didn't leave with the young lady who was here. In fact, she's standing directly in front of me and she's worried sick. Do you think you might look into this for Trinity Studios? The insurance company is having a conniption fit."

"Tinkie and I are taking a little vacation. I can help you find another PI to take the case."

"I've heard you and Delaney Detective Agency are the best. I'll make it worth your while. You have to understand that the film will shut down if the insurer pulls out. That would be terrible for all of us and Greenville."

He was putting pressure in all the right places, though I was still reluctant.

"Please help me out. I'll give Maylin a role in the movie."

The final straw. "Sure." I put my hammer down. "I'll need some basic information about this missing man."

"Right. If you could come back to the set, I'll give you everything I know. And Ms. Williamson, the woman Jules was dating, will tell you what she knows. They were supposed to meet yesterday evening but he never made it to the restaurant. Also, expect a call from Jane Bernardo with the insurance company. She'll have some questions for you."

"Let me get the details on Mr. Valiant before I talk to the insurance people. How about Mrs. Richmond and I meet you tomorrow at eight? We can get the facts and explain our plan to search for Jules." The day was drawing to a close, and it would be easier to start the search for Jules in the morning. "Just be sure you file a report with the local sheriff. That's something you don't want to skip."

"Ana has already done so. In fact, the sheriff is concerned. When Ms. Williamson showed up looking for him, she made me extremely worried. I shouldn't have assumed he flaked out and went home."

"You haven't had any trouble on the set, have you?" I remembered the rumors that the movie had upset some town residents.

"No, it's been mostly quiet. No one should object to the film. It's an action-adventure story of bravery."

"Okay. Be sure and call any contacts you have for Jules. The more you can do to find him, the quicker Tinkie and I can get results."

"You've got it."

4

The vista of Delta sky, most often a lovely blue, was draped with gloomy gray clouds. The wind gusted and kicked up. The Roadster, so solid and heavy, snugged the road as we drove to Greenville. I pulled up directly at the movie set, which, to my shock, was crawling with workers at eight o'clock in the morning. Down by the dock, they were filming a sequence with Marlon boarding the riverboat. He wore suit pants, a white starched shirt, suspenders, and a vest. He hurled orders at a ship's crew who raced around the paddle-boat preparing for the oncoming storm. While I hated the gray days, this was a gift to the movie people. They could get a lot of preliminary flood shots now, before the rain came down. Marlon, with Ana at his side, was making the most of it.

When the scene concluded, Marlon signaled Tinkie and me down to the trailer where we could talk privately. We'd just been seated when a tap came at the door. He opened it to reveal a beautiful young woman in her mid-twenties. "This is Jennifer Williamson," he explained.

"Can you find Jules?" she asked.

"We hope so." I didn't want to make any promises I couldn't keep.

"What's your fee?" she asked, twisting her hands nervously.

"Don't worry about that," Marlon told her. "Trinity Studios will cover that. The important thing is finding Jules."

"Let's work on the timeline," I told them both. "Who saw Jules last? Have you asked the crew?"

"It was me," Jennifer said. "I was sitting on the dock with him while he worked on the raft. He said another guy was coming to help him set the mast so the raft could have a sail."

"We're going to float down the river to Vicksburg on the raft once the movie is shot," Marlon explained. "We'll film a documentary about the river, the raft, and the fabulous tradition of Huck Finn. We'll use the documentary to promote the feature film." He was clearly excited about the prospects of a river adventure. "The Mississippi River has tickled the American imagination for decades."

So that explained the raft. "Let's walk down to the dock," I suggested.

"I have to go to work. Please call me when you find something about Jules," Jennifer said. She headed up the hill, head bent in worry.

As Tinkie, Marlon, and I sauntered down to the water, Marlon talked about the film and how the Brandon family had lost all of their downtown properties in the flood, but had rebuilt with cotton, hard work, and a toe in politics. "Everybody in Greenville knows my grandpa," he said.

"Of course they do," Tinkie said. "He was a U.S. senator from Mississippi for six terms. He was instrumental in getting bridge projects, agricultural help during hard years, and better schools. Senator Brandon was an old-school politician. He went to Washington to bring back help for his state, and he did. That was his primary focus, and he was good at it."

"Yes, he was," Marlon agreed. "He has a great love for this state."

"Why aren't you staying at the Brandon plantation?" Tinkie asked.

"How do you know he isn't?" I asked her. She knew too much about Marlon. She was sounding like a stalker.

"I make it my business to know about handsome men in the Delta," Tinkie answered tartly, and we all laughed.

"I'm flattered," Marlon said. "I'm staying in a B and B to be closer to the set. Also, I didn't want to drag Grandpa into this film. Folks around here are suspicious of anyone different, anyone who comes in with ideas and attitudes that aren't . . . traditional. Folks have crazy ideas such as movie people are deviants. There have also been rumors that my script bends the truth too much. False, of course. My movie tells the truth."

I knew exactly what he was talking about, and so did Tinkie.

"Do you really think people suspect you of an ulterior motive?" Tinkie pressed.

I wondered if she was looking for a reason Jules Valiant had disappeared, or simply being nosy. I hated to admit it, but I was nosy, too.

"Do you happen to know Lamar Bilbo?" he asked.

Judging by Marlon's frown, Lamar Bilbo was not a friend. "I know who he is." I didn't much care for the man myself.

"Old Mississippi name, entitlement upright on two legs." Tinkie summed it up perfectly.

Marlon grinned. "He's expressed opposition to the movie and he's doing his best to make an issue of it. When I was in a bar off Washington Street, I got a surly greeting from several guys who looked like bikers. They told me to get on a plane back to Hollywood before they had to hurt me."

"You said some opposition. You didn't say you were getting threats," I said.

"I don't take them seriously," Marlon said. "Talk is cheap, and Bilbo doesn't even have a clue what he's talking about."

"Most of those guys are blowhards," Tinkie said, "but be careful. Sometimes their brawn overpowers their brains."

"I've seen more guns in Greenville in the past week than I ever saw in Los Angeles," Marlon said. "I sure don't want to upset the locals and get them riled. I just want to shoot the film and get back to California to edit it and prepare for release."

"I see you're directing the project," I said. I'd also done a little research.

"Yes, I wrote it, too. And because I'm directing, I can withhold the script from the actors until they need to see it. It keeps the twists and surprises fresh." He pointed at Ana McCants, who was working with a wardrobe team to outfit a very beautiful young woman dressed as a flapper. "I couldn't do any of this without Ana. She's the executive producer on the film and she got all the financing. She's also exceptionally good with the cast. She knows how to make them feel like they're the most important thing in the world. Actors love that. I know because I love it." He laughed at himself.

"Is that actress Cindy Devlin?" Tinkie asked. "She was terrific in her last film."

"She's a talent," Marlon answered, pleased. "I was lucky to get her. Her role isn't huge in the film."

"Romantic interest?" Tinkie probed.

"There's not a lot of romance in the film, but she is my character's love interest."

Ana signaled to Marlon that she needed him. It didn't take me long to see why. Lamar Bilbo had come on the set with a pretty red-haired woman I recognized as Mary Dayle McCormick, the owner of the local bookshop in Greenville. She was an authority on the history of Greenville and came from a long-established family. The McCormicks had once owned thousands of acres of farmland, but the Depression had hit the family hard. Mary Dayle had left the Delta for several years but had returned to bring the bookstore back to life. She had a reputation for scooping the biggest, bestselling authors up and getting them at her store by means fair or foul. Behind her back, she was called the boss of the Mississippi Literary Mafia. She was a woman used to having her way, and she did not look happy.

"Uh-oh," Tinkie whispered to me. Her blue eyes twinkled as she watched Lamar and Mary Dayle sail into Ana and Marlon. Whatever they were upset about, they intended to make sure everyone within three miles knew about it.

"Let's get closer." I was dying to hear what the hubbub was about.

"You can't continue with this film!" Lamar Bilbo shouted. "We're here to shut you down!"

"Why?" Marlon was low key and calm.

"Because we said so," Lamar huffed. "You're going to make fools out of the people of Greenville, and I won't stand for it."

"Are you nuts?" Marlon asked in a tone far more reasonable than I would have used.

"You have no right to portray my ancestors as brutal, cruel racists."

"Who said I was going to do that?" Marlon asked.

Ana slipped behind Marlon and slowly backed away. She motioned to a cinematographer to start filming. A smart move if Lamar took any physical action. She'd have it documented. Judging by Lamar's very red face and sputtering, he was on the edge of a total emotional collapse. He'd either cry or fight. I was hoping for tears.

When I glanced down at Tinkie, she was filming the whole encounter. "Remember how Cece helps us with our cases? Now I have something she is going to want for her digital page. With Marlon's approval, of course."

"You are brilliant," I told her, meaning every word. This would boost readership of Cece and Millie's column yet again. I wouldn't be surprised if the two didn't get an offer to syndicate.

"Double uh-oh! I think Lamar is onto me." But she didn't put the camera away. When the angry man strode toward us, I stepped in front of Tinkie. "Best leave before you do something you'll regret," I told him.

"You can't push us around, Sarah Booth Delaney." Mary Dayle came straight at me. "Your mama and daddy were good people, but all you do is consort with lowlifes and criminals."

"Why don't you write a book about it?" Tinkie jeered.

"I just might do that," Mary Dayle said, unflustered. "Tinkie, I'm shocked your husband allows you to socialize with people like Sarah Booth. Common folk."

"I always wondered what your specialty in the book business was," Tinkie said. "Now I know. Meanness and hopes for a rigid class structure." She stepped toward Mary Dayle and lifted her hands up in a dramatic gesture. "Be gone!" she said, pushing out with her palms.

To my amusement, Mary Dayle stepped back. So did Lamar. They pivoted abruptly and left. Several feet away I could hear Marlon laughing.

"That was great," he said. "'Be gone!'" He mimicked Tinkie. "Badass."

We all started laughing and Lamar turned back to shoot us the bird.

"Sore loser," Tinkie called out. Then she turned to Marlon and Ana. "What's going on with those two? What are they talking about?"

"There are differing versions of the truth regarding the flood," Marlon said.

"Care to explain?" I asked.

"Some of the flood victims were hemmed up on the levee and not allowed to leave. There was a fear that the poor people, the field-workers and day laborers, would flee the area once the floodwater receded and there would be no one to work the fields." His face was grim.

"Folks were deliberately stranded?" I asked.

"Yes, though it isn't often discussed. My film isn't about that," Marlon insisted, but he looked uncomfortable. "Now let's get back to work. We're burning daylight hours and there's too much to get done." He turned to us. "Ladies, if you wouldn't mind vacating the set for a bit. Perhaps we can reschedule our talk for in the morning." He checked his watch. "The day is getting away from me."

Marlon was struggling to regain his composure. Despite his jocularity, it seemed that Bilbo and Mary Dayle had gotten under his skin. "Sure, but that's another day Jules is missing," I pointed out.

"Then start looking for him, if you would. I'll touch base with you tomorrow. The insurance company can cut you a check and send it for your retainer. But please be discreet. We don't want any more trouble with locals. If they think the set is dangerous . . ." He blew breath out. "Insurance for a film is expensive. We don't need rumors."

"I understand." And I did. "We'll talk tomorrow."

Tinkie and I walked up to stand on top of the levee. From there, we had a view of some of Greenville. "Let's eat," I said. "I'm starving."

"Me, too. This was a wasted trip here." Tinkie was a little annoyed. "I realize Marlon is a big cheese and busy, but so are we."

"Let's check into Mary Dayle and Lamar. I think they may play a role in the disappearance of Jules Valiant."

"Like, they kidnapped him?" Tinkie bit her bottom lip. "That could be incredibly effective. They could kill the movie with gossip."

5

We decided to have lunch at Kingfisher's, a local eatery that specialized in home-cooked meals and soul food. We were not disappointed with the food or with the talkative waitress who served us. Orie Ruth was petite and full of energy as she filled orders, carrying up to six plates at a time. She could have had a circus act. She also knew almost every person in Washington County and their family pedigree. And she loved to talk.

"What do you know about Lamar Bilbo?" I asked when she stopped to refill our iced teas.

"His family once owned a large mansion right on the river. Had the best dock for miles, and they charged for the supply boats to load and unload and pick up the cotton."

"Didn't all the docks charge for tying up the ships to be loaded?" I didn't really know how life on the river had worked.

"I guess, but the Bilbo dock charged big. There were a lot of benefits, though." Her grin told me this was delicious gossip.

"What kind of benefits?" Tinkie asked.

"Whores and fine food and drink. There was a gaming house on the bank above the dock. A fancy place, not just a backroom joint." Orie Ruth glanced around the restaurant to be sure all of her customers were satisfied. She slipped into a chair, sighing. "My feet are killing me."

"Take a load off," I said. "What happened to the Bilbo gambling den?"

"The flood. I'm hoping there's at least a nod to it in the movie they're making. It was hot stuff back in the day."

"Was it totally destroyed?"

"Swept away," she said. "My grandmother worked there." Her grin was impudent. "Someone had to feed the family and let me tell you, the planters didn't pay a living wage for farm labor. Granny made more money in a night than her husband made in a week."

"That just pisses me off," Tinkie said.

Orie Ruth gave Tinkie an amazed look. "You get it. For a rich bitch, you really understand."

"I do," Tinkie said. "I'm sorry that people are so greedy."

"Hey, not your fault." Orie Ruth didn't hold any grudges. "The Bilbos come from a long line of racists and people who like to step on the necks of the poor. That Theodore Bilbo, the one who was elected governor and U.S. senator, was a member of the Ku Klux Klan and did everything he could to keep Black people from voting."

I knew this part of history. "Theodore Bilbo wasn't a nice man."

"Understatement of the year." Orie Ruth laughed. "True to form, he was never legally punished."

"You're well versed on Mississippi history," Tinkie said. We both knew that most of the horrible racial injustices in the state had been erased from Mississippi history books. "Where did you learn it?"

"A few years back I worked as a photographer for a civil rights attorney who came to town to sue about voting practices. I learned a lot. In fact, I started working toward my law degree. I'm here because of the movie company. Good tippers. Then it's back to Clinton for more law school."

Her high energy would serve her well.

She stood up. "You ladies need more cornbread or anything else? Maybe some peach cobbler for dessert?"

I shook my head and gave Tinkie the evil eye. Before Maylin she had willpower to resist dessert. Now she wanted to eat everything she could reach. The rub came from the fact that I had no willpower. Whenever Tinkie ate dessert, so did I.

"Not today," Tinkie said, glaring at me. "But next time for sure."

"Does Lamar Bilbo live in Greenville?" I asked before Orie Ruth got away.

"He does. He's still at the old family place."

"Does he work?" I asked.

"He's a substitute teacher at the high school. The kids hate him." She laughed. "Even they see through his soft-spoken, pretentious Southern accent. I think he studied the Mississippi archives and patterned himself after Byron De La Beckwith, the murderer."

In the summer of 1963, Beckwith had shot a field operator for the NAACP, Medgar Evers, in the back in his own garage. It was an ambush. That coward Beckwith was hiding in the shrubs near his home. "Beckwith was finally convicted," I reminded her.

"Yeah, third time's the charm, right? Hung jury in the first two trials and years passed before he was tried for the third and final time."

I gave her one of my business cards. "If you're up around Zinnia, give me a call. I'll treat you to a drink."

"Great!"

"Before you go," Tinkie said, "what about Mary Dayle McCormick?"

"Good family. Nice people. Smart. The bookstore carried a lot of books about real-life events back in the day. But she's prickly as a hedgehog in heat."

"She's not a racist?" I asked.

"She didn't use to be. You know she had a bad break when she was working for a marine entertainment center. Her assistant was killed by a shark. It kind of took the wind out of her sails and she came home."

"She's hanging around with Bilbo," I said.

"Well, in the last few years, Mary Dayle changed. I think it was the death of her assistant. I heard he was bitten almost in half right in front of her."

That would be enough to change a person's outlook forever. "Was she held responsible?"

Orie Ruth frowned. "No. No charges were brought. From all accounts it was a terrible accident. But you know folks. They hounded Ms. McCormick. She just came back to Greenville and threw herself into the bookstore."

"Why is she hanging around with Bilbo?" Tinkie asked.

Orie Ruth waved at her supervisor. "Time to go. I heard Mary Dayle and Lamar were involved. Like a romance. Bad taste is the only taste some people have in relationships. It's sad if you think about it."

After we paid the check, we walked into the fresh air to find Jennifer Williamson waiting for us outside the restaurant. She came forward with a folder and handed it to Tinkie. "Ana said you were here. You have to find Jules. This isn't like him. I put together all of his contact information, some friends who might help, the last job he was on. Things like that. Jules would never just leave. He was so excited about this job and hoped that the crew would sign him on and take us both to Los Angeles with them. I want to design costumes. I can't stay any longer. I'm due at work, and I'm in trouble already."

"Thank you," we both said. "We'll let you know if we find anything to report."

"I really care about Jules." Her composure broke and tears leaked down her cheeks. "Please find him." She turned abruptly and hurried away.

When we pulled up in front of McCormick Book Inn, we both lingered in the car. The place was hopping. A Jackson author, Miranda James, was hosting a signing and the readers of the town had turned up to buy his new book, *Hiss Me Deadly*. Tinkie and I went in. We were both fans of Diesel, the Maine coon cat in the series.

When we had our autographed copies, we lingered in the stacks to watch Mary Dayle interact with her customers. She was completely gracious, a far cry from her surly demeanor at the movie set earlier. And the woman knew books. She was better than a card catalog.

"What does she see in Lamar Bilbo?" Tinkie asked. "She has breeding and humor and intelligence."

I only shook my head. When the shop was empty, we approached the counter.

"Mary Dayle, we're looking for a gaffer who went missing from the movie set. We're asking around, hoping maybe he talked to someone locally and said where he was going."

"I have no idea, but I'd like to give him a present for leaving that horrible movie set. Marlon Brandon is going to burn the people of Washington County. He's going to make his family of crooks look good and everyone else look like racist thugs."

"Now wait a minute." Tinkie leaped to Marlon's defense. "How do you know this? Have you seen a script?"

"My brain can put two and two together. Marlon never cared for Mississippi. He's a narcissist. He took on that ridiculous name, Marlon Brandon—like he was already a movie star. Honestly, that family and their vanity. Anyway, I remember him when he was a teen. He'd come in the store and buy inflammatory books. He never wanted to read anything good about his home state."

"What is an inflammatory book?" I asked. Mary Dayle was strangely overwrought by a kid reading.

"Those books that say all Southerners hate Black people. That's not true and you know it."

I did know that generalizations were always untrue, but the burden of history couldn't be ignored, either. "The truth is the only answer to what happened in the past. Eventually, there needs to be an accounting. Building a life or country on lies is just wrong."

"The whole system of slavery was an aberration. It should never have happened. I totally agree. But is there really a point in digging all of this up again?"

"We're not trying to right the wrongs of the past. We're looking for a missing gaffer," Tinkie said. "Wouldn't Marlon's family qualify as participants in the system you think he is going to reveal?"

"Of course. He's a hypocrite. Just like the rest of his family. You can ask Lamar Bilbo. He's known the Brandon family for years. He said that Brandon Brandon, the senator, made millions while he was in the Senate. Feathering his own nest. He helped the state, but he helped himself first."

"Like so many other elected officials," I said.

"You know, you should run for office, Sarah Booth." A hint of humor hid in Mary Dayle's smile.

"Right after I drink my strychnine tea," I answered.

Tinkie's eye sparked. "That's a great idea, Mary Dayle. I'll talk Sarah Booth into it. I will. I'm very persuasive. I can see it now. Senator Sarah Booth Delaney."

"It doesn't hurt to dream," I said on a yawn. "Now let's get crack-a-lacking. By the way, why is the retired senator's name Brandon Brandon? Really? A name so nice they used it twice?"

"Originality wore thin in the Brandon family, I guess." Tinkie was pulling my leg. I could tell. Mary Dayle, too, seemed to enjoy the joke.

"Why would they do that? It must have been hell for him when he was a kid."

"Brandon is a family name and a first name. Heck, I don't know. I'd hate to be Tinkie Tinkie. It sounds like I have to pee."

On that, I closed the discussion on names, and we headed to Bluebeard's Bar, a quiet place where we could peruse the file on Jules.

6

The notes Jennifer Williamson had compiled held a lot of helpful information on the missing gaffer. Jules was a hardworking young man who'd traveled the Southeast taking jobs with various movie companies. He had letters of praise from cinematographers, some of them famous. He seemed intent on building a career in the business. Walking away from a movie set would not be strategic. I was beginning to believe something bad had happened to him.

There were photos in the file of Jules, a handsome guy with a wide smile. He'd also done some work on set locations and had even found the site that Marlon Brandon was now using. He didn't appear to be a guy who'd simply walk off on a whim.

We sat at Bluebeard's Bar, going over the file. Tinkie was

absorbed in reading when I nudged her under the table. "You could work here. Look, they have wench costumes."

"Yes!" Tinkie was instantly taken with the little plaid skirts, black corsets, and white scoop-neck blouses. Oscar Richmond, her husband, would have my head on a platter if I let his wife put something like that on and serve drinks.

"We're leaving," I said as I threw some money on the bar and grabbed her wrist before she could ask for a server's outfit. "Let's get busy here or head back to Zinnia. Maylin is waiting for you."

That was the magic sentence. "Yes, Maylin is waiting. What are we going to do about the missing man?"

I had a photo of Jules on my phone, and I showed it to the barkeep. "Have you seen this man?"

"He was in here two nights ago. Had a couple of girls hanging all over him."

"Did he leave with them?"

He shook his head. "He left alone. Said he was working on a raft or something like that. Didn't make sense to me, but a lot of things leave me flummoxed these days."

"Thanks." I put an extra twenty on the bar for a tip and we were out the door.

"To the movie set?" Tinkie asked.

"Yeah. With this new information Jennifer gave us about Jules, I have some questions for the crew." We walked along, enjoying the warm day and the energy the movie people had infused the entire town with. It made me wonder what Greenville had been like when cotton was king and the river city was a major distribution point to send the "white gold" downriver to the Port of New Orleans and off to Europe.

As we stood at the top of the levee, below us the movie set buzzed with motion. I could see the riverboat at the dock and the raft beside it. No one was working on the raft.

"It looks like everyone is busy," Tinkie said.

"Too bad. They'll have to talk to us."

"Remember, Coleman can't back us up in Washington County," Tinkie reminded me.

"If a man is missing, the Washington County sheriff will have questions of his own." I knew that Sheriff Nelson and Coleman were friends. I didn't like to trade on Coleman's sterling reputation in law enforcement, but I would if I had to.

"True enough," Tinkie said as we headed down to the heart of the movie set.

While everyone was busy, we found a young woman who took five minutes to talk to us about Jules.

"He was a terrific gaffer. The best one here. The cinematographer is upset that he just disappeared. But they couldn't force him to stay, you know." She pushed her dark bangs out of her eyes. "The crazy thing is he didn't tell anyone he was unhappy. He seemed to love the work and he was really into the raft. Marlon was going to take him on the raft ride downriver. He was to be the cinematographer. It was a big step for Jules. It makes no sense that he just walked away."

The young woman, part of the costuming team, had an excellent point.

"We spoke to his girlfriend, Ms. Williamson. She is extremely worried." Tinkie put a hand on the young woman's shoulder. "Do you have any idea where Jules could be?" she asked. "The bartender said he was with a couple of young women. Is he a player? Maybe holed up with a girl somewhere?"

The costumer broke into tears. "Jules isn't like that at all. He's friendly, but he was stuck on Jennifer. Everyone is saying he fell in the river and was swept away. We've been searching since he disappeared. There's no sign of him, but his tools were left on the raft where he was working to set the mast."

"Could he swim?" I asked. Surely he could, if he was going to build and float on a raft.

"I don't know," the girl confessed. "We all play in the water after we finish shooting for the day. Jules was always working on the raft, but he seemed comfortable on the water." Tears slid down her cheeks. "I just don't know what to think."

"Thank you," I told her before I drew Tinkie aside. "We should call the river search and rescue."

She sighed heavily. "I agree. It's not looking good for Jules. The river current is so treacherous. Non-locals wouldn't have any idea how dangerous it can be."

"Maybe we're wrong. But we must resolve this one way or the other."

"Let's tell Marlon what we've learned."

Marlon was both shocked and contrite. "It never occurred to me he could have fallen into the river," he said. "We should have been looking for him there."

"The search and rescue team will be here in about fifteen minutes," I said, checking my watch.

"Thank you for calling them," Marlon said. He looked physically ill. "I should have thought of this. It's just that if he fell off the raft, he is right there by the dock. He would have climbed out or swam to shore."

"Hey, there's no proof he went in the water," Tinkie reminded him. "The costume woman said that a lot of the crew cools off in the river after work, though. You might warn them about the currents. Just to be on the safe side."

"The hotels have pools. My B and B has a pool. I wouldn't get in the river. It is dangerous," Marlon said. "With the current, and also how much fertilizer has washed into it. I did tell them about the dangers of poisoning from those chemicals, but they're young. They think they're invincible."

"And stubborn," Tinkie said with a gentle smile. "I'll warn the crew right now. They might listen to an older woman."

Marlon gave her a brilliant smile. "You're right. They'll listen to a beautiful Delta belle," he corrected her.

"Enough dishing out compliments," I said. "The rescue team is here." I was a little startled to see that Coleman was with them. I hurried over to him while Tinkie did her best to make the crew see the dangers of the Mighty Mississippi, or as the Native Americans called it, the Father of Waters. "What are you doing here?"

"And it's good to see you, too." He chuckled. "You look surprised."

"I am. This isn't Sunflower County, in case you didn't notice."

"I'm a certified diver. They needed me to help with this search."

It was true. Before we started seeing each other, Coleman had completed all the training to be a certified rescue diver. It had always been a hobby—one he didn't get to pursue often. But he knew what he was about in the water. He loved the crystal blue-green waters of the Gulf of Mexico. The Mississippi River was a murky mess for diving. And just because a person had air tanks and flippers, it didn't mean the current was any less dangerous.

"I know you'll be careful." Both Coleman and I faced

danger at times in our careers. I had to trust him and accept he knew what he was doing, just as he did me.

"I will." He gave me a quick kiss on the cheek and caught up with the rescue team at the dock. I watched as they assessed the shore and then suited up to dive into the water. Several boats had appeared to search the shoreline of the lake and farther downriver. They'd put the whole operation in gear very quickly.

"That's Sheriff Nelson," Tinkie said, pointing to a man in one of the boats.

I'd met him before, but it had been awhile. "He must be taking this drowning business seriously."

"I hope it isn't true." Tinkie linked her arm through mine.

"Me, too. Jules seems like a young man with a lot going for him." We turned around to see the film crew back at work. The daily cost of production was high. There was no time to waste.

I checked my phone for the weather. "That storm front is still due to come in later this week. If Jules is still alive, they need to find him before he truly is swept out to the Gulf."

"I know," Tinkie said. "I don't have a good feeling about this, Sarah Booth."

I didn't say it, but my gut echoed hers. "Look, isn't that Lamar Bilbo about to get in a fistfight with the cameraman?"

"It is." Tinkie grabbed my hand and tugged me behind her as she racewalked toward Bilbo. "We can't let any of the movie people punch his lights out," she said. "It will stop production."

She was right. I quit lagging behind and raced along with her. We got to the confrontation just in time.

"You need to get off the set," the cameraman said. He

handed the camera to another worker. "Now. Or I'll put you off the set."

"This is public property, and you can't make me do a damn thing," Bilbo said.

Bilbo's face was red with anger. Tinkie stepped between the two men.

"Enough," she said. "This is a movie set. If you aren't working here, you need to leave," she said to Bilbo.

"Well, well, if it isn't the busybody wife of Oscar Richmond. Does your husband know you're down here frolicking with communists and the likes?"

I inhaled deeply. We'd just stepped into another world of crazy.

"If you were my wife, I'd tan your hide and lock you in the bedroom until you came to your senses."

"If you were my husband, I'd kill myself," Tinkie replied. She was teasing, but Lamar Bilbo wasn't a man who understood that.

"Break it up." I stepped right into the middle of it. Since I was a good foot taller than Tinkie, I was eye level with Bilbo. Bullies normally didn't like to pick on a person the same size they were. I was counting on that. "The film company has a permit to shoot here. For the time that permit is in effect, you have no right to be here. Leave."

I didn't know if what I said was true or not, but neither did Bilbo. He backed up a step and I pressed my advantage. I pointed to one of the crewmembers who was filming the encounter. "We have all of this recorded," I told him. "If anyone is pressing charges, it will be us."

He took another step backward. "This isn't over."

"Yes, Lamar, it is."

The deep baritone voice came from behind me. Tinkie

and I, along with everyone else, turned to face a tall, white-haired man in an expensive suit. I knew him instantly, Senator Brandon Brandon.

"You can't boss me around, Brandon," Bilbo said. "My family served the state just like yours."

"Not exactly," Brandon said with a tight grin. "Not anything like mine, as a matter of fact. I, for one, was never banned from the Senate. Now you should move along and let these people do their jobs. Otherwise, you'll be sued for the loss of a day's production. That's a lot of money, sir."

"Here you are, still thinking you can boss everyone in Mississippi around because you once got elected senator."

"It was a few times more than once," Brandon noted with wry humor. "Now skedaddle before you get in financial trouble, Lamar. Leave these people in peace to tell their story."

Lamar Bilbo turned on his heel and stalked away.

"Thank you, Senator," Tinkie said. "I don't understand what's wrong with Lamar Bilbo. He's acting like a nut."

"Unhappy people do unhappy things," Brandon said. "It's a pleasure to see you, Mrs. Richmond. And you, Ms. Delaney."

I was shocked he knew me. Knowing Tinkie was understandable. She was a power of Delta society. I was a nobody. "Are you here to see your grandson's movie?"

"I am. Marlon is going to do our state proud, don't you think?"

"I do think," I said.

"You bet," Tinkie agreed. "It's going to be a swashbuckler, from what I hear."

"Any news on the missing crew member?" the senator asked.

The news of Jules's disappearance had traveled fast.

"Search and rescue are looking for him in the river and along the banks. He may have fallen off the raft into the current when no one was around to hear him."

"That would be a shame," Brandon said. "If that's the case, do they think his body is still in the lake? Or do they feel he's been swept downriver?"

"Hard to tell," I said. "The river has been high with all the spring rains." I shook my head. "I'll know more once the rescue team reports back."

"Are you and Mrs. Richmond working his disappearance?" the senator asked. "I hear you're very successful at solving disappearances and other mysteries."

"We've been asked to look into it," Tinkie said.

"By my grandson?" he pressed.

"No, technically, we're working for the insurance company. Why?"

"I want to take this burden off Marlon. He has enough to worry about." He reached into his beautifully tailored suit jacket and brought out a checkbook. "How much?"

"We've already been paid," I said. "Thank you, but we're set. We'll do our best to find Jules Valiant."

He put his checkbook away. "If it turns out you need more money, let me know. I realize there will be expenses and so forth. And thank you both. I hope we can find the missing crew member. I don't want a dark cloud over Marlon's big project. This means the world to him."

"He's lucky to have your support," Tinkie said.

"There are people around here who really want to stop this project." The senator scratched his chin. "I don't get it. But those who have a little power here fear any change.

This is a movie, not an invasion of wealthy corporations. Marlon and his friends will be here for a few months, bringing a lot of money into Greenville, and then they will be gone. I don't understand this resistance, but you two be careful. Folks who are afraid are dangerous."

He wasn't lying, and I was glad to see he had his ear to the ground regarding Lamar Bilbo. It was odd because both the Brandon family and the Bilbo family had served the state as high elected officials. With very different agendas. Theodore Bilbo's reign of racism was long before I was born, but his legacy lingered. Brandon was a politician's politician—polished, conciliatory, championing the forward progress of the state and leaving the past behind. He wasn't exactly my cup of tea, but he had brought a lot of federal contracts and jobs to the poorest state in the union.

"We'll keep our eyes open," Tinkie told him. "We have Marlon's best interests at heart."

"As I said, call me if you need more funds." He held out a business card to Tinkie.

She put it in the back pocket of her leggings. We watched the senator walk away.

"That's fortuitous for Marlon," I said. "Family support means a lot."

"Family is everything to the Brandons. It always has been. I'm actually surprised they let Marlon head off to Hollywood. I'm sure they hoped he'd run for political office and carry on the family tradition."

Tinkie linked her arm through mine again. "Your parents would be very proud of you, Sarah Booth. Carrying on the family tradition of seeking justice. But they would also be proud if you took up acting again."

"You have easy standards for me, Tinkie."

"Not at all. When you love someone, their happiness is the most important thing ever."

She was right about that.

7

When the day drew to a close, Tinkie and I met up with Coleman and Oscar at Doe's Eat Place. I was eager to hear what the search and rescue team had discovered, but the news wasn't good. It wasn't even news. They'd found no evidence of Jules or what might have happened to him.

"He's simply gone," Coleman said. "We searched the deep pockets of the lake and down the banks of the river. If he went into the water, chances are the body is on the way to the Gulf of Mexico."

That was disheartening news. "Can you say positively?" I asked. We'd be returning the insurance company's check if the rescue team had done our work.

"There's no evidence that allows me to say positively that Jules drowned," Coleman said. "But Sheriff Nelson is ready to unofficially label it an accidental drowning. I don't think he's going to spend county resources on a drawn-out search."

"He's calling it quits? Without a body?"

"The movie is insured by a big Hollywood company. They'll pay Jules's family something. The thought is to get the payment out as quickly as possible before the disappearance becomes a big story in the newspaper. The producer of the movie, Ana McCants, appealed to Nelson to end this fast before the rumor mill makes it worse."

Tinkie and I exchanged glances. It was too late to keep the press from running with the story. We'd already spilled the beans to Cece. "I suspect there'll be a story tomorrow in the *Zinnia Dispatch*. And on the internet."

Coleman looked at both of us. "Cece?"

We nodded. "We didn't realize it would be an issue," Tinkie said. "It was just a fact we reported to her. The young man is gone."

Oscar put a hand on Tinkie's hand. "Don't fret about it. It is news. Whether the film people like it or not."

We finished our dinner and headed back to Zinnia. Coleman and I were listening to Mississippi public radio on the way home. They sometimes had the best blues music and also interesting stories. The current one was on the history of the boll weevil, a pest that had decimated the cotton crop for years. The story brought up a lot of memories for me, and I was quiet as we raced through the night.

The weather report came on. "Storm warnings from Tunica down to Jackson are in effect this coming weekend. Prepare for potentially dangerous weather. High winds, hail, heavy rainfall."

"Great," Coleman said. "It's going to make it hard even to search for the body."

"Maybe he isn't dead," I said, holding on to a slim belief Jules wasn't hurt.

"Let's hope you're right," Coleman said.

Coleman and I were still in bed Wednesday morning when the phone rang at daybreak. Coleman answered and I could tell it was business for him. I slipped into jeans and a sweatshirt and ran out to feed the horses. We wouldn't have time for a ride this morning. We both had work to do. I'd just let the horses out of the barn after they finished eating when Coleman brought me a cup of coffee.

"I've got some bad news."

I took the steaming cup and held it, waiting for him to continue.

"Marlon Brandon disappeared from the set last night. He was supposed to be in makeup this morning at five o'clock. He didn't show. When they checked the B and B where he was staying, his bed hadn't been slept in."

"Could he be with Ana? They were an item once."

"She's the one who called the sheriff, who called me."

"What do you think happened?" I asked. Coleman had great instincts, and I had a really bad feeling.

"I don't know, but it's suspicious that two people from the film crew have disappeared, and Marlon has a lot to lose. Production costs will eat him alive if he doesn't get back to work."

"Do you think someone is trying to sabotage the movie?"

"I honestly don't know what to think. Nelson has asked

for my help. Things are calm here in Sunflower County, for the moment. DeWayne and Budgie can handle things. I'm going down to talk to Nelson."

Coleman didn't have a lot of funds to fight crime, but he was exceptionally lucky in the two deputies who worked for him. They were solid investigators, each with unique talents.

"Okay." I hated for Coleman to go back to the river, but it had to be done. "Tinkie and I will follow. This is bad news."

"Don't jump to conclusions. Let's see what the circumstances and facts are. Marlon has a reputation as a womanizer. Could be he's having a tryst and didn't want to let his crew know."

Marlon might be a ladies' man, but first and foremost he was a writer/director/actor of a film with a huge budget. If he was being a layabout, it was nonsensical.

I watched Coleman drive away with cold dread in my heart. Something was very wrong on the movie set. Tinkie and I had to find out what it was—immediately.

Millie made us biscuits and sausage to go, so we hit the road with hot coffee and chow. I hated leaving the pets for another day. I dropped them off at Hilltop to play with Pauline, Maylin, Chablis, and Gumbo. They were probably happier there than with me—at least I tried to console myself with that thought.

We'd just turned onto the highway when my cell rang. I answered and put it on speaker. The California area code told me it was about our investigation. My supposition was correct. Word of Marlon's disappearance was already out in Hollywood, and the insurance company had doubled our fee to find Marlon and Jules. We agreed to do the job, but when I glanced at Tinkie, she was clearly worried.

"I hate taking money when I think something terrible has happened. Two people who just disappear—that's not coincidence. We have to search for Marlon," she said. "I like him. I mean, what could have happened to him? It doesn't make any sense."

The situation troubled me greatly. Two men from the movie missing within two days. But, as Coleman said, it was important not to get ahead of ourselves. "Let's just see what's what." The movie set was total chaos. Ana McCants was doing her best to keep people working on the things that could be accomplished without Marlon. Since he was the star, the writer, and the director, his absence touched every aspect of the film, but there were still scenes that could be shot with other characters. Locations and setting shots were also good to have in the can.

When Ana took a breath, we approached her. "Any idea where he might be? Tinkie and I are looking for him." I told her about the call from the insurance company. "Do you think he's off with a honey?"

"This isn't like him at all. He's serious about his work. About this movie." She threw up her hands in surrender. "I'm worried sick." Tears rimmed her eyes, but she blinked them away.

"Did he say anything the last time you talked to him?" I asked.

Before she could answer, Senator Brandon rushed onto the set and came straight for us. "Where's Marlon?" he demanded. "That boy can't play around like this. Time is money. I talked to the head of Trinity Studios and they're worried and angry. They called the house looking for him. What should I tell them?"

"How did they even hear he was missing so fast?" Tinkie asked.

Ana's mouth set in a grim line. "There's a rat in the crew. Someone had to call and tell."

"Who would do such a thing?" the senator demanded.

"I don't know, but I'm going to find out," Ana vowed.

The senator grasped Tinkie's hand. "Will you search for my grandson? Please. Right now? I'll give you whatever it takes. Name your amount."

Tinkie looked at me and I shrugged. "We've already been hired to find Jules. We'll look for Marlon at the same time," Tinkie said.

"Maybe they're together somewhere," I added.

"If my grandson is screwing around, you can tell him he's dead meat. Dead meat. I'll make him regret this."

Senator Brandon was angry, and I didn't blame him, but he was too willing to believe Marlon and Jules were merely goofing off or something equally unprofessional. It was curious because as far as I knew, Marlon had never given anyone a reason to think that. I figured it was likely a defense mechanism to prevent the dark thoughts of what else could have happened.

I repeated the last question I'd asked Ana. "Did Marlon say anything the last time you saw him?"

"We'd shut down for the day. He was headed to town to meet some women for dinner and drinks."

"What women?" Tinkie pressed.

"Some locals. I didn't ask. There are women all over the set, as you well know."

We did know. And Marlon was very popular with the local ladies. "Did he mention where they were eating?"

"Asiago's, I think," Ana said. "They have a nice bar with great specialty drinks. Marlon knows the ladies like that kind of thing."

It was a lead; so far the only one we had. "Tinkie? Are you ready?"

"I am."

It didn't take long to get to the restaurant, and it was very elegant, as Ana had hinted. The bar wasn't open this early, but the manager was helpful. He called the bartender at home and gave me the phone. It took only a few minutes to find out Marlon had been there with a Bitsy Sue and Carmella. Ten minutes after that I had phone numbers and addresses. The joy—and pain—of a small town often came from such intimacy. Folks knew who you were, and they knew your business.

I called one number and Tinkie the other and the two young women agreed to meet us at a local coffee shop. I'd had plenty of breakfast, but another cup of coffee would be perfect.

Bitsy Sue was a short brunette with a wide smile. Carmella was a dark-eyed model type. Both were concerned when they realized Marlon had disappeared.

"This doesn't make sense. We had a nice dinner, a few drinks. Then he wanted to walk along the levee," Bitsy said. "That's just not something I want to do. You know there are alligators around. Not to mention mosquitoes big enough to carry a short person off."

I doubted alligators would live around that many boats and people, but I couldn't say for certain. The mosquitos were a real concern. Any minute now they'd hatch out and be all over everyone.

Carmella continued, "Last summer when I went down to the lake after dark, I was almost eaten alive."

"Yeah, I'm just not one of those nature freaks who like to be out in the mud. Or sand. Or grass," Bitsy said. "I like carpeting and air-conditioning. And champagne."

"Well, it's good to know what you like," I said. "So what time did you part company from Marlon?"

"About eleven," Carmella said. "We spent a lot of time with him. He's fun and easy to talk to. He was just determined to go to the movie set and check on the raft. It was almost like he thought something was waiting there for him."

"I think this is going to be a great movie, but I wish I'd been around when they filmed that Carol Baker movie in Benoit," Bitsy said. "Some people say I favor her. I would have loved to play Baby Doll."

I'd forgotten all about the Elia Kazan film based on a Tennessee Williams short play. In 1956, the movie was considered too sexual and a scandal. It was long before I was born, but my mother, who had heard all the stories from the Delaney relatives, had talked about it. Mama told me about how the film crew had partied with some of the old Delta families in Greenville and other towns.

"Bitsy, you would have made a perfect Baby Doll," Tinkie said.

"Yeah, that was an indoors film. A big old mansion. Beautiful furniture. I could have even slept in a cradle. That would have been so cool. And no sweating. Marlon's movie is all about the river and rain and storms and floods and people dying. I like movies about sex and money and people living the good life."

"Well, there it is," I said. "Maybe next film will be more your style. Girls, did you see where Marlon went?"

"We walked out of the restaurant with him, and he did go down to the water," she said. "Last I saw him, he was headed to the levee, just as he said."

"Did you see anyone else? Maybe someone following him?" Tinkie asked.

"No, the town was totally dead. You know Greenville isn't exactly a hopping place after ten o'clock. As they say, the sidewalks roll up at nine."

She was right about that. "Thanks. If I have any more questions, I'll give you a call."

"Sure. That's fine," Carmella said. She turned to her friend. "I hear there's a great blues band at Ground Zero Blues Club. Why don't we plan on going there tonight? No telling who we might run into."

"Good idea," Bitsy said as they walked away. "I love the blues. Harmonica players. They do it for me."

Tinkie grinned as they left. "Two ladies looking for fun."

"Indoor fun," I specified. "No outdoor, bug-biting, sandy, or sweaty fun."

8

We talked with a couple of patrons from the restaurant, but Bitsy and Carmella appeared to be the last people to see Marlon in town. He seemed to have walked into the night and disappeared. A lot like Jules. It was more than disturbing.

I called Coleman to see if he and Sheriff Nelson had come up with anything new, but they'd drawn blanks as well. And there didn't appear to be new leads. How did a movie star disappear in a small town?

We went back to the movie set to continue questioning the crew. Someone had to have seen something. Jules might not have been familiar with the river, but Marlon had grown up in the Mississippi Delta. He knew to beware. I asked several of the younger crew members about swimming in the dangerous water, and they told me that Marlon had sent a memo telling everyone to stay out of the river since Jules had disappeared.

"He wouldn't be swimming alone, would he?" Tinkie asked as we stood beside the water.

"No, but he might have been working on the raft." I pointed. Someone had put up the mast.

We checked with Ana, who said it had to have been Marlon who'd done the work before he disappeared. "He said yesterday he'd set the mast for a small sail. He was determined to have that raft ready to go," she said. "The idea of a documentary to publicize the feature film is a great idea, but no one was getting me on a raft in the middle of that river. I know how dangerous it can be."

I understood her reluctance. And judging by Tinkie's face, so did my partner. "Ana, has there been anyone making threats about the movie?" I asked.

"Only that Bilbo character and that bookstore woman. They have been all over it doing everything they can do to stop us. I don't get it. We're bringing thousands of dollars a day into town. Marlon told me to downplay it, so we have, but I'm worried. These people seem unhinged."

"In case you haven't noticed, some people just aren't very bright." I hated to be mean, but sometimes I couldn't stop myself.

"Who is that?" Ana asked, pointing to a woman walking toward us.

"That's Delilah LaRue," Tinkie said. "Head of the Mississippi Film Commission. I'm surprised you haven't met her."

"Marlon handled all of that."

Delilah waved. "I need a word with Marlon."

Tinkie and I kept silent. This was Ana's problem.

"He's not available right now. Can I help you? I'm Ana McCants." She held out a hand and gave a warm shake.

"I have some great news I wanted to share with him. The film commission has a grant for the documentary. Marlon assured us it would show Mississippi in a favorable light, and we're delighted to be a part of all this. The whole resurrection of Huck Finn and adventure on the river is a great idea."

"He's going to be so excited," Ana said, acting as if everything was perfectly fine. But what else could she really do? Grant money was on the line. And Marlon might show up at any minute.

Ana and Tinkie were talking nice with Delilah, but I saw double trouble headed our way. Bilbo and Mary Dayle were streaking toward us with a set of papers. This didn't look good at all.

"Halt all filming!" Lamar said as he shoved the papers at Ana. "This is a ruling that you must stop filming right now. This instant."

"Why?" I asked.

"Marlon failed to get the proper paperwork signed," Bilbo said gleefully. "He screwed up big time. And you have to stop everything, or I'll have the sheriff impound your cameras and equipment."

"Are you insane?" Delilah asked them. "This movie is great for Greenville and the whole state. What the hell are you trying to do? We've worked hard for years to attract film companies to our area."

"Then you're a stupid woman," Bilbo said. "This is what happens when you put a woman in charge of anything. This film is going to make Mississippi the laughingstock of the world."

"What?" we all said together.

"What are you talking about?" Delilah demanded.

"This isn't about how heroic people were able to save drowning folks, it's about how certain people were left on the levees." Bilbo cleared his throat. "You know, so they'd be there to work when the floodwater receded. It's another poke at Mississippi and the past."

"Yeah," Mary Dayle echoed him, though the look on her face struck me as curious.

Tinkie's nostrils flared and her blue eyes sparked lightning. "If that's what happened, then maybe that's what needs to be told."

"Another bleeding heart, aren't you, madam?" He thrust his face at Tinkie.

Oh, how I wanted to throat punch him. I settled for coughing right in his face.

"I'd love to see the raft," Delilah said, trying to divert us all away from Bilbo.

"It's down here." I was just as eager to get away from the dotard.

"The riverboat is beautiful," Delilah said. "I heard some of the paddle wheelers rescued a lot of residents."

"They did," Ana said. "The current was so strong. And when the levee broke and all that water whooshed into the land, a lot of folks were caught unprepared."

We walked out onto the little dock to allow Delilah to admire the raft. With the mast set it looked more impressive.

"As long as the weather is good, that should be some adventure." Delilah bit her lip, clearly hankering for an invite.

"Want me to ask Marlon if there's room for you?" Ana asked.

"Would you?" Delilah jumped up and down. "I would

die. I would just die to participate, even for such a short distance."

"I'll be sure and tell Marlon when I see him," Ana said.

"And when will that be?" Delilah pressed.

"Should be soon. I'm not exactly certain where he is, but he shouldn't be gone long."

"Do you mind if I wait?" Delilah asked. "I want to give him the good news myself. It's a substantial grant."

"You're giving that renegade troublemaker state money?" Bilbo demanded. "My tax dollars?"

"It's federal money, Mr. Bilbo. So back off and mind your own business." Delilah really had his number. The grin on my face faded, though, when Bilbo, face red with anger, stepped toward Delilah and pushed her so hard she fell off the dock and into the river. She went down and disappeared.

"Oh, no!" Mary Dayle wailed. "Get her out right away. It's dangerous. Find her."

"Where is she?" Tinkie asked, rushing to the other side of the dock to look. There wasn't a sign. Not even bubbles. The film commission employee had totally disappeared into the murky water. For a long moment we stood frozen. Finally, I whipped out my phone and called 911.

"We're at the movie set on Lake Ferguson. A woman was pushed into the water. She never came up. Send help now, please."

I hung up and began stripping off my boots and jeans. If I was going in to look for Delilah, I didn't need to be hampered by wet clothes.

"No!" Tinkie put a hand on my arm. "It isn't that deep. She should come up."

"But she hasn't."

Right at the place she fell in, the water churned, and Delilah popped into the air, gasping and cursing like a sailor. "Lamar Bilbo, you wait until I get out of here. I'm going to beat your ass so thoroughly you'll never forget it."

I leaned down from the dock to offer Delilah a hand. The bottom in the low areas was mushy and gross. Slimy weeds were on top of her head and hanging in her face. The beautiful suit she'd been wearing was ruined.

Bilbo backed away from the dock. He held Mary Dayle's arm and moved her with him. He kept looking over his shoulder. He was going to take a runner as soon as he got off the dock.

"Stay your ass right there," Delilah warned him. "If you run, I'll charge you with attempted murder. And you, Mary Dayle McCormick, as an accomplice."

"I didn't do anything," Mary Dayle said truthfully.

"You have crappy taste in the people you hang out with. That's a crime in my book."

Tinkie turned away to hide her smile and I had to bite my cheek to hold back the laughter. Delilah took my hand and I braced for her to find footing on a piling and climb back onto the dock. It was slow work, but I got her to safety. We were both panting from exertion.

"Thank you, Sarah Booth," she said.

Thick, oozy mud covered her shoeless feet. Her glam shoes had been sucked off her feet. Her blouse was ripped and torn. She looked like she'd been in a battle with Neptune. "Call the sheriff," she said to me.

"I already did. And 911. Are you okay?"

"There was something in the water with me. Something grabbed at me. It was cold and disgusting." She looked over the edge of the dock cautiously.

"Probably slimy weeds," I said. "The lake bottom is sandy in some places but oozy in others." I personally hated the feel of slimy mud between my toes.

"No, it wasn't like that. It was big and it nudged me. Like fingers sliding over my skin. I don't know what it was, but it scared me silly." She walked closer to the edge of the dock to look into the water.

"Oh, my. Holy shit." It was the soft way the words slipped from her that made me rush to stand beside her. I didn't know Delilah, but she didn't dress like a person who cursed a lot.

I joined her, peering into the murky water. I could see something caught in a slow eddy. It swirled, floating ever closer to the surface, a flash of white in the brown water. It took me a moment to recognize what it was, but when I did, I backed up instinctively. "No!" I couldn't think of anything else to say.

"What?" Tinkie demanded. "What are y'all having a fit over?" She came to the dock's edge. When she saw it, she gasped. "That isn't right. Is this a joke?"

The understatement of the year. We all watched in horror as a severed foot floated on the water. It spun gently in a soft current, the toes pale lavender and the ankle bone raw and jagged.

Ana McCants joined us. Her exhalation was an expletive. "What in the name of Satan is going on here? Get a net from the riverboat," she said. "Hurry."

I rushed to the riverboat and got a net on an extension pole from the utility closet. I hurried back to the dock, where they all stood transfixed by the severed limb swirling gently in the current. I quickly had it in the net and hauled it up on the dock. It made a terrible, sodden plop when I dropped it out of the net. I couldn't look at it. It was just too awful.

"Find something?" Sheriff Nelson came toward us, seemingly amused at us all on the dock like zombies. He was taking in Delilah in her sodden disarray and the rest of us standing, stunned. Maybe he thought we were stoned. "Everyone okay?"

"Everyone but him," Tinkie said, pointing at the foot. The size of it clearly indicated it belonged to a man. A tall man. "I think it may be Jules Valiant. Or at least part of him."

"Could it be Marlon?" Ana choked back a sob. "No! It can't be."

"What the holy hell?" Sheriff Nelson said. "Now someone tell me how this happened."

No one standing on the dock had any answers for Sheriff Nelson. And no one said what we feared the most. That we had found a part of one of our missing men. Either Jules Valiant or Marlon Brandon.

9

Delilah, swaddled in clean blankets, was seated in the sheriff's office. Tinkie and I were waiting our turn to tell the same story we'd already told four times. Dread had set up residence in the pit of my stomach. One of the two men we'd been hired to find was likely dead. Bitten by something big, like an alligator. Or maybe chopped by a propeller. Whatever the cause of the severed limb, it was horrid. Coleman was there with Sheriff Nelson. He gave me a wink to cheer me up.

He came over to put his arm around me. "This is almost over, and I can tell you that it isn't Marlon. The foot has been in the water at least forty-eight hours," he said.

"Is it Jules the gaffer?"

"Maybe," he said.

"What cut his foot off? What could do that?" Boaters

were out on Lake Ferguson all the time. If Jules had accidentally drowned it was possible he'd floated into the deeper waters and been hit by a boat propeller. The boater might have thought it was a log or some other natural hazard.

"They're taking the foot to Zinnia for Doc Sawyer to examine. If he doesn't have any answers, they'll either take it on to Memphis or down to Jackson where there's more lab equipment to analyze the tissue and bone destruction."

"Great. More waiting."

"Patience is a virtue, Sarah Booth."

I didn't bridle at his gentle teasing because he was right and also because I was reminded of Aunt Loulane and the great love she'd shown me. She had a million adages and old sayings. "How long will it take Doc?" I asked.

"It shouldn't be forever. When this is done, we'll grab a bite and hang around to see if the sheriff gets any results."

"Excellent." I wouldn't wait for the sheriff to tell me. I'd call Doc Sawyer directly. He'd been my doctor since I was born, and he had a soft spot for me and Tinkie. More than once he'd patched us up from our misadventures.

At last Sheriff Nelson called me back and I repeated, once again, the sequence of events that had led to the recovery of the foot. Coleman was there and while he didn't interject anything, he gave me encouragement with glances and nods. Tinkie was up next, and Coleman and I waited for her. Oscar was going to join us for some food when we were done.

Sheriff Nelson thanked us and let us go. We slogged out of the sheriff's office, exhausted from a long day of emotional upheaval. When we stepped outside, I had no sense what time it was. I was a little shocked to see the sun moving down the western horizon. My stomach complained loudly.

Tinkie and I had picked up biscuits from Millie's, but we hadn't eaten since. I was all in for the idea of an early dinner. And a drink. A dirty vodka martini seemed like a necessity after the day I'd had.

Sheriff Nelson had given Coleman some information on the "official" search for Marlon, and he shared it with us over dinner. Nothing of any use had been found so far. When dessert was served, I excused myself and went outside to call Doc. He answered on the second ring. "How was the foot severed?" I asked.

"Shark."

"What?" I thought I'd misheard.

"Shark. I've never seen anything like it. Do you think someone transported that body part to Greenville and threw it out in the river?"

"I don't know. Surely there can't be sharks in the river. It's fresh water. Sharks are saltwater creatures."

"I did a little research," Doc said. "Bull sharks, one of the more aggressive and dangerous types, can survive in fresh water. In fact, it's been documented that one navigated from the gulf to St. Louis. It is possible there's a shark in the river and therefore in Lake Ferguson."

"This can't be true." I thought of Delilah floundering in the water by the dock. Sharks were sometimes known to hunt around areas where people swam.

"I think this foot had sunk to the bottom, but when the film commission woman fell in, she stirred the currents, and it floated up."

"If there is a shark, how will they drive it back to the Gulf of Mexico?" I asked.

"I'm not a shark wrangler," Doc said with a hint of humor. "You know who worked with marine life?"

"Who?"

"The bookstore owner in Greenville, Mary Dayle Mc-Cormick. She had a degree in marine biology. She's smart as a whip. It was when she was working on the big marine exhibit planned for Gulfport that her assistant was accidentally killed. She was never charged with anything, though there were plenty of rumors."

"That's right. I heard about this. Do you know how it happened?"

"He fell into a tank with a shark they were transporting. Didn't stand a chance. It was a huge scandal. Awful photos in the newspapers. You were likely up in New York."

There had been a time, after Aunt Loulane's unexpected death, that I'd avoided all news from the state of Mississippi. It was too painful. I believed I'd never return to my home, and I blocked everything related to Zinnia, the Delta, Dahlia House, and the entire state from my mind. Survival tactics.

"McCormick was never charged? Maybe she wasn't at fault."

"The gossip centered around the way she drove her employees, forcing them to work long hours. I heard the young assistant was exhausted from days of work and simply fell into the tank."

It was a fine line between being responsible for a death and contributing to one. "What happened to the marine exhibit?"

"There's one in Gulfport but they don't have sharks."

"And that's when Mary Dayle returned to the bookstore?"

"She did. Never underestimate her intelligence, Sarah Booth. She's set against this film. I don't know her reasons, but folks up here in Sunflower County are talking about it. A lot of the local residents think the film is going to mock them or make fun of them or reveal unpleasantries. Greenville is struggling to survive. No one wants bad publicity."

"She's not so opposed she'd bring a shark upriver, is she?"

"You'd best ask her that question," Doc said. "Just be careful. I don't think I can fix you and Tinkie if they cut you up for chum."

"Cheerful, Doc. Really cheerful."

He laughed. "Now I need to report to the sheriff. Don't let on I told you first."

"Not a problem," I said. "Thanks. I think." He'd given me a lot of information, but it was more disturbing than helpful. Coleman had been diving in that river looking for Jules. And now Marlon was missing, too. This would impact the ability to search for him.

Most importantly, how in the hell had a shark gotten all the way upriver to Greenville?

When I returned to the table, everyone knew I had news. They signaled the waiter for coffee and Coleman nodded. "Out with it, Sarah Booth. You look like you're going to pop if you hold it in any longer."

"I guess my poker face needs work."

"Just give up poker. You'll lose everything you own," Tinkie said. "Spill it."

I told them about the foot and the shark, and I didn't have to go on with the possible repercussions.

"How can we search for Marlon in the river now?" Tinkie asked. "No one should be in the water if we know there's a shark."

"It is going to complicate things." Coleman waved for the check. He was ready for action. My news about the shark had motivated him, and I was curious what he was up to. When we stepped outside into the falling dusk, I slipped under Coleman's arm.

"Ready to go back to Zinnia?" I asked.

"I need to speak with Sheriff Nelson first," he said.

Tinkie and Oscar drew abreast of us. "We're going home to Maylin," Tinkie said. "I've missed my baby."

"It's been a long day," I agreed. "Give her a kiss and hug from me and another from Coleman."

"Will do. Are you two okay to be left alone?" Tinkie teased.

"We are," Coleman assured her. "We'll be behind you shortly. We have horses to feed, and we'll stop by and pick up the critters. I know you're eager to get some sleep, so we won't be long."

"You're acting like an old man, Coleman," Tinkie said. "Be careful or Sarah Booth will be looking for one of those young movie stars."

"Not a chance," I corrected her.

"We'll settle this in Zinnia," Coleman said, trying to sound threatening but failing.

The Richmonds left together, and Coleman and I walked to the sheriff's office. It was a lovely evening, the sky shaded from lavender to navy, with the stars popping brightly in the darker hues of the night. A half-moon hung over the river. I couldn't help but feel a chill when I thought of Jules, bitten by a shark. And Marlon, missing in action.

"Did Doc say if the shark chomped the foot before or after the person was dead?" Coleman asked.

"He didn't. I didn't think to ask."

"He's certain it wasn't an alligator that maybe got him?"

"He said bull shark. Doc's pretty particular with his details. And no one is certain yet if it is Jules." I tried for a positive spin, but even I knew I was fooling myself.

"I heard stories of bull sharks running the river," Coleman said. "But I never heard of anyone being attacked by one."

"Will they cancel the dives to search for Marlon and Jules?" I asked, fingers crossed that Sheriff Nelson would do that once he learned of the lurking shark.

"I don't know. We'll see. I'm sure Doc's had a chance to talk to Nelson by now. I'd like to participate in the decision if they want my advice."

"And if they want mine, I'll be happy to chime in."

Coleman snuggled me close against him. "That won't be necessary. Our priority is to evaluate the risk to the divers against the possibility that Marlon—or Jules—is injured and alive somewhere. It's a lot to sort through for the best approach."

Coleman and I had come to a determination early in our romance. We would not lie to each other, and we would not try to boss each other away from danger. Law enforcement and private investigation were dangerous professions and getting more dangerous by the week. Heck, teaching grade school had become treacherous, but at least there weren't sharks in classrooms.

We caught Sheriff Nelson just as he was leaving to do a shore search with volunteers and Q-Beam lights. Those intense lights would pick up eyes in the dark. If Marlon was somewhere along the shore, they might find him. It was a long shot, but I couldn't argue against it. We had to try everything.

Sheriff Nelson motioned me to his private office. "Have you been hired to find Marlon?" he asked. "Did the senator hire you?"

"Not the senator. Actually, the insurance company for the movie hired us. They'll lose heavily if Marlon isn't found alive and able to finish the film. With the gaffer missing, too, it's not a good situation."

"The actor grew up around here. He knows better than to be in the river."

That was indisputable. "Do you think he fell in or went in voluntarily?"

"I think he was pushed. Just like the other one. I think there's a murderer on the set of this movie." Nelson didn't mince any words. "I can't make you and Mrs. Richmond leave the area, but I can tell you that it would make my job easier if you did."

"We have a case." I blew out a breath. "We'll be careful, and we won't get near the water. The whole shark business is insane. Did you know Mary Dayle McCormick was a marine biologist?"

"I know. I've actually called her to consult."

I wanted to react, but I stopped myself. Why on earth would he rely on a woman who'd publicly stated she intended to stop the film one way or another? Next he'd be hiring Lamar Bilbo to advertise the film.

"You think I'm being duped by Mary Dayle, don't you?"

"Are you?" I thought it best to answer with a question.

"No. But if anyone can help us, it will be her. She can advise us on when those sharks feed and the best way to avoid them. Or what to do if we encounter one."

"You're going to continue with the dives?" My heart sank.

"We have to. The foot indicates someone is dead, but there are two missing men. Maybe we can recover one alive, and I believe it will be Marlon."

"You really think Marlon might be alive?" It was difficult to contemplate the handsome actor dead. But if he was alive and had fallen in the water, Nelson was right. He needed to pull out all the stops and take help wherever he could get it.

Nelson nodded. "I do. Mary Dayle's expertise with marine life may give us the information we need to find Marlon. We can use her."

It was a cut-and-dried way to look at it. "Thanks. Coleman and I will go back to Zinnia so he can get some rest. I'm sure he'll be here early in the morning."

"I'm sure he will," Nelson said, waving me back into the main office. Coleman was waiting by the door and I joined him, recounting what Nelson had said as we drove back to Dahlia House.

10

In the morning Coleman had no time for a horseback ride, but I took off on my fine black gelding as soon as he was gone. I needed the brisk morning air to clear my muzzy head. And to help me firm up my resolve to do whatever was necessary to find the missing men. My faith in Coleman's abilities was on an equal par with my fear of a predator shark's lust for human body parts. I feared the foot belonged to Jules, and if so, he was dead. Marlon's disappearance was confounding and scary. Tinkie and I needed to find him—now. But we had so little to work with.

When Tinkie got up, I'd talk with her and express my anxieties. She found the bright side of things and always made me feel better.

The day had bloomed into another spring bonanza. The

warming earth left no doubt that old man winter was in the rearview. I was untacking my horse and rubbing him down when my phone rang. Hollywood. It had to be the insurance company that had hired us.

Sure enough, Jane Bernardo had drawn up a contract for us and was sending it via email. Tinkie and I were to sign it, scan it, and send it back. Then our first payment would be sent to the bank. I wondered if I should tell Jane what we'd learned, but I didn't. We'd gather more facts first. If she knew about the shark, it was possible she'd cancel the insurance and then the movie would be dead if Marlon happened to be found. I had to balance the truth with the potential consequences. It wasn't fair to Ana, the other backers, and the crew to kill the film. At least not yet.

Sweetie Pie and Pluto were eager to jump in the car. They loved going to Tinkie's. In fact, it seemed they'd rather be there than at home. But I didn't begrudge them time with Pauline and Maylin. The nanny took them for walks around the grounds of Hilltop. She played ball with Sweetie Pie. And Maylin lavished them with smiles and gurgles. It was better than being alone.

"What's on the agenda for today?" Tinkie asked when the animals were inside, and we were in the car.

"We're paying a visit to Senator Brandon."

"Why?"

"I need to know how much Marlon knew about the river, the dangers, etc. And if there is anywhere else he might be. Maybe the senator is covering for him."

"Okay. We'll stop by the movie set first to see if they've heard or found anything."

"Good plan!"

"I hate to say it, Sarah Booth, but I'm starving. Could we grab a bite first?"

Time really was of the essence, but sustenance was equally important. "Why don't you go down to the set and talk to Ana, see if there's any new information? I'll run over to Bluebeard's and pick up some breakfast to go. I'll call in some BLTs, and we can eat them on the way out to the Brandon estate."

"Perfect. And some coffee."

"You got it."

Bluebeard's wasn't a breakfast place, but it was open and they served sandwiches and coffee. I called in my order as I walked toward the bar. I was hungry, too, but I felt pressured to get on the road to the Brandon plantation.

I pushed open the door of the bar as my phone rang. Hollywood again. I told the insurance agent I had nothing new to report. They were terribly antsy about the film and if they were going to lose millions. And they made me even more anxious. I went to pick up my order and pay when I noticed a beautiful woman sitting alone at the bar, drinking out of a golden cup. She waved me over.

Her chestnut hair sparkled with golden highlights. Huge blue eyes gave her pale face a look of innocence. She wore a formfitting blue dress and watched me with an unflinching gaze.

I walked over. When I stood beside her, I realized she had no reflection in the mirror behind the bar. Jitty! Damn it. And I'd almost talked to her—the perfect way to demonstrate insanity in public.

"Come outside," I hiss-whispered to her. "Now."

"I can't. I'm waiting for someone."

"Another haint?" I was talking softly without moving my lips. Enough of this and I could be a ventriloquist.

"No, Miss Smarty-Pants. A god. Odin, if you must know. We drink together often, and I offer him wisdom. Sometimes even a glimpse of the future."

"Delusions of grandeur, much?" I asked.

She sipped from her golden goblet and a drop of crimson red wine trembled on her lower lip before she caught it. She spoke with great dramatic skill:

"River! that in silence windest
Through the meadows, bright and free,
Till at length thy rest thou findest
In the bosom of the sea!
Four long years of mingled feeling,
Half in rest, and half in strife,
I have seen thy waters stealing
Onward, like the stream of life . . ."

"Hold off!" I recognized the Henry Wadsworth Longfellow poem. "That's about the River Charles, not the Mississippi," I told her.

"A wise person can apply beauty and poetry wherever he sees the need."

"What is going on with you?" I was trying hard not to draw attention to myself, but the barkeep was giving me the hairy eyeball. He poured a cup of coffee and brought it over to me.

"You okay?" he asked.

"Of course. Just gathering my thoughts. I have a few lines in the movie and I'm trying to calm myself and get it right."

"You're rehearsing to be in the movie?" He was relieved.

"Yes, sorry. I know I must look like a kook."

"A little," he agreed. "I thought you were arguing with yourself."

"Nope. I'm not that far gone. Yet." I gave him a perky smile. I gave Jitty a glare in the mirror. It only came right back at me.

"Have the coffee, on the house," he said as he went to see about a table of businessmen.

I turned back to Jitty. I had to get out of there before they called for a straitjacket. "And just what are you and Odin up to? And who are you?" I knew a bit about Odin, the Norse god who had his finger in a lot of pies, including poetry, healing, and battle.

"I am called Saga, protectress. As a water deity, I guard the rivers and streams, the waterways. With my poetry, I help the flow of emotions that water represents."

"Your poetry?" I sipped my coffee. "Right. You're a poet like I'm van Gogh. You stole that poem from a famous poet."

"Imitation—or larceny—is the highest form of flattery." Jitty, as usual, was unrepentant.

"Are you here to tell me something?"

"Even if I were I couldn't say so. You know the rules."

"No, I don't. That's the problem. I think you make them up to suit yourself." My nerves were frazzled and Jitty was stepping all over them.

"That's the number-one rule," Jitty said, and then cackled. It was good no one could hear her but me or otherwise she'd be burned for a witch with that laugh.

"What do you want?" I had to address her issue, or she'd follow me to the set and then I'd be in real trouble, talking to thin air in front of Tinkie.

"Even the creatures of the water need protection," she said.

I didn't have time for a lecture on pollution of the water-ways by herbicides and fertilizer, or Jitty's particular dislike of loud motorboats and Jet Skis. Thinking about it, I realized she did have a real concern for the waters of planet Earth.

"Who are you meeting?" I asked. I didn't for a minute believe it was Odin.

She nodded toward the door. "Him."

An old man in a cloak and pointed hat came toward us. He looked like a wizard. "Is that Odin?"

"He seeks to consult me about the future. Saga is a seeress."

I didn't doubt that Jitty could see the future. And the past. But whatever she saw, she'd never share with me. It was time to boogie. I picked up the bag of breakfast and coffees. I had to get out of there. The barkeep was watching me and so were the businessmen. "If you want to talk to me, come outside."

"Maybe later," she said. "It's not every day I get to drink with a Norse god."

Another golden goblet had magically appeared on the bar. She picked it up and handed it to Odin. In a moment there was a flash of golden light and the sound of rain pummel-ing the roof. The sound was almost deafening, and when I looked out the window, I saw the sunny day was now gray. A storm had been predicted but it wasn't raining yet. I'd been victimized again by Jitty's sound effects from the Great Be-yond. As I looked at the sky, it was another reason to get after finding Marlon and Jules, or at least their remains.

When I turned back to the bar, it was empty. Jitty and Odin were gone, and I hurried out the door before the bar-tender could ask me any questions. One day, Jitty was go-ing to be the death of me.

11

I heard the altercation at the set before I was able to visually track it down to a cluster of angry people behind one of the trailers.

Ana, Bilbo, and Mary Dayle McCormick were arguing while Sheriff Nelson looked on. Tinkie was also a rubber-necker to the fight, which looked as if it might come to fisticuffs. My money was on Ana. She was tiny but tough.

I trotted toward the arguing, picking up some shouted phrases as I drew closer. The entire film crew had stopped work and was gathered on the fringes watching. Several of the crew looked as if they wanted to punch Lamar Bilbo into next Sunday.

"This paper right here states they have to stop filming,"

Bilbo said to the sheriff. "You're required by law to enforce this. They don't have the proper permits."

Bilbo and Mary Dayle had tried this once before. But now the sheriff was looking at their documents.

"We have every permit we need," Ana countered. "This," she slapped the paper in his hand, "is total bullshit and you know it. Sheriff, this is absurd."

"If you allow them to continue filming knowing the paperwork is not in order, you and the film company will be liable for any damages if something goes wrong," Mary Dayle warned the sheriff and Ana. "The reason there are laws governing these things is to protect people."

"More like to give asshats the power to stop what they don't like," Ana said. "We have scenes to shoot today, and we're moving forward."

"What happens if your big star is dead?" Bilbo asked. "What are you going to do then?"

"We'll cross that bridge when we come to it," Ana said, but her face had paled, and her voice broke. She was worried about Marlon, too. Maybe it was personal, but there was certainly a business angle to her worry. Without Marlon, the money already spent would be lost, unless they recast the film and started over. But who would care enough about this Mississippi story to pump more money into it?

"Sheriff, it's your duty to stop the filming," Bilbo said.

"Is it now?" Nelson asked. He didn't cotton to being ordered about by Lamar Bilbo.

"Ms. McCants, I need to see your permission slips." Nelson wasn't thrilled with his job at the moment. "Let's get this done. I have a manhunt to organize."

"Marlon had all the paperwork," Ana said. "When we

finish shooting today, I'll check at the B and B to see if I can find it."

"You have to stop her now," Bilbo said. "Now."

Nelson sighed. "Ms. McCants, I need to see that paperwork now or I'll be forced to temporarily shut you down until I see it."

I hadn't seen Senator Brandon approach, but when I realized he was bulldozing his way across the set, I quickly understood that the thundercloud on his forehead was as dangerous as the gray, churning sky had become. Jitty was hanging out with Odin, but Zeus was about to throw some lightning bolts. I looked around to find the nearest cover if the clouds opened up.

"Nelson, ignore these fools," he ordered. Looking at the sheriff's face, I realized he didn't like being bossed by Brandon any more than Bilbo.

"Stay out of this, Brandon," Bilbo said. "Your grandson is going to make fools out of my town. I won't have it. He pretends this is all about an action thriller, but I know he has an agenda. An agenda that makes the old planter families look like murderers."

"You have lost your mind, Lamar," Brandon said with restraint. "Now get off this set and let these people work before it starts to rain."

"Sheriff Nelson," Mary Dayle said. "Do your duty or risk the ire of the voters."

"Mary Dayle, I don't know how Lamar Bilbo hoodwinked you into participating in his vendetta against the Brandon family, but wise up. You're being used. I'm going to give Ms. McCants the opportunity to bring me that paperwork at the office, but I want both of you off this set and don't come back. You want to complain about the film crew, you come to me."

"This is public property," Bilbo said. "You can't order us off a public space."

"Maybe not, but I can arrest you for aggravating the snot out of me." Nelson reached for his handcuffs and brought them out. "Leave on your own, or you'll leave in the back of my squad car."

Bilbo stepped back. "This isn't over," he said.

"Yes, it is. And you're not innocent here, Bilbo. If Ms. Delilah decides to press charges against you for assault, I'll be only too happy to lock you up. Now scat!" He waved his arms and Bilbo backed up again. Mary Dayle backed away with him.

Ana signaled for me to come over. When Bilbo and Mary Dayle were fifty yards way, she grasped my wrist tightly. "Any word on Marlon?"

"No." It was best to be blunt. "He seems to have disappeared without a trace." I didn't want to continue, but I did. "It isn't looking good."

"Did the shark get him?" Ana sounded almost hysterical.

"We don't know. We're doing everything we can," Tinkie added.

"I need to talk to Senator Brandon," I said, but I realized I was too late. The senator had disappeared.

"Ms. McCants," the sheriff said, "you have to stop filming. I'm sorry, but without the proper paperwork I can't risk the city or county being responsible for any accidents."

"We did that paperwork," Ana said. "Marlon has the copies. Why isn't it on file with the city or county?"

"That's a good question," Nelson said. "Likely the answer

is Bilbo. His family has a lot of ties to local officeholders. A lot of favors given and taken."

"You think he stole it?" Tinkie asked.

"I'm not making an accusation. I'm just mentioning a possibility. I'll check it out." He sighed. "How could something as fun as a movie turn into this kind of nightmare?"

"Sheriff, do you think there's anything to Bilbo's concern that the movie will make certain families look bad?" I asked.

"Folks died during the flood. People left stranded on the levees suffered. There was talk it was deliberate, to keep the local pool of labor from leaving. If that's true, today it would be a murder or at least manslaughter charge. Back then . . . I don't know about the movie or whether Marlon is trying to stir up trouble from the past. The Brandon family profited from the flood. That's something Marlon should take into account."

Ana stepped forward, her face flushed. "We've said it again and again. There is nothing in this film that should upset locals. Wait here. I'll get the script I have and show you."

"I thought Marlon was keeping the script a secret," I said.

"He is. But I need an idea of what's coming so we can plot out the least expensive way to shoot. Scenes with the same background, setting, etc., are shot out of sequence."

It made sense. "So why wouldn't Marlon allow other people to see the outline of his script?" Tinkie asked.

"Because no one likes to be bullied by people who might want to restrict their right to tell whatever story they choose to tell. Bilbo is a prime example of someone who wants to control the narrative," Ana said. "He only wants what he likes or believes to be out there for public consumption. He's the worst kind of hall monitor."

I didn't disagree with her, but it would be so much easier to just show Bilbo and Mary Dayle that their precious family histories weren't going to be skewered. Now it was going to cost the movie several days of sorting out paperwork. Unless we found Marlon safe and sound and he had the necessary copies of it.

"We're going to interview the cast and crew about Marlon's activities last night," I told Ana. "You look for those papers." We weren't moving fast enough. None of us.

"Do you think Marlon is still alive?" Ana was about to cry. "We're finished if something has happened to him."

"There's no evidence he isn't," Tinkie said soothingly. "Let's focus on that and keep the movie going."

"Thank you both. I'm so glad the insurance company hired you two to find him. The locals will talk to you. If he is safe and doing God knows what, you can tell him that I will personally kill him. As soon as the film is done."

I didn't blame Ana at all, and I didn't take her threat seriously. She was frustrated and worried. The knowledge that a shark had bitten someone's—presumably Jules's—foot off was terrifying to everyone.

It didn't take long to talk with the cast and crew. There were plenty of them, but most of them had been hanging out together, drinking, when Marlon and Jules went missing. They'd seen Marlon having dinner and talking with the young women, but they hadn't thought anything about it and had gone on to party among themselves. It was a daily routine for most of them. The few exceptions were early to bed, early to rise folks who'd returned to their various hotel or camper quarters. No one on the set late had seen anything unusual or suspicious. None had been threatened in town by any locals. They were as puzzled about what had happened to the star as we were.

"This doesn't make sense," Tinkie said. "He's there one minute and gone the next."

Unless he'd stumbled in the water and the shark had eaten him. I didn't say that, though. No point in painting that mental picture.

"What next?" Tinkie asked.

We'd settled at a small picnic table that was part of the Lake Ferguson recreational area. The movie set was north of us, and we were blocked from their view by tents and trailers.

"Let's go find the senator. He may know special places where his grandson could be."

"Seems like he would have said something earlier," Tinkie said. "He's not helping Marlon if he knows where he is and doesn't say. If this film is shut down, it will probably never get made. Since the Brandon family is featured prominently as heroes, that would be a bad thing for the senator."

She was right, but I didn't have any other suggestions. We could canvass the businesses in town, but that seemed a waste of time. Word was out all over Greenville that Marlon was missing. If someone knew something about the actor surely they would have come forward. It did remind me to ask Ana to offer a reward, or perhaps the senator would. This was the perfect reason to visit the Brandon plantation.

"Let's get on the road." I stood up and turned to face the movie set. "Look," I said to Tinkie. Senator Brandon and

Lamar Bilbo were in a heated discussion behind one of the trailers.

"What the hell?" Tinkie said. "They look like they're going to kill each other."

She wasn't wrong about that. Both men were red in the face and gesticulating with their hands in a wild fashion. Any minute one might grab the other's throat. "I guess the senator is sick of Bilbo interfering."

As we watched, Bilbo stomped off. But not for long. He met Mary Dayle on the set where filming had stopped. She was in a heated set-to with Ana. "What the hell now?" Tinkie asked.

We were about to go find out when a young man called my name. I looked at Tinkie. "See if you can get Mary Dayle to leave. I'll take care of this."

"Sure thing." Tinkie was off on her mission.

"What can I do for you?" I asked the young man who was dressed in clothing from a bygone era. Obviously, he was one of the cast members of the movie.

"That woman down there—the one trying to kill the movie. She was with Marlon the night he disappeared. I heard them. He was working on the raft and she showed up, kind of sneaking onto the set."

"Sneaking?" It was a loaded word.

"That's what it looked like to me. She didn't make a sound and kind of ambushed Marlon. He was on the raft; she was on the dock. They were arguing."

"About what?"

"I don't know. I was coming out of that trailer up on the south end. I could see the dock and raft, but I wasn't close enough to hear."

"Are you one of the local actors?"

"Yes. I have a bit part. Marlon said I was pretty good. He encouraged me, and this movie could be my big break."

"If Mary Dayle and Lamar are able to stop the film, you won't get your chance."

"That's right. Not a lot of film companies come to Mississippi. I write, too. Marlon was going to read one of my scripts and evaluate it for potential. He said if it was good, he'd help me. We have to find him."

"What's your name?"

"Robert Davis, but I go by RoDa. That's going to be my professional name."

"Just RoDa?" I couldn't help it. I remembered when I was mulling over stage names and a million different aspects of my big dream to be on Broadway. I'd never achieved my goal, but I still had all the memories and joy of those heady years of dreaming.

"I want to be iconic. One name is enough."

"I wish you the best of luck, RoDa. How about I get your phone number? I think Sheriff Nelson will want to speak to you."

"I'm not sure about talking to the law. That's why I sought you out."

"If what you tell Nelson helps us find Marlon, then you'll be a real-life hero. That could only help a film career."

His brow cleared. "You're right. I honestly want to help find Marlon. Not just because he's helping me, but because he's a decent guy. His word is good."

RoDa's testimonial touched me—something I hadn't anticipated. My jaded view of movie stars and Hollywood almost tripped me up. Everything I'd learned about Marlon led to the conclusion he was a decent guy with a story he passionately wanted to tell. Had someone harmed him because of that story? There were questions I needed to ask.

I took RoDa's information and texted it to Sheriff Nelson. When I looked down at the set, Tinkie seemed to have everything sorted. The film crew had disbanded with some of the cast and crew headed toward downtown Greenville. Mary Dayle and Lamar had been successful in blocking filming, at least for today. I joined my partner, who rolled her eyes.

"I didn't believe Sheriff Nelson would actually stop the movie, but he did."

"He might not have had a choice," I pointed out. "Mary Dayle and Bilbo have some power in town, it seems."

"Bilbo is a blowhard, but Mary Dayle has plenty of brains. They call her the boss of the Literary Mafia."

I had to laugh. It was an unlikely juxtapositioning of words. "What? She whacks people who use adverbs improperly?"

Tinkie chuckled. "Always the clown, Sarah Booth. No, Mary Dayle seems able to get the biggest literary names to come to her store to do book signings. People have Bake-Offs and prepare cuisine to match the featured book and author. It's a big deal."

"But that's a nice thing, isn't it?"

"Not if you're one of the other bookstores in the area. She snags all the bestsellers and big names. She sells all the books. She makes money and the other bookstores suffer."

"Exactly how is it she manages to procure the big names?" I wasn't seeing this as a crime.

"Blackmail and bribes, from what I've heard."

"We need to prove that if it's true. She wants to shut down the movie. Maybe we want to shut down her store."

"Good plan," Tinkie said. "I know just the person to ask."

"Me, too. Mary Dayle McCormick. Evidently she had a fight with Marlon right before he disappeared."

"You talk to Mary Dayle, and I'll call Janet Malone and Sandra O'Day. If there's been any funny business with booksellers having authors sign, they'll tell us."

"And all the juicy gossip to boot." The two authors Tinkie mentioned were former clients. Janet was still dating our close friend Harold. I was all in for that relationship. She made Harold laugh.

12

The bookstore was not in the downtown area but on a tree-lined street of older homes. Solid, serene, perfect for those who indulged in reading. I parked and left Tinkie in the car still on the phone with Janet Malone. Mary Dayle was behind the counter, and that surprised me.

"So, a private investigator who reads," Mary Dayle said. "How shocking."

"A sarcastic bookseller. Equally shocking," I replied. Despite her crankiness, there was something about Mary Dayle that I liked. She was sharp, and almost funny.

"Looking for a book on how to accessorize blue jeans?" she asked.

"I'm not really interested in fashion," I said.

"Oh, do tell!"

I had walked right into that one. "I have some business questions for you. Since you've made it your job to oversee the filming of a movie, I thought I'd oversee your business as a bookseller."

"Do go on." She lounged against the counter.

"How do you get all the big-name authors to come to this store?"

"Let me see. How do I do that?" She held her pinky against her lips like Dr. Evil. She was having a blast with me. I looked out into the parking lot hoping Tinkie would come inside soon.

"Do you blackmail them?"

"Most of the time." She smiled. "Sometimes I resort to physical threats."

She was having way too much fun with me. "I'm serious, Ms. McCormick. There are rumors that your tactics are unethical and likely illegal."

"And the spreaders of these *rumors* would be whom?"

I shrugged. "I'm not at liberty to disclose my sources."

"And I'm not stupid enough to fall for that old tactic. What are you doing here?"

"Looking for leverage." I put it out there.

"At last, an honest answer."

"Why are you so opposed to this movie?"

"I'm opposed to the people of Mississippi being sold a pig in a poke." She dropped her gaze, which made me wonder what her real motive was.

"And you're certain that's what Marlon Brandon is up to? Shooting a mega-million-dollar movie just to make the state look bad?"

"I love Mississippi," Mary Dayle said. "And we've been on the receiving end of a lot of bad publicity for exactly the same things that happen in other places."

I started to jump on that with both feet, but she held up a hand, stopping me.

"I'm not saying the things that happened here are right, but they happened in many other places. Those places have been allowed to heal."

There was an element of truth in what she said. "Citing that bad things happened in other places is no excuse for what state and national elected leaders allowed to happen here. And you're hanging out with a man who is the walking epitome of what's wrong here."

"No one controls who I associate with or what I do."

Normally I would support that stance, but Lamar was beyond the pale. "Exactly how did you avoid being charged with your assistant's death when the shark bit him in half?"

Mary Dayle turned white. I'd landed a well-placed blow. "How dare you?"

"You can dish it out, but you can't take it," I relentlessly pressed her.

"I had nothing to do with my assistant's death. He was told to stay away from the tank. I have no idea what he was trying to do when he fell in. The situation was investigated, and I was absolved of all guilt."

Those facts were true, as I understood the sequence of events. It was obvious that Mary Dayle still felt guilt, though. "Why did you quit your job and give up your work as a marine biologist if you were innocent?"

"Some bad things are so bad that the only way to survive them is to leave everything connected behind. That's what I had to do, and I'm not ashamed to admit it."

I unexpectedly felt for her. It was clear I'd ripped open an old wound. I couldn't stop now. "Are you involved with that bull shark in the Mississippi River now?"

That took the wind out of her sails—for about thirty seconds.

"Absolutely not!"

"The law officers believe Jules Valiant was killed by a shark."

"I heard that," she said. "But it has nothing to do with me."

"You were transporting a shark to Gulfport for an exhibit when your assistant died."

"That's true. That happened a long time ago, and I haven't been back to the coast since then. I don't even swim anymore. I was so disturbed by what happened that I gave up my identity, my career, a life that I'd worked hard to achieve."

"You came home to be a shark in the world of books and authors."

I thought it was a clever remark, but Mary Dayle laughed out loud. The color returned to her face, and she pointed to a chair. "Have a seat. I like you."

"I'm not so certain I like you," I said bluntly.

She waved me into the chair and went behind the counter to get two glasses and a bottle of Irish whiskey. She poured us each a shot and handed me a glass before she sat down across from me. "You want to know about my assistant?"

"No," I said, sipping the whiskey. "I'm more interested in the shark now swimming around in the Mississippi River."

"They have the ability to swim up from the Gulf," Mary Dayle said. She was relaxed in her chair, as if she were enjoying the conversation.

"I know they *can* do this. But I don't think this one did."

"What exactly do you think brought this shark to Greenville waters?"

"Not what, who," I countered. Before I could continue, the bookstore door opened and Tinkie came in.

Mary Dayle rose, fetched another glass, and handed Tinkie a libation. She took the third chair in the small reading cluster near the front window.

"Our hostess was just explaining to me how the shark got up here in fresh water," I said to Tinkie.

"Excellent. I have lots of questions," Tinkie said.

"Fire away. I don't know what really happened but I'm happy to talk about the needs and behavior of bull sharks," Mary Dayle said. "I'm what some would call an expert."

"Are you actually bragging about the creature that likely bit Jules Valiant's foot off and probably killed him?" Tinkie put into words the things I was thinking.

"I'm not bragging. I'm educated in marine science and sharks are part of that. I had nothing to do with that shark being anywhere close to Greenville, but I've heard people talking. That's the thing about a small town. Nothing is ever forgotten. I knew this when I moved back home from the coast to a failing business and the reality of selling most of the family land."

I'd walked a mile in those shoes. I came home from New York and faced a harsh set of financial facts. I'd sadly neglected my business in Mississippi, just assuming that somehow Aunt Loulane would take care of things. She did until she couldn't. I almost lost Dahlia House.

"How did that shark get all the way up here?" Tinkie asked.

"Either it swam—and bull sharks have been spotted all

the way to St. Louis before—or it was brought here and set loose."

"How would someone bring a shark that distance?" Tinkie asked.

"Two possible methods. In a cage behind a ship or in a tank over land."

"That doesn't sound healthy for a shark," I said.

"It isn't. They're wild creatures. They aren't meant to be exhibited or on display. I think the practice should be illegal. I quit my work because of the death of my assistant, but I was already fed up with the way marine animals are exhibited and displayed. I couldn't stand the idea of imprisoning these innocent creatures in tanks for the entertainment of fools. Believe it or not, I care about marine animals. It's why I studied them. I made the mistake of going for a big salary in a job I grew to loathe."

I wasn't certain I believed her, but she did sound sincere. "What can you tell me about the shark that bit off Jules Valiant's foot? And we do believe it's his foot."

"I saw the foot. My best guess is that this shark is a female, between eight and ten feet in length. She probably weighs in at four hundred pounds at least. If she's pregnant, she'll be even more aggressive, preparing her young for birth."

"What else do they eat besides feet?" Tinkie asked.

"Smaller sharks, fish, turtles, birds. They're aggressive hunters and will eat anything they sense is food."

"How long can they live?" I asked.

"A decade or more. Fourteen is an old age for one. If this shark is pregnant, she'll give birth in the summer. If her pups live, they will hunt in a pack."

"We have to get her out of here," Tinkie said. "If word

gets out, you know every redneck with a gun will be trying to shoot her."

I gave Tinkie a long look. I had a tender heart for animals, but sharks were predators.

"She may not be in this river by choice," Tinkie said stoutly. "If someone brought her here to use her as a pawn, she doesn't deserve to die, and I won't let that happen if I can stop it."

"She's right," Mary Dayle said. "The shark is innocent. It is only doing what sharks are designed to do. Swim and eat. It's up to us to capture and remove it."

"I had no idea they could survive in fresh water," I said.

"There are several species of shark that do fine with less salt concentration. They adapt well to fresh water and are in numerous rivers around the world. Keep in mind they have fifty rows of teeth. When a shark loses a tooth, the ones behind move forward to replace it and then new teeth are grown."

"Efficient killing machines," Tinkie said.

And Coleman and his buddies were in the river with this bad girl. "Do they attack unprovoked?" I asked.

"Sharks aren't moral or immoral. They swim and eat to survive. They don't know the difference between a dolphin or a human. They shouldn't be punished for doing exactly what nature designed them to do."

"If we can't figure a way to catch and remove that shark, they will kill it." I wasn't being dramatic.

"I know, but the mayor has asked us not to make a big issue about the shark until a plan has been put into action." Mary Dayle turned slightly away. "They want to kill Betty and gut her to see if any human body parts are still inside."

"Betty?" Tinkie asked.

Mary Dayle shrugged. "I named her. It helps to humanize her to the people who want to kill her."

Mary Dayle knew a lot about human nature as well as sharks.

"Do you know who brought Betty upriver?" I asked.

"I know you think I might have hurt Marlon or that gaffer, but I didn't. I will tell you, honestly, if I can find the person responsible for that shark, I would be happy to feed him or her to Betty." She gave such a wicked grin that I wanted to check how many rows of teeth she had.

"Thanks, Mary Dayle." I stood to leave. Tinkie was at the door before I could blink.

When we got outside, she looked at me. "Do you believe she's innocent about the shark?"

"Hell, no. Do you?"

"Not for a red-hot minute," she said. "If anyone brought that shark up here, she had a hand in it. She just knows too much and every fact she gave us was designed to make us more afraid of the river."

"Yep. She's working hard to destroy the film."

"But why?" Tinkie asked. "That's the only thing I don't get. Why is this so important to her?"

"I don't know yet, but I hope we find out."

13

Tinkie had just called Oscar for directions to the Brandon plantation when my phone rang. Coleman. I answered breathlessly. "Are you okay?"

"What's wrong?" he asked.

"Mary Dayle just gave us the lowdown on bull sharks, and I can't help but be concerned that you're playing Esther Williams to a shark."

"We're done for the day. That storm is slowly coming our way. I'm going back to Zinnia, so I'll pick up the critters and take care of the horses. I'll feel better if they're in a stall if it's lightning."

"Me, too. As long as someone is there to let them out if the barn gets struck."

"I can work from home. I've got reports to catch up on

and I need to write that speech for the sheriffs' association meeting. While I've got a minute, catch me up on what Mary Dayle said about the shark."

I filled him in. When he didn't react, I asked, "Did you see the shark?"

"No, but I did find something else."

The way he said it made my ears perk up. "What?"

"A stainless steel cage. One that could transport a shark upriver. It's designed to be hauled by a boat with the cage submerged."

I swallowed back an outraged reply but finally said, "Someone did bring the shark up here. This is deliberate. Whoever did this is guilty of murder." I knew it wasn't that straightforward but, in my book, the person who released a killing machine in an area where a movie was being filmed was responsible for what the shark did.

"I can't say for certain that the shark arrived in the cage, but it's a ninety-nine percent probability."

"Where's the cage?"

"We left it in the river. The boat that hauled it is long gone."

"Mary Dayle said the two ways to transport a shark are in a cage like that or in a tank like on an eighteen-wheeler."

"This was the easiest and less obvious method," Coleman said. "Someone is playing a very dangerous game. Who do you suspect?"

"Mary Dayle is the obvious answer. Maybe too obvious. Because of that, I'd say Lamar Bilbo. He has zero ethics, and he'd do anything to achieve his goals. I'm sure he's familiar with all the marine people Mary Dayle knows. He acts like he's nearly bankrupt, but I doubt that's the truth."

"Keep an eye on Mary Dayle, Sarah Booth. Did she

mention she was down on the Gulf Coast a week ago talking to the manager of the marine entertainment center? Sheriff Nelson told me about it."

"She did not. In fact she said she hadn't been back to Gulfport." And I hadn't pressed her. Dammit. "She's sly, isn't she?"

"I don't have any evidence, but she's an authority on sharks. The good and the bad. Who else would have thought of using a shark to halt production on a movie?"

"Do you think she has Marlon hidden somewhere?"

"Sheriff Nelson is getting a search warrant to go over her home and the bookstore. We'll know by the end of the day if he's there."

"Do you think you can catch the shark and take it back to the Gulf?" I was actually worried about the man-eater. I liked the shark a lot better than some people I'd recently talked to.

"We're coming up with a plan. There are several agencies offering to help. Some of them want to take it captive and put it on display."

"No!"

"That was adamant."

"Shooting it would be kinder, Coleman. I mean it. Putting animals in prison for stupid humans to gawk at them is worse than death."

"Don't tell anyone, sweetcakes, but I agree." He chuckled because he could clearly imagine the lightning shooting from my eyes.

"Sweetcakes? Forget you know that word. That was demeaning."

"Only a little. Now what are you going to do?"

"At long last we're going to the Brandon plantation to

see if the senator knows where Marlon might have gone."
I didn't say it, and I tried not to show it in front of Tinkie,
but a rising tide of anxiety sloshed around in my brain. No
one had seen even a hint of Marlon. He'd left two women
after a nice dinner and disappeared. Jules was likely dead
from a shark attack. The movie seemed cursed. And worst
of all was that Tinkie and I had nothing solid to investigate.

"Check the movie set. I heard they were loading up the
camera equipment."

"What?" Coleman's tip snapped me back to the moment.

"What?" Tinkie had rejoined me. "Wait, what?"

I put the phone on speaker. "We have to go down to the set
for a minute. Coleman says they're packing up all the equipment, calling it quits."

"Marlon hasn't even been gone twenty-four hours," Tinkie pointed out. "That's ridiculous."

"I'll bet Lamar is behind it." I was going to have to kick
him in the shins. Hard enough to lay him up for a few days,
the meddling asshat. "Gotta go, Coleman."

"Let's go." Tinkie grabbed my arm and tugged me toward
the car. "Next time we'll bring the Caddy. You drive all the
time. It isn't fair."

I wasn't worried about the fairness of driving. I pressed
the accelerator hard, and we spun out for the set. Just as
Coleman had said, the crew was packing up equipment.

"What's going on?" I asked.

"That old busybody blowhard has shut us down. The
company where we rented some of the cameras in Jackson
was called and they're on their way to pick them up." The
young man looked almost in tears. "We don't have tickets
or a way to get back to Hollywood."

"I can take care of that." Senator Brandon spoke from

behind us. He looked very worried. "You folks don't fret. I'll get a bus to take you to the New Orleans airport and I'll book direct flights back to Los Angeles—if that becomes necessary. Know that I'm going to fight this stupidity that Bilbo is pushing. I believe victory will be ours, but I understand if you want to leave since no one will be paid after today." He cleared his throat. "Until my grandson returns to finish his film."

"Senator, we'd love to speak with you."

"I'm going to Jackson to speak with my law firm. I intend to file an injunction against Bilbo to keep him away from this set."

"Maybe just speak to Sheriff Nelson," I suggested. "Seems like he could do that."

"I'd rather let my lawyer handle it. I've learned the benefit of legal representation in matters such as this. Perhaps we can talk tomorrow."

"That's good." It was another little twist of the worry knife in my gut. I didn't want to delay another day, but I had no choice.

"So where is that lowlife Bilbo?" Tinkie asked. She was wearing heavy Doc Martens boots. She should be the one to kick him in the shins.

14

In record time, the cast and crew drifted away from the set. The frenzy of activity had disappeared, leaving an eerie silence all around. Another few days of this and the movie would be permanently shut down due to cost overruns. We had to find Marlon, and fast.

"Let's grab a cocktail at Bluebeard's," Tinkie suggested. "We might find some locals who saw Marlon on his way to the raft. Since the senator is out of town, all we can do is canvass the people who are out and about in town late at night."

We pushed into the bar, which had a mellow atmosphere. The tables were filled with people eating sandwich specials and drinking iced tea or an alcoholic concoction. Tinkie and I took a seat at the bar.

"Any luck with your case?" the barkeep asked.

I didn't recall telling him we were working a case, but it was a small town. Gossip could spread faster than Covid. "Not too much," I admitted.

"I hear you're looking for Marlon Brandon," he said.

"We are. Without a whole lotta luck," Tinkie said as she plopped on a bar stool. "I'd like a vodka martini, dirty, with three olives."

"The same," I said. It was just one of those days. I couldn't shake the idea of Coleman flopping around in the river with that damn shark trailing him.

"What's our next move?" Tinkie asked.

"I'll call the insurance company out in LA and give them an update. Then we go to the Brandon plantation. I still believe the senator might know something about Marlon's whereabouts."

"Why do you say that?" Tinkie asked.

"He doesn't seem as frantic as I would be if my grandson had disappeared and a shark was hunting prey in the river. He's cool, calm, and collected."

Tinkie nodded. "It's possible he knows Brandon is safe and caught up in a romance doing the double nasty. You're right."

"If that's the case, then I'll bet the insurance company will sue him to recover our expenses."

"That's not the half of it," Tinkie said. "Big money is being lost every hour that movie isn't shooting. Rentals, salaries, food, hotel expenses—all of that will add up fast. I'm sure the cast and crew have contracts. They'll be paid up to a certain point no matter if the film is shut down. If Marlon is being irresponsible, he could be liable for all of it."

Marlon hadn't struck me as a lowlife loser or someone willing to put so many people's livelihoods on the line. I liked him, yet I wouldn't swear he wasn't at fault. He could easily be hiding at Muscogee Plantation, his grandfather's spread. We'd hoped to explore the place when we went to talk to his grandfather, but now could be an even better opportunity, with Senator Brandon out of town.

It seemed like I'd spent half my life trying to get to the Brandon property. Every time Tinkie and I tried to go, something interrupted us. This time, we would not be deterred. We finished our drinks and loaded up.

Tinkie had the directions, and she guided me perfectly. Five miles southeast of Greenville found us slowly traveling down a lonely tarmac road that ended in a gated driveway. A cast iron arch reading MUSCOGEE PLANTATION hung over the road. The gate was open, so we drove through. Only empty fields greeted us on either side of the narrow road.

"You would think they'd be out working the fields on a day like today," Tinkie said, pointing at the fallow soil.

"I don't think the senator has a huge interest in agriculture. Planting and reaping are for the hired hands. He probably leases the land."

"At one time Muscogee was an incredible operation," Tinkie said. "Oscar has books detailing the cotton produced per acre, the number of bales shipped downriver, the amount of labor. The number of enslaved people needed to harvest the cotton still makes me cringe."

I knew exactly how she felt. How were the settlers of this land able to convince themselves that owning, working, breeding, and selling human beings was justified in any way?

"Sometimes, I can look across the fields and see the ghosts of the field-workers." I couldn't confess about Jitty, but I did tell Tinkie about the haunted past that was always with me. "I watch them work, hear the field chants, the sadness and longing. It chills me to the bone."

"I know."

I barely coasted down the road that was now shale and sand. In the old days, oyster shells from the Gulf Coast would be crushed for driveways. Now that material was too expensive and hard to come by. "How far back is the house?" I asked.

"I haven't been here in ages," Tinkie said. "I came with my parents once, for a party. I was maybe five, so I don't have clear memories except the house was like a fairy tale. So beautiful and lights in all the trees. A small band played dance tunes from the 1940s and people in glittery evening gowns held champagne flutes, laughing and having fun. My father waltzed with me. I felt so grown up."

I shared the glow of Tinkie's memory with a twinge of melancholy. I felt as if I might drive off the ends of the earth into the past. At last, a line of tall narrow cedar trees came into view. They hid the house, but when I cleared them, the plantation was a vision of architectural opulence. Muscogee, named for a Native American tribe, showed nothing of the indigenous culture. The design was neoclassical. Balanced, symmetrical, and well maintained. The triple stories of the house concluded with a widow's walk. The design brought a birthday cake to mind.

"Do you think the senator will be mad at us for coming here?" she asked.

"Depends on whether he's hiding Marlon or not."

"True. Oscar was telling me that the senator has a reputation for pushing for what he wants until opposition collapses."

"He's a politician. I think that's in the DNA."

She laughed. "What's the worst he can do?" she asked. "He can't kill us. Everyone knows where we are."

"Let's not tempt fate." I parked and killed the engine. We got out and walked up the flower-lined sidewalk to the front porch. Tulips, daffodils, paperwhites, and hyacinths were ready to meet the warming sun. Before we could ring the bell, the door opened. To our surprise, the senator stepped outside.

"Ladies, I was just going down to Jackson. I thought I was clear that I didn't have time to visit today."

In for a penny, in for a pound, as Aunt Loulane would say. "We're looking for Marlon," I said. "It occurred to us he might be hiding out here and you wouldn't even know. It's a huge place."

"You think Marlon is deliberately absent from his movie?" He sounded amused and a little angry.

"We have to check everything," Tinkie said. "The insurance company that hired us expects us to do no less. If you help us, it'll go a lot quicker."

"Marlon hasn't lived in the Greenville area in years. He went out to Los Angeles to make his fame and fortune. All of his friends have moved away or started businesses and families. I don't have the foggiest notion where he might be and, frankly, I don't believe he's voluntarily absent from the film set. I find that insinuation to be ignorant."

"Where do you think he is?" I asked.

"If I knew where he was, I'd drag his ass back to the movie set and make sure he didn't leave again. That's assuming he is not injured or dead. I hope he's being a fool. At least that would mean he isn't hurt."

"Women, gambling, drugs—which vice do you think he's indulging?" Tinkie asked. Man, she went at it head-on.

"I didn't say he was indulging in vices." Brandon was getting angrier.

"Then what do you think he's doing? Singing lullabies to sick babies?"

Something about Brandon had set Tinkie on edge and she wasn't holding back. She, as his social peer, could get away with it far easier than I could.

"You are a crass young woman." Brandon pierced her with a steely look. For an old man, he still had a lot of presence.

"I'm a realistic young woman," Tinkie countered. "And Marlon comes by hanky-panky honestly. Senator, there have been rumors for years that you were involved with one of your young aides. One of many liaisons, as I understand. I'm not judging, I'm just saying the apple doesn't fall far from the tree sometimes."

"Leave my property. Now."

Tinkie had pulled out the big guns of old gossip—stories we'd all heard but that had never been proven. "Can we have a look around?" I asked. The senator had lied to us, saying he would not be here. It stood to reason he might be hiding something. But why? Would he possibly try to destroy his grandson's film? Nothing about this case made sense. I just knew we needed to search for the actor. "You can send the butler with us to make sure we don't steal anything."

"I don't know what's gotten into you two, but look all you want. You won't find Marlon here. James!"

The butler was at his side in under ten seconds. "Sir?"

"Show them around the house, the outbuildings, the fields, the ditches. Wherever they want to look. And then make sure they leave the premises. I'll be very late getting in."

He went down the stairs with a firm step. A car whipped into the driveway and a chauffeur opened the back door for him. In a moment there was nothing but a dust trail.

"Ladies?" James stepped back from the door. "Go wherever you wish but I must accompany you."

"Sure." I didn't mind a hall monitor checking on us. "Let's try the bedrooms first."

We took our time and covered the house from attic to root cellar. We checked the sheds, the old barns empty of livestock but filled with hundreds of thousands of dollars of equipment. We walked the fields around the house. Nothing. If Marlon had been there, he was long gone.

"Have you seen Marlon?" I asked James. There was something about him that led me to believe he might answer truthfully.

"When the movie first came to town, he stopped briefly to see the senator. They don't always see eye to eye. They've never been close."

"Was there something specific?" Tinkie asked.

"Marlon asked the senator for papers about the flood. Senator Brandon wasn't interested in sharing the family story."

"But the Brandons were heroes, rescuing dozens of people from drowning. That's what the movie is about."

James didn't reply. I looked at Tinkie. She gave a slight nod. She felt it, too. James was withholding a lot.

"Do you know where Marlon might be?" I asked him.

"The young sir was fond of a few establishments down-river," he said slowly. "Vicksburg has some entertainment spots he used to take his dates to."

"Can you remember the names?"

"The Hornet's Nest and Jojo's. But I don't think he's there. You can call them. They know Brandon well and will tell you if he's around."

"Where do you think he might be?" Tinkie asked.

"If he doesn't want to be found, he could be over the river at the rice plantation on the Arkansas side. I don't have a sense he is willingly absent from the movie, though. This is a passion project for him."

"The Brandons own another plantation?" I was a bit surprised. The family had acquired thousands of acres of land and property.

James smiled but quickly dropped back to a neutral expression. "They do. And hunting lands. And downriver docks. After the levee broke, the family was able to purchase a lot of land that had been flooded. Prices were dirt cheap. It was the perfect time to buy, and the older generation acquired an excellent nest egg for future initiatives."

James was a wealth of information, and he was speaking of the Brandon family with great pride, as if he were part of it. I didn't get the sense that he was attempting to betray them in any way.

"Who farms the land now?" I asked.

"Agri-Co. It's a company that's buying up the farming rights to a lot of land. Senator Brandon doesn't care about farming. He needs the land to produce crops for money. He's very satisfied with their performance."

"That's good to know," I said. "Tinkie and I both have

land we lease. We'd like to find the best bargain." Which wasn't true at all. Sustainable farming was more important to me than a big paycheck. I wanted the land to be used, but not poisoned and destroyed.

"If you're satisfied with your search, I have duties to attend to."

"Thank you, James," Tinkie and I said in unison. We left Muscogee Plantation in lockstep.

When we were back in the car, Tinkie put a hand on my arm before I started it. "Did that feel strange to you?"

"It did. But I didn't grow up with a butler."

"James was friendly. Helpful, even. I get a sense he is very fond of Marlon. Proud of him, even."

"Yes, there seemed a strong bond. Especially since Marlon lives in Los Angeles and, as far as I know, never comes home. This movie is the first time he's been back in several years."

"Depends," Tinkie said. "All the cooks and maids at my house favored me. My mother was cold and bossy. She never said when something was done well or right, only criticism. Senator Brandon strikes me the same way."

"A lot of people are like that." I'd seen it in spades in the acting business. Artistic people were often super critical and seldom gave praise. It wasn't necessarily a system that got good results.

"Do you think we missed anything?" Tinkie asked.

"No." I was confident we hadn't. There wasn't a trace of Marlon in the house. If he'd even been by to visit his family home or share a meal or cocktail with his grandfather, there was no evidence of it. He'd booked a room in a downtown B and B—because he didn't have a desire to be at the plantation? Or to protect his grandfather from repercussions of the film he was making? Or maybe because his grandfather's criticism brutalized his spirit? It was impossible to tell anything from the few solid clues we'd unearthed.

"Let's get our hands on a copy of that script," Tinkie said.

"Marlon said he was only giving it out as necessary."

"Ana has the master copy. Maybe the dialogue isn't written, but the scenes will be on the page. No investor would contribute to a film without a solid idea of what it would be about."

She had a point, and Ana had offered to let Bilbo and Mary Dayle look at some versions of a script. "Call Ana and tell her we'll be by for a copy."

Tinkie made the call and instantly got pushback from Ana. It took Tinkie three minutes to sort out the situation before Ana agreed to give us copies of what she had. We arrived back in town and I whipped by the front door of the hotel where she was staying. She came out to give us a large envelope.

"I know you've been taking photos for that journalist friend of yours, Cece Dee Falcon. If you share this, I will sue."

"Cece has only given you good publicity," I said. I *had* planned to share the script with Cece and Millie.

"It's not good or bad publicity that concerns me. Marlon has been emphatic that no one sees the script or knows the twists and turns he has planned. Of course, I had to have the outline to get financial backing, but Marlon wants a more organic approach. I'm going to let you have this, but you are honor bound not to reveal any of it. Do you get it?"

"We do," Tinkie said, taking the envelope. "You have our word."

"Have you found any leads as to where Marlon might be?" Her abrasiveness gave way to worry.

"No," I said. "Have you heard anything from the sheriff or any of the search crews?" There were boatloads of volunteers searching downriver and all along the shores of Lake Ferguson.

"Your boyfriend spotted the shark while he was in the river." She said it like she was saying the coffee was good.

"What?" I was ready to jump out of the car. "Did they catch it? Did it hurt anyone?"

"Catch it?" She laughed out loud. "Catch it and do what with it?"

"Release it back into the Gulf," Tinkie said. "It's not the shark's fault it's here."

"Tell it to Jules Valiant and his family. The DNA matched. The foot belongs to Jules and the local coroner has ruled him dead. How would you like to plan a funeral for a foot?"

I blocked a burst of laughter with a snort and quickly turned my face away to hide my expression. I couldn't help it. It wasn't funny at all. Not at all. But it was the way she said it and the grisly image of a solitary foot in a coffin that was nearly my undoing. I struggled for control.

"That must be terrible for the family," Tinkie said, covering for my awfulness. She put a hand on my shoulder. "Don't cry, Sarah Booth. We're doing all we can to bring justice for Jules."

I leaned on my arm on the steering wheel. My face was hidden, and my shoulders shuddered, as if I were crying. Only it wasn't tears.

"Well," Ana said, backing off a little. "I'm counting on you to be discreet with this foot—I mean script."

It was nearly too much. I boo-hooed to cover my inappropriate behavior.

"We should leave," Tinkie said.

I pressed the gas and sped off. When I turned a corner and was out of sight, Tinkie whipped off her shoe and hit me with it. "You are a horrible person, Sarah Booth. Really! That. Was. Inexcusable."

I pulled to the curb and stopped the car before she knocked me unconscious. I looked at her and she bent over double, laughing. "See," I said. "It isn't funny but it's impossible not to laugh."

She wiped her eyes. "We are not nice people."

"I won't argue that."

"God is going to punish us."

"No, she won't," I countered. "It was spontaneous laughter. Sort of like spontaneous combustion but not so messy to clean up."

Tinkie hit me with her shoe again. "Just drive," she said. "I worry that your lack of social etiquette is going to wear off on me. Then it's a downhill slide into wearing my underwear on the outside of my clothes."

"I don't do that," I protested.

"Not yet, anyway." She pointed down the road and I put the car in motion. "Where are we going?"

"Let's head to an office printing store. We can copy that script so we each have one, then we can go home and read it. I hate to say it but we are striking out on every front." She bit her bottom lip, a sign she was frustrated or manipulating a man. This time it was frustration. "Marlon may be somewhere slowly dying, and we can't even find a lead," she said. "And we are horrible people. I need some Maylin affection to counteract laughing about a funeral for a—"

"Don't say it. You'll set me off again."

"Just drive." She leaned back in the seat and tilted her head. "You exhaust me, Sarah Booth. There are days when I think about Loulane dealing with you during that awful time when your parents died. You were a handful."

"That's an understatement." I was an awful delinquent. I slipped out of the house at night, disappeared, skipped school, and basically nearly killed Aunt Loulane with worry. She was never anything but kind and loving. "She should have tanned my hide."

"She knew how wounded you were. She didn't want to break your spirit. Conformity is overrated, as you well know." She turned to me. "But don't laugh about a foot funeral!"

I'd gotten myself under control. "I promise."

"Good. Now let's get this copied and get home."

15

By the time I'd finished the script, Coleman was home. A mist of rain had begun to fall, a precursor to bad weather waiting to pounce.

I built a small fire in the parlor, eased Coleman onto the sofa, and handed him a drink. He looked worn and discouraged.

I tried not to lead the conversation with questions about his shark sighting, but I couldn't help myself. "Did you really see that shark?"

He shook his head in amazement. "News travels fast."

"You had to be pretty close to see it in that murky river water."

"Too close for comfort."

I checked my first response of worry. I didn't want Coleman to lie to me, but I hated to be afraid for him. "What happened?" I swallowed half of my neat Jack Daniel's. I had a feeling I was going to need some liquid courage to hear what came out of his mouth.

"I was in the water with a team of divers. We were exploring the cage I told you about. The river is dense, so it's hard to see anything, and the shark is dark on top and light on the bottom, so it has pretty good camouflage."

I gulped the rest of my drink and felt the fire hit my belly. "Is it big?"

"Yes. And smart."

Coleman loved animals and often said animals were far superior to humans because only humans had worked so hard to destroy the planet that gave them life. "Are you going to have to kill it?"

"Maybe," he said. "Public safety comes first, but I didn't have a weapon when I saw it. We were working on lifting that cage from the bottom of the river. The shark was just suddenly there. Watching us. Almost like it was treading water, though I know sharks can't do that. Creeped the hell out of me."

"Damn." I didn't want to say too much because I might fly off the handle and spew my fear all over Coleman. Restraint. That was what Tinkie had been harping about. "Mary Dayle says the shark is dangerous. Really dangerous." I said it calmly.

"That's what she told Sheriff Nelson. She also offered to help us capture it if we agreed to return it to the Gulf."

That was news. "She did?"

"I happen to agree with her. I'd love to save it if we can."

"How close did it get to you?"

"Close enough that it could have caught me if it had been hunting."

"That isn't comforting, Coleman."

"I know. People in Greenville are getting riled up. They're demanding that something be done about it. The weather is warming up and folks want to be on the water for recreation. The searches for Marlon haven't yielded anything, and Jules Valiant's family will be here tomorrow, demanding action, I'm sure. There's a lot of pressure to kill the shark and be done with it."

"Can you open the cage thing and draw the fish in there?"

"Maybe. I want to try."

I refilled our glasses and sank onto the sofa so I could lean against him. His strength was a comfort. Coleman had evaded being a shark's lunch today, and he acted like nothing had happened. "Bilbo and Mary Dayle shut down the movie. Something about permits and all of that." My news wasn't as exciting as a shark encounter, but it might help him and the sheriff.

"Those fools claim Marlon is going to make the rich people of the Delta look to be murderers."

"I just read the script." I pointed to it on the coffee table. "There's no indication of that. It's pretty much what Marlon said all along, an action thriller. He's the hero. Happy ending."

Coleman picked it up. "Then why doesn't Ana just distribute the screenplay so people can see for themselves?"

"It has something to do with the authenticity of the actors. Marlon likes to put them in a position where they react. Real reaction; not manufactured. That's how Ana explained it."

"And he's shut down because of that." Coleman finished his drink and drew me closer, kissing my neck and ear.

"That's not entirely fair. The movie is shuttered because the star, director, and screenwriter have disappeared."

"I can't believe his absence is voluntary," Coleman said. "I'll bet the insurance company pulls the plug any minute. I suspect Bilbo will win by default."

"They haven't removed all of the equipment yet," I said. "Since the equipment was leased and Marlon missed a payment, the rental company got cold feet and took some of the lighting. But there's plenty of equipment to continue work. Tomorrow, I'll see if Ana can bring in enough crew to start filming something if she has those permits. Better to put up a solid front and show that she isn't going to quit without a fight."

Coleman's nibbling on my neck and ear became more insistent. "Tomorrow is another day," he whispered.

I gave in to the sensations he created, the building desire. Tomorrow was indeed another day.

The next morning, I dropped the pets at Tinkie's and picked her up. Coleman had gone an hour earlier. He intended to bait the cage with chum and see if he could lure the shark inside. I had to stay busy, or I would drive myself crazy with worry.

We headed to the movie set and knocked on the door of the trailer where Ana worked. She opened the door with a frazzled expression. "Any word on Marlon?"

"No." I hated to say it, but it was true. "You?"

"Nothing. Not one clue. And the Valiants will be here today. It's going to be bloody awful."

"I think you should keep filming." I just said it. "If Bilbo and Mary Dayle think they've cowed you into submission, they won't give up. We have to find those permits, Ana. You have to keep filming if you want to save the movie."

She looked at me like I had two heads. "And how will I pay the cast and crew?"

"The promise that money will come if the film is saved. You can do set shots of the area, crowd shots of the fake town you built—before-the-flood shots. I know you can't flood the set or pay any of the bigger name actors, but a lot of locals would act for nothing."

"That should be interesting," she said sarcastically. "Maybe I could give acting lessons while I'm here."

Tinkie stood to her full five-foot-two height. "If you'd been raised a Daddy's Girl, meaning a woman with breeding and class, you would know that appearances are everything. You must keep up the appearance that the movie will be made. If you fold your tents and leave, you'll never get this project started again and it could easily taint your reputation for other projects."

I almost stepped back from the blast of Tinkie's anger. She'd taken this case to heart. "What Tinkie means is that you'll kill the movie before we have a chance to really hunt for Marlon if you give up so quickly. We can't give up."

"What about the permits?" Ana asked. "They aren't in the office here."

"You said Marlon had all the paperwork. We'll search his room and see if we can turn them up. You call back the cast and crew and just explain things to them. I'll bet you'll be surprised who's willing to work and who isn't."

"Do you really think we can fight this? I've never been in a situation where the town didn't want us. Most places are in love with the movies and the money we bring to local merchants."

"I believe the majority of folks in Greenville support you. The problem is just two big blowhards with an axe to grind," Tinkie said in a much friendlier tone. "Look, I was just trying to stiffen your spine. I can't believe a California woman would let a couple of bumpkins run over her."

"I agree with Tinkie. If you truly care about this movie, and Marlon said you did, then stand up for it. Fight." I put a hand on her shoulder. "We'll help. I'm pretty sure law enforcement will be on your side, once you get the permit situation fixed. The townspeople we've talked to are delighted you're here, and Marlon has a legion of fans who would be willing to help, I'm sure."

She inhaled and nodded vigorously. "You're right. I just got depressed and let Bilbo intimidate me."

"Did he threaten you?" Tinkie asked.

"Not in so many words, but he implied bad things would happen if I didn't pack up and leave. I'm responsible for all of these people. Look what happened to Jules. Nothing like that can occur again. The guilt will kill me."

I understood how she felt, and I also understood her desire to pack up and quit. Thank goodness Tinkie had stepped in and put a little starch in her underwear. "Okay, we'll check Marlon's room for the paperwork and report back. If the insurance company calls, don't answer."

"I can get by with that for a day, but they'll send someone here if I don't talk to them tomorrow."

"Maybe by tomorrow we'll have the permits in place and a lead on Marlon."

"Have you talked to RoDa about Marlon's hangouts? They were close."

"We will. Thank you," Tinkie said.

"Please find those papers and bring them back. You're right. We have to fight."

I gave her a thumbs-up.

We were familiar with Marlon's suite at the B and B. It didn't take us long to go through the bedroom, sitting room, and bathroom. We found nothing—until I thought to check with the owner to see if Marlon had left any paperwork or packages.

"That sweet young man, he asked me to hold on to this messenger bag for him." Nancy Aldren reached under the front desk counter and pulled out a handsome leather bag. "I'm so worried about him. Where could he have gone?"

"We're searching for him," I said, trying not to show the depth of my worry. "The company insuring the movie has hired us to find him, but in the meantime the movie needs to keep filming and we need those permits if you have them."

She was about to hand over the bag when she reconsidered. "He told me to keep this and not to let anyone else have it."

"We can get Ana McCants, his producer, to come over and ask for it, but that will just slow her down. We'll take it straight to her. You've probably heard there are people who want to shut the movie down. The papers in that bag could help save the movie."

"Really?" Nancy said. "I want to help. I do." She put a hand over her mouth as she considered her options. "I just don't know what the right thing is."

Tinkie put a hand on top of Nancy's hand. "The right thing is to help Ana keep the movie going so that when we find Marlon, he can get right back to work. If the set is closed down, the movie will die and likely never get resuscitated."

Tinkie wasn't lying. "She's right, Mrs. Aldren. Help us help Marlon. We're on his side."

"Who is on the other side?" she asked cagily.

"Lamar Bilbo." I put it out there. No prevaricating.

She pushed the bag toward Tinkie. "Take it. If I'm doing the wrong thing, then I'll face that when Marlon is found. And he will be found alive. My heart tells me that." She put her hand on Tinkie's shoulder. "Please find him. Please. He's a wonderful young man. Reminds me of my grandson, so full of energy and ideas."

I was itching to get my hands on the bag and see what was in it but snatching it away from her probably wouldn't be the right move. Tinkie must have read my mind because she stepped between us and gently took the bag.

"Thank you, Mrs. Aldren."

"Call me Nancy, please."

"Thank you, Nancy. You may have played a major role in saving the movie."

Before she could reconsider, we rushed out the door and drove away.

"Whew," I said as we pulled into the parking lot at Bluebeard's. Before we gave Ana the bag, I wanted to know what was in it.

Tinkie had the bag and she pulled out a leather folder and files. "I think this is it," she said.

I tamped down my impatience and watched as Tinkie opened the first two files. "Here!" she said when she dug into the third. "These are the permits."

I started the car and we drove straight to the set where

Ana was marshalling the cinematography team and some actors in costume. She'd taken on the chore of directing a few of the scenes.

"We have the permits," Tinkie said, waving them as we hurried to the set.

"You are lifesavers," Ana said. "Would you mind taking them to Sheriff Nelson? Better yet, make a copy in the trailer so I have my own set of permits."

We happily obliged with a set of papers for Ana, for us, and for the sheriff. I was happy to deliver them to Nelson. That would give me a chance to check on the dive team and Coleman. He wasn't the only person in the water with a predator, but he was my person. Hopefully, there would be some good news about Marlon, too.

16

Sheriff Nelson was out with Coleman and two other divers, still on the lake. We left the papers for him at his office and drove down to the boat ramp to wait for the searchers to return. Being so close to the water, knowing that Coleman shared the underwater space with a bull shark, made me even more antsy.

The rescue boats were visible. I could make out the sheriff and two other men, but Coleman was obviously in the water.

I paced and stared into the glare of the water.

"Want me to get some coffee?" Tinkie asked. "I hesitate to offer caffeine when you're already revved up, but it might help pass the time."

"No, thanks." I didn't want anything except to see

Coleman climb into the boat. I'd been able to push the worry to the back of my mind until now. Standing on the edge of the lake made it all too real. Coleman in danger; Marlon missing, maybe eaten; Jules dead.

"Maybe we should go back to the movie set," Tinkie suggested. It was clear she was trying to break my fixation on the water.

"I'm okay." I started to turn away from the lake and stopped. A gray triangular dorsal fin broke the surface of the river. "Tinkie!" I gasped.

"Oh, no." Tinkie grasped my wrist, and I realized I was surging toward the river. "You can't go in the water, Sarah Booth. There's nothing you can do."

"I can't just stand here and do nothing." I pulled out my phone and called Nelson. He answered on the second ring.

"Do you see the shark?" I asked.

"I do."

"Can you get the divers up?" I found it hard to breathe.

"I'm not sure that's the best move."

"Can you warn them?"

Nelson looked toward the shore and lifted a hand. "Coleman and the others are on the lookout for the shark," he said. "You have to trust that they know how to handle this."

"Are they armed?" I asked.

"Spear guns, yes. I know you're worried. I'm worried, but the smart move is to let those men do what they know how to do. Now I have work to do. Just be patient." He left us at the water's edge.

Easy for him to say. Tinkie was hanging on to my arm as if she thought I'd hurl myself into the water. She was right, though, I couldn't do anything to help, and interfering would only put me and the divers in more danger.

"Do you think the shark can't get back into the river and make its own way down to the Gulf?" I was talking to Tinkie to keep from screaming.

"I did some research," Tinkie said. "They generally have pups in the hot months, and they often seek safer waters. In the open gulf and ocean, the pups frequently don't survive."

Pups seemed like such a gentle name for killing machines. But in every species, mothers tried their best for their offspring. Even sharks. "Do you think it's a pregnant female?" I asked.

"I don't know." Tinkie led me away from the water.

The dorsal fin had disappeared. The wind gently skimmed the smooth surface of the lake. To my utter relief, I saw one of the divers break the surface, then two others. They climbed on the boat to safety.

"My heart can't take a lot of this," Tinkie said. "Do you think we'll ever find the remains of Jules?"

"I hope so. For his family. It must be awful for them."

"Yeah." She gave me a sidelong glance, checking to see if my insane giggling would return. I was over that moment. I couldn't imagine the anguish the Valiant family was feeling—until I imagined how I'd feel if Coleman was attacked. It wasn't funny at all.

It seemed to take forever for the rescue boat to make it to the ramp, but Coleman was the first one to shore and I rushed into his arms. "I saw the fin," I said.

"Yeah, we were aware of the shark. That's why we called it a day." He released me. "We can finish our trap tomorrow. Mary Dayle said she'd come help."

I turned to Sheriff Nelson. "Copies of the permits for the movie, signed and in order, are on your desk."

Coleman had some clothes in the sheriff's office, and we went there for him to change. Tinkie and I went over the permits with Nelson.

Once Coleman was changed, he headed back to Sunflower County. Someone had burglarized a hardware store on the outskirts of town. DeWayne and Budgie, the deputies, could handle it, but Coleman's presence was always expected and appreciated by the local businesspeople.

"Tomorrow we'll get that shark," Coleman told me. "Mary Dayle's expertise will be invaluable. What will attract the shark, how to lure her, that kind of info. Tomorrow is just a matter of finding the shark and herding her into the cage."

"Just a matter of" made it sound so simple and safe. I wasn't buying it at all, but again, my lips were zipped.

Tinkie and I headed to Vicksburg, which was south of Greenville and still on the Mississippi River. The high bluffs of the city had been perfect for the Confederate forces to set up artillery and retain control of the river during the Civil War. The Mississippi proved to be a vital supply route for the rebel forces. General Ulysses S. Grant surrounded the city, pounding it with artillery and cutting off supplies. Civilians and soldiers both starved. When Vicksburg fell, it was the beginning of the collapse of the Confederacy.

"I love Vicksburg," Tinkie said.

"Me, too. Daddy told me plenty of stories about the town along the river." I was a kid, but my daddy talked to me like I was grown, and important. He'd shaped my view of who I was and who I could be with our nightly walks. Morality and ethics were important to him. He didn't give a hoot about drinking or sex or a million small personal choices people made. His eye was on the bigger spiritual and soul questions. To participate or support people, activities, or institutions such as slavery was a moral failing of the worst kind. Yet he'd always been quick to point out that many of the Confederate troops had been duped into identifying with slaveholders, even though the soldiers were dirt poor and had never owned slaves. Still, they put their lives on the line to defend the rights of the wealthy to hold another human in bondage.

"I'll never be able to understand this," he'd often said. I could almost hear his voice, so sad.

"Hey, Sarah Booth!" Tinkie nudged me. I'd been sitting at a STOP sign for a full two minutes while I strolled down memory lane.

"Sorry." I hit the gas and sped toward Vicksburg. We were in luck that both bars were a little north of the city. The Hornet's Nest was high on a bluff overlooking the river. We went there first, checking with the manager and waitresses. Tinkie was instantly taken with their little plaid skirts and white button-down tops. They looked like naughty and rebellious teenagers.

The manager remembered Marlon from days gone by, but he hadn't seen the actor lately. "He was down here a couple of years ago," he said.

"Doing what?" I asked. I'd been under the impression Marlon hadn't been in Mississippi for nearly a decade.

"He met with some men. They had a heated discussion. That's what I know."

"Was it about the movie he's making?" Tinkie asked.

"I wasn't privy to any details," the manager said. "Marlon is a friendly and well-liked young man. I enjoyed knowing him, but I wasn't a buddy or close friend. His secrets were his own, but I will say that they were acting secretive.

I guess it's why I remember it after all this time. They were huddled up discussing something."

I would give my eyeteeth to know what they'd discussed and who he'd met with.

"You haven't seen him this year?" I asked.

"No. I haven't. Hold on." He threw a dish towel over his shoulder and went into the kitchen. He was back in a moment with a middle-aged woman who looked tough as nails. "This is Bianca."

"Why are you asking about Marlon?" Bianca asked. She patted the cigarette pack in her shirt pocket.

"He's missing from a movie set in Greenville and we've been hired to find him," Tinkie said. It was the simplest explanation.

"Why don't we step outside?" I suggested.

When we were on the back deck, she turned to me. "I was best friends with Marlon's mother growing up."

This was an unexpected turn of events. I'd always known of Senator Brandon. He was a fixture of my childhood. Marlon was just a little younger than me and had attended private or boarding schools after his folks decided the Washington County public schools weren't up to snuff. Where in the heck were Marlon's parents? A generation was missing, and I'd hardly remarked on it. Neither had Tinkie.

"Who are Marlon's parents?" I asked Bianca. "I never knew them."

"Jackie was a great gal. She was Marlon's mom, married to Jacob Brandon, Senator Brandon's only child. It was like a fairy tale when Jacob asked her to marry." Bianca's face softened with the memory. "They were so in love. So desperately in love. Bianca wasn't exactly the type of woman his family wanted for him, but they swallowed the situation with grace. Since Jackie was pregnant, they always felt that she'd trapped Jacob into a marriage. That just wasn't the truth. They truly were in love."

"What happened?" Tinkie asked.

"Jackie died before Marlon started school. Lord, they were two peas in a pod. Wherever she went, he was with her. He was a smart and funny kid, even as a toddler. He had charisma."

"And his father?"

"Shortly after Jackie died, Jacob drowned in the river."

"Oh, dear."

"I know," Bianca said. "I felt like half my heart had been cut out. Jackie and I were that close. She was so happy, so excited about the future and how she and Jacob would raise Marlon to be the change, to be one of the leaders that brought Mississippi into the future."

"His movie will certainly help show Mississippi in a different light."

"He always wanted to be an actor. He comes by that naturally. Jackie wanted to move to Hollywood. She felt that both she and Jacob had a chance in TV or film." She paused when the manager brought out a round of drinks for all of us. "Thanks, Tom," she said. She lit a cigarette and sighed.

"I guess the senator raised Marlon," Tinkie said. "I know my folks knew the Brandons socially, but I never recall my mother or father discussing all of that loss."

"Senator Brandon shipped Marlon off to that private boarding school as fast as he could after Jackie and Jacob died. Jacob had been a disappointment to him, and he wasn't going to invest anything emotionally in Marlon."

That explained a lot, including why Marlon wasn't staying with his grandfather.

"When he was little, I took a job working in the house to be near Marlon, so I could tell him about his mother and father. I knew the old man wouldn't do it, or if he did he would only tell negative things. I wanted Marlon to know what good people his folks were. How much they loved him and this world. How they were fighting to be sure he would have a good future." She laughed softly. "He was a character. That kid was too smart for his own good. Is that butler, James, still working there?"

"He is," Tinkie said.

"After I left Greenville and came down here to work, Marlon would get the butler to drive him to see me. I was cooking at the Duff Mansion then, and Marlon would show up, rent a room, and stay a day or two so we could visit."

"His grandfather let him do that?"

"The old man was gone a lot. James was in charge, and he adored Marlon. He'd loved Jacob and Jackie, and he did what was right for the boy whenever he could. Despite what the senator said."

Marlon had earned the devotion of James and Bianca. Ana and the crew, too. They were people willing to go out on a limb for him. "Do you have any idea where Marlon might be?" Tinkie asked.

"I don't," Bianca said. "I haven't seen him for a couple of years. He was down here asking about some paperwork his grandfather had when I worked in the house. I told him where I saw it last, but not to get his hopes up because I hadn't been there in two decades. Even an old roach like the senator has to clean up sometimes."

Bianca clearly had an active, long-held aversion to Brandon.

After she lit another cigarette, I asked her "What were the papers about?"

She shook her head. "The senator has an extensive collection of old articles, papers, and books that deal with the history of the Delta and particularly Greenville. It was something to do with that."

"Maybe research about the flood," Tinkie suggested.

"Maybe." Bianca shrugged. "I didn't care about that kind of stuff. Neither did Jacob, and a good thing because Jackie sure didn't have a pedigree."

"Did the senator actively dislike Jackie?" I asked.

"Oh, yeah, wholeheartedly. Every time he looked at Jackie it was clear he would vaporize her if he could. When she started showing the pregnancy and Jacob married her, I thought the senator would stroke out."

"Was Jackie unhealthy or did she suffer from some chronic illness?" I asked.

Bianca shook her head. "That's the thing. She had excellent health. Her death was a shock to me, and I would swear to Jacob, too. The rumors swirling around town were that she had a chronic illness that she kept hidden." She looked beyond me for a moment, transfixed as if she'd caught sight of the past. "She never said a thing to me, and we were close as sisters. She made the best of living at Muscogee, though she dreamed of California or at least a little house of their own away from the senator." She sighed. "James and the staff were good to her. They made it bearable for her."

"And Jacob? Was he good to her, too?"

"He loved her more than life. When she died, it took him down along with her."

"How did she die?" Tinkie asked.

"The senator had sent Jacob off on some fool's errand downriver on a barge. That's when Jackie died. She had a weak spell and fell. The senator said, and Jacob confirmed, that she'd been having fainting spells but wouldn't go to the doctor. They found her at the bottom of the staircase. It was horrible. Marlon found her and when she wouldn't get up, he curled up beside her. He thought she was asleep. She was cold so he was trying to warm her up."

I blinked back tears at the tragedy of Marlon's loss. "And how did Jacob die?"

"He loved the river. And more than that he loved escaping from his father's constant criticism. After Jackie died, Jacob was low. He started drinking hard. The senator sent him to New Orleans with a barge company. The ship's captain said Marlon was on the upper deck, drinking at dusk. When they went up to get him for dinner, he was gone. They never knew if he'd slipped and fallen overboard or jumped because his grief was too much to carry."

"And what do you think?" I asked Bianca.

"He didn't kill himself deliberately, though drinking the way he was going at it is a form of suicide. No, he didn't jump. He would never have left Marlon to fend for himself with that controlling old fossil, the senator. The senator loved Jacob, but there was no pleasing the man. He never gave Marlon a chance. Nothing was ever good enough no matter how hard folks tried to please him. And Marlon did try. For a number of years."

"Thanks, Bianca. If you happen to see or hear of Marlon, tell him he needs to get back to the film set. A lot of people are counting on him."

"Will do. And you tell him to come see his old Bianca. I love that boy."

"I will."

She gave me an impulsive hug, and I wondered if that was the most honest, freely given love Marlon had known as a child.

17

We stopped at Jojo's since we were in the area, but the atmosphere was completely different. The crowd, young and loud, looked at the photo of Marlon we showed them on our phones but weren't interested. Music from a heavy metal band blared. We asked the bartender and the waitresses, who wore Daisy Dukes and checkered halter tops, but no one even remembered Marlon stopping in. That he was a movie star slipped right by them. The patrons of Jojo's were all about the music.

"I'll bet I could snag you one of those waitress outfits," I said when we were outside and I could actually hear again. "They look more practical than a pirate wench's getup."

"No, thanks," Tinkie said. "We wore those in high school. Remember? Especially you. I clearly remember you sitting on the tailgate of a truck in jeans so short the hot metal of the tailgate burned the backs of your thighs and maybe a little of your butt cheeks." She gave me a side-eye. "You were quite the fashionista."

I had to laugh. Yes, I'd worn cutoffs so tiny Aunt Loulane had sneaked them out of my room and taken them to Goodwill. I'd gone to the thrift store and bought them for fifty cents. It made Aunt Loulane laugh because she said there wasn't even fifty cents' worth of material in them. She had a point.

"Fine, pick my golden memories apart. I won't mention the high school dance you showed up at in a frothy ballerina gown carrying a magic wand. I still remember you shaking a leg to Madonna's 'Like a Virgin.' You had the boys foaming at the mouth."

"Oh, stop it!" She held up a hand. "Mother made me wear that."

"I suspected as much."

"Who made you wear the Daisy Dukes?"

"No one. That was my own exquisite taste at work."

We both laughed as we rolled down the highway toward Greenville and ultimately home. We'd managed to keep the movie filming for at least another day, but we'd failed to turn up any leads on the missing actor. Marlon's strange disappearance was like a giant eagle flew over the river, swooped down, plucked the actor up in its talons, and carted him away to another land.

"Each hour that passes makes me think we won't find Marlon," I admitted. The humor we'd shared only moments before had evaporated as we both confronted the reality.

"I've been waking up in the middle of the night," Tinkie admitted. "I think I hear Maylin crying, but when I go to check on her, she's asleep. Sometimes out of the corner of my eye I think I catch a glimpse of a shadowy child, a little boy, looking so lost and alone."

That fit perfectly with what Bianca had told us. But if Marlon's childhood ghost was showing up at Tinkie's place, did that mean Marlon was dead? I didn't want to voice that concern and give it weight.

"What do you think happened to Marlon?" I asked.

"We don't have any evidence to support a theory." Tinkie dodged the question.

"What do you *think*?" I pressed.

"Okay. I think someone knocked him out and pushed him in the river. Maybe he drowned. Maybe the shark got him."

"You think he's dead."

"I do." Tinkie's jaw clenched. "I think some moron who wants to protect the mythic bullshit of the glorious past did him in to shut him up."

"But the movie isn't negative about the past."

"I know that. You know that. But in case you haven't noticed, there's a strain of kooks oblivious to facts running around."

She was dead right. And that same theory had crossed my mind. Someone of Bilbo's ilk could have killed him. Because they assumed he was going to tarnish the past. To an awful lot of people violence now seemed like the answer to every problem.

"How are we going to catch them?"

Tinkie inhaled and blew out her breath. "We may not be able to ever prove anything, Sarah Booth. If the shark ate his body, there's no way to know this unless the shark is killed, and the gut opened up. Even so, I don't have a clue how long it takes a shark to digest something."

That was a question to ask Coleman, for sure. "Okay. What's next on the agenda?"

"Last night Oscar suggested that we talk to some of the fishermen in the area. The old-timers and the real dedicated fishermen who know the lay of the land. He said they would know if there was any place Marlon could be laying low, but he also didn't think our guy would sabotage his own movie."

"We don't have any other leads," I agreed. "Let's do it." Anything was better than sitting around worrying about Coleman and the shark.

There were several catfish restaurants along the lake and farther south or north on the Mississippi side of the river. We stopped at several, showing a photo of Marlon and Jules, and asking questions. Two hours into it, we hadn't had any luck at all. Plenty of people had seen Marlon in town or on the set, but none had seen him on the night of his disappearance.

A few people mentioned the senator's hunting lands and the rice plantation across the river in Arkansas. If we didn't turn up a lead in the next hour, Tinkie and I would have to check out the rice plantation.

We finally stopped at a tiny little dock on the lake not too far north of Greenville. We would never have known it existed except for one of the old fishermen who recalled that it was a favorite spot of the Brandon family. Long ago, they'd owned the land and a small cabin where they held summer parties for fishing and skeet shooting.

"Let's check it out," I said, trying hard not to keep glancing at my phone, willing it to ring or ding or something to let me know Coleman was safely out of the water.

"Call him," Tinkie said. "I'll check on Maylin, too."

She was only doing that to give me comfort, but I didn't

hesitate. I sent my honey a text. When he didn't answer, I texted the sheriff, too. Nelson responded immediately, saying that Coleman was still in the water but there'd been no sign of the shark. They were about to call it quits for the day. The operation would be repeated tomorrow. It wasn't exactly what I wanted to hear, but at least I knew Coleman would soon be in the boat.

Maylin was doing fine, and Tinkie did her best to keep her deep longing for her child from her expression. "Let's check out the fishing shack and then call it a day," I said.

"I agree. We're near the turnoff."

We'd been driving along the lake for most of the afternoon. It made sense to finish this lead before we packed it in. Tinkie pointed out the road and I turned down it, aware that it was in rough condition. When I bought a vehicle—which would have to be soon—I'd consider a pickup truck. I didn't haul or tow a lot of things, but I sure beat the hell out of a car on the washboard and muddy roads we had to travel in some of our investigations. The Roadster had a fine motor, but the car was old. Everything needed more delicate treatment when it got older, including me. Pickups had once been work tools. Now they were luxury vehicles with a lot of power. I'd never sell the Roadster, but a stripped-down, non-luxury pickup or rugged SUV was absolutely in my future.

We easily found the old fishing shack, complete with cane poles, floats, and hooks, a few nets and stringers, some ancient ice chests—the basic things needed to sit on the bank and fish. I could see why the location had been popular. The camp was on a little inlet of the lake where the water was smooth and calm. The sunlight played on the surface, casting sparkles into the trees that grew down to the dock. A rotted old rope showed that once a vessel of some type had been moored there. Back in the day when the river hadn't been so polluted, this would have been a haven of family activity. Fishing, swimming, picnicking—the staples of country spring and summer.

The door of the shack was ajar, and we went in, looking for any trace of Marlon. Dust coated everything. Vines had grown up the outside of the camp and in through cracks in the windowsills. They'd intertwined on the roof of one room, creating an artistic and very creepy atmosphere.

"I don't think anyone has been here in a long time," Tinkie said. She didn't bother to hide her disappointment. "Damn. I thought for sure we'd find something. Anything to move us to our next action."

I felt exactly the same, but we couldn't manufacture something that wasn't there. "Let's go back to town," I said. "We'll check in with Ana one more time before we go home."

"Good idea." We walked back up the drive where we'd parked the Roadster and stopped.

The car tilted slightly on the right side—with flat tires. Someone had let the air out of two tires.

As aggravating as the flats were, at least we had phone reception. I called triple A because I only had one spare. Tinkie pressed me to call Coleman, but I resisted. It would be better to tell Coleman in person where he could see we were both fine. This wasn't dangerous, only frustrating.

"You know someone had to have followed us to this isolated place." Tinkie wasn't being dramatic, only accurate. Someone had followed us and acted to impede our movements. Why? And who?

"We've made someone uncomfortable," I agreed. "Was it the trip to Vicksburg or going to Muscogee plantation?"

"Do you think we got too close to whoever made Marlon disappear?" Tinkie asked.

"I can't say." I ran through our latest moves in my mind. Our trip to Vicksburg, the search of Muscogee, our interference in finding the filming permits. The motive for flattening our tires could be almost anything we'd done. "Don't you think the butler at Muscogee was behaving oddly?"

"Yes, but Bianca explained he was very close to Marlon. You know he's worried, too. And why would Senator Brandon be upset that we're trying to find his nephew?"

"Your guess is as good as mine. Maybe it was Mary Dayle or Bilbo who sneaked back here and did this."

"Good possibilities," Tinkie said. "Except Mary Dayle wouldn't be deep in the woods. She's not one for the challenges of the great outdoors."

I had that same reading of Mary Dayle, but then again, she'd been a marine biologist. She had a yen for the great aquatic outdoors. Maybe we weren't giving the devil his due. "Flattening our tires is just an inconvenience. It won't stop us, and if the people who did this had a clue about who we are, they'd know this will only make us six times more determined to find Marlon." I sincerely disliked being underestimated.

"Let's look around," Tinkie suggested. "We have time to kill, and we can at least do a good search."

The cabin held nothing incriminating or even of interest, so we set out to canvas the grounds. We worked off grid patterns, looking through the tall weeds and boggy places.

"If I get Lyme disease from a tick bite, I'm going to sue someone."

"Who?" I asked, a little tickled at her dire threat.

"Whoever I can pin the blame on," she said. "Except for you."

"That warms the cockles of my heart."

We were both chuckling when I came across the first marijuana plant. It was a handsome plant about a foot tall. Beside it were several others. They were scattered in a pattern that led us deeper into the woods. Wherever there was plenty of sunshine, another few plants could be found.

"Damn," Tinkie said. "It could be the owner of these plants that flattened our tires. The vandalism might not have anything to do with our case."

"Could be. But why would the owner want us to hang around and poke into things more? Seems getting us moved along would be a top priority."

"Just because someone can grow weed doesn't make them Einstein," Tinkie said.

I had to laugh. She had a point. "I'm sure Sheriff Nelson will be glad to learn about this."

Tinkie cleared her throat. "Maybe we can just let it go."

I looked over at her. Tinkie was law and order, more so than me. "What?"

"This could be for someone who is sick."

"I don't think it takes thirty plants for one sick person. This is pretty much a cash crop for someone."

She shrugged. "Who cares? It doesn't hurt anyone. Maybe we can just pretend we didn't see it."

"What's going on?" I asked.

"Ever since Lydia and Bethany got involved in growing medical marijuana, I've rethought my feelings about the plant. There are so many illnesses it helps. Why is it even illegal? Think about it. Tobacco is legal and tobacco kills people. Alcohol is legal and it destroys livers, kidneys, and families. Dope smokers are generally nonviolent."

I didn't know where Tinkie was getting her facts, but she'd done an about-face. I had never been anti-grass because my college friends who smoked were compassionate and decent people. It had never been the boogeyman that some people saw. And I knew for a fact that weed was a tool for racial discrimination in the hands of lawmen who chose to apply it that way. "I'm fine with ignoring it," I said.

"Good. There are so many more serious things for lawmen to pursue."

I couldn't disagree. "Let's pull a few leaves and roll one."

"What?"

"You know, we have time to kill. We can turn on the car radio and blow some smoke."

"You were a wild child in college, weren't you?"

Actually, I wasn't, but I had a persona to uphold. "You know it."

"I know better than that, Sarah Booth. You were so focused on getting to Broadway and New York you didn't waste a minute smoking or drinking." She gave me her smug look.

"I can't fool you, Tinkie."

"Only because you don't really want to. Now let's go back to the car and wait for help. I think your tires aren't damaged. Someone just let the air out. But you told them to bring new tires, right? Just in case."

"I did. And an air compressor. I just hope they hurry up and get here."

18

By the time the repair guys arrived, deduced the tires were fine, and aired them up, it was late. I'd texted Coleman to let him know where we were and what had happened. Tinkie decided to let Oscar slide. I didn't blame her, but that bill was eventually going to come due.

The day had grown hot—one of those rare April days where the temperature soared into the upper eighties and the humidity was low. The perfect day for a dip in the creek, yet when we got to the movie set, I was a little shocked to see some of the cast and crew dog-paddling around in the water. It was Lake Ferguson, not the Mississippi River, but it was still dangerous, and the shark continued to roam free, coming and going through the ship channel that connected the lake to the river. Cooling off wasn't worth the loss of a limb, at least to me.

I didn't see Ana anywhere on the set, and when we checked the office trailer she wasn't there, either. No one we asked knew where she was. The hot sun baked into my shoulders and back. Tinkie and I sauntered toward the water, talking about the swing set Tinkie was having built for Maylin. We were about fifty yards from the water when raised voices caught our attention.

Down on the tiny little dock, Ana and Mary Dayle McCormick were going at it with real gusto.

"Get off this movie set," Ana said, pointing toward Greenville.

"You can't order me off this land. This is public property. I have as much right to be here as you do."

"Not according to the permits I have," Ana countered. "You and that mush mouth Foghorn Leghorn Bilbo did your best to shut this movie down, but you failed. Scram!"

"Make me." Mary Dayle put her hands on her hips.

"Oh, nothing would give me greater pleasure," Ana said.

Going by size, they were equally matched. Ana had righteous indignation on her side, but Mary Dayle had pure gall. The outcome was unpredictable.

"Ladies," Tinkie said. "Let's stop this. Someone is going to get hurt." She looked over the side of the dock at the water. "This is dangerous. Let's go back to the trailer and talk this through."

"She has to leave," Ana said, pointing at Mary Dayle. "She's a jinx and an interfering bit—"

"Enough!" Tinkie clapped her hands sharply. "This isn't getting us anywhere. Stop all this arguing and get off this dock before someone is hurt."

It was almost as if Tinkie had a premonition. The water beside the dock ruffled and not five feet from where Delilah had fallen in, the big gray dorsal fin of a shark rose. It was aiming directly for the dock. I had a terrible flashback to the 1970s movie about a killer Great White that chomped the back end off a big boat and sucked one of my favorite actors, Robert Shaw, into its maw. All those rows of razor-blade teeth were still frozen in my memory.

"Get off the dock!" I yelled. "Now!" I had visions of the shark rising up from the depths of the water and snatching us. "Run!" I grabbed Tinkie and started to drag her toward land.

The crew members in the water screamed bloody murder and churned toward the shore. That would excite the shark plenty.

In my hurry to get Tinkie safely off the dock, I wasn't aware that Mary Dayle and Ana were still locked in mortal combat. The two women were struggling, each trying to land a blow on the other. I stopped dragging Tinkie and just gawked.

"Ana! Get off the dock!" I called to her. "The shark is right there."

"Mary Dayle! Stop!" Tinkie yelled, warning them of the danger. "You two are going to fall in and get eaten."

Ana landed a solid blow on Mary Dayle's ear. The bookseller howled in pain and struck back with a hard kick to Ana's shin. "You're going to die!" Ana countered, hopping on one leg as she tried to rub her shin without giving ground.

Mary Dayle saw her opportunity and gave Ana a push. The producer stumbled backward, the heel of her right foot off the edge of the dock. Her momentum was going to dump her into the water. Her arms windmilled as she fought to regain her balance. Just as she started to fall backward, she grabbed Mary Dayle's arm. She pulled hard, trying to keep herself on the dock. The momentum sent her stumbling onto her face on the dock, but Mary Dayle went over the side into the water.

Everyone gasped. Tinkie and I rushed to the dock to try to find Mary Dayle when she surfaced. The water was eerily calm, as if the lake had swallowed her whole.

"Where is she?" Ana asked. She was pale, distraught. "I wasn't trying to throw her in, I just didn't want to go in myself. I grabbed her to regain my balance."

That was exactly what I saw, but I had no clue what Sheriff Nelson would do about this. "Stay calm, Ana. Look for her. We can get her back up here and out of danger."

"We can if she surfaces," Ana wailed. "What if she doesn't?"

"Just look for her," Tinkie said. "She has to come up. We'll save her."

Members of the crew came forward to help. We lined the small dock, each peering down into the murky water. At least the dorsal fin was no longer in evidence. Maybe the shark had scooted away from us.

"Where could she be?" Tinkie whispered to me.

"Maybe under the riverboat?" I didn't have a clue. She couldn't breathe under the boat, so it was a stupid answer.

"Sarah Booth, what are we going to do? I think she's gone. Just like Marlon and the rest of Jules."

The shark had been frolicking right beside us. Coincidence? I didn't think so, but I was reluctant to say it. It would sound insane to think that the shark had been programed to hang out waiting for Mary Dayle. "Call 911,"

I told one of the crew members. "Get someone here fast. Search and rescue. It's possible she's caught on something."

"I'll look," the crew member said.

Before I could stop him, he dove into the lake.

"Not another one," Tinkie said. "He shouldn't have done that."

When he surfaced, I felt a weight lift. "Get out of the water." I sounded like a goddess demanding to be obeyed. It was effective. The young man scrambled up on the dock with the help of his friends.

"Did you see anything?" Tinkie asked him.

He wouldn't meet her gaze. "Just one of her shoes on the bottom. That's it."

"Am I going to be charged with murder?" Ana asked us.

"I don't know. It looked like an accident to me. A lot depends on what everyone else saw."

"We were fighting, but I wouldn't deliberately do this. Not with a shark in the water."

I wasn't the person she had to convince. Sheriff Nelson and Coleman were coming toward us at warp speed.

19

Sheriff Nelson didn't cuff Ana, but he led her away and put her in the back of his patrol car as we all watched.

"I think this movie is cursed," Tinkie said. "I've heard of such things, where an artistic endeavor results in multiple deaths or bad luck. Maybe the movie set is on top of a Native American burial mound. The Winterville Mounds aren't far from here."

Tinkie had a point, but I was caught in a mental loop. The video of Ana almost falling backward, reaching out, grabbing Mary Dayle, and ultimately hurling her into the water played over and over again in my head. It looked like an accident. But was it? Mary Dayle had been a thorn in Ana's side for several weeks now. Had the producer simply given in to bottled-up rage and intentionally knocked Mary

Dayle off the dock? And as intriguing as that question was, what in the heck had happened to the bookseller? She fell into the lake, went under, and simply never came back to the surface. It didn't make sense. The water wasn't all that deep near the little dock. The cast and crew had been swimming in the area only an hour before. What happened to Mary Dayle beneath the lake's surface? I wasn't sure I wanted to know.

The search and rescue team, including Coleman, dove into the water and began the search. She'd only been gone an hour, but it seemed clear enough to me that she was permanently gone. I didn't care for Mary Dayle's high-handed behavior, but I also didn't want to think of her as shark chum.

Even if Mary Dayle was found, I didn't see a future for *Hero at the Helm*. Ana would likely find herself behind bars. Without Ana and Marlon to lead the charge, the movie was well and truly shuttered. Even the cast and crew members seemed to accept it. The movie that had burst into town on such high hopes and anticipation was clocking out with just a whimper.

I couldn't stay at the water's edge, waiting to see if the search and rescue team met with a Peter Benchley fate. I had the bizarre notion that my anxiety was like a beacon and would draw the shark toward the first responders I wanted to protect.

"Let's head to Bluebeard's. I need a drink."

Tinkie nodded. She looked as done in as I felt. "What could have happened to Mary Dayle?" she asked, her gaze lingering on the smooth surface of the lake.

"I wish I knew." Or did I? The things I imagined were not pleasant. "Keep in mind that Mary Dayle is trained to work with sharks." I said it more to bolster myself than Tinkie. "If anyone can face down this shark, it's her."

"The shark is a worry, but lack of oxygen is what I'm truly concerned about." Tinkie pushed her hair out of her face. It almost never happened, but Tinkie looked disheveled. "She can't breathe underwater. She went straight under, and there wasn't a sign of her. I must accept that either the shark got her and dragged her down to the deepest part of the lake, or she simply drowned and is floating around the bottom. Old-timers say it takes three days for a body to float up to the surface."

"If she's actually down there."

"What do you mean?" Tinkie asked. "We both saw her go in. And she hasn't come out."

I couldn't disagree with my partner, so I only sighed and signaled for her to walk with me. The episode was so distressing—it was as if the lake and river had been magically cursed to swallow people whole. A tequila shot at Bluebeard's would give me a little liquid courage.

We'd barely gone ten yards, though, when a Mercedes sped onto the set. Lamar Bilbo got out, slamming the door with real force. "Where is she?" he demanded. "Where is Mary Dayle? What did you do to her?" He reached to grab Tinkie's shoulders, but I slapped his hands away. The bullies always went for the smaller person.

"Back off, cretin," I said.

Bilbo looked shocked that I had ordered him to do anything. "You can't tell me what to do."

Oh, yeah, I loved this part. Tinkie walked up to him and pushed him in the chest hard enough to make him stumble backward. "Who are you talking to?" she asked. "Her?

Me? I am telling you what to do. Get the hell off this movie set. You've been told more than once. *Vamoose!*"

She was small but mighty. I didn't bother to hide my grin. "Beat it, Bilbo. We don't know where Mary Dayle is."

"They said Ana McCants pushed her into the water and she never came up."

I felt a twinge of sympathy because he truly seemed to care about the bookseller. But my compassion wasn't big enough to tolerate his awfulness on the movie set where everyone had gathered around to watch the exchange.

"Ana didn't push her," I said. "So put that out of your mind."

"If McCants laid a hand on Mary Dayle, I'll make sure the DA prosecutes to the fullest extent of the law."

"Get out of here," Tinkie warned him. She looked down at the pointy toes of her shoes. I knew exactly what she was thinking—that he needed a good kick in the butt.

"You can't push me—"

Before he could finish, one of the crew hit him in the face with an overripe tomato. It smacked him hard, the wet, red guts covering his face and falling onto his starched white shirt. "How dare you?" Bilbo's face was so red I thought steam might shoot out from his ears and ketchup would be made.

The response was another juicy tomato hard against his chest. He stepped back two feet and put a hand on his chest. Tomato goo ran down his shirt, dripping on his polished shoes.

"You will be sued for this personal attack," he proclaimed, puffing his chest out.

The tomatoes came from all directions. I recalled that

the food services for the movie had set a large basket of tomatoes out on a table for snacks and sandwiches. The crew had found a much better use for them.

I tried hard not to laugh, but I couldn't help myself. It was like some comedy skit. Tomatoes whacking into Bilbo and his howls of outrage.

"Should we stop this?" Tinkie asked.

"Eventually." I wasn't quite ready to pull the plug on Operation Bilbo Ejection.

"Stop this behavior immediately!" The clipped, angry voice of Senator Brandon made everyone freeze. He had a commanding presence when he chose to use it. He'd sneaked up behind us and no one had seen him approach.

I saw one of the crew draw back to hurl a tomato at Senator Brandon and I lightly grabbed his arm. "Don't. That's Marlon's grandfather. He wouldn't want you to."

The young man looked at the tomato and then at Brandon. I realized I was talking to RoDa, Marlon's friend. He pressed his lips into a thin line. "Marlon has no warm feelings for this man. The senator never had the time of day for Marlon. Even now, with a big-dollar movie in production, the senator can't be bothered."

"I know," I said. "But don't make it harder for Marlon. The movie is in a real tough spot. The senator may be the only person who can pull enough strings to save it. If we find Marlon."

"If I knew where he was, I'd damn sure fetch him and drag him back."

"No idea what happened to him?" I pressed. All around us the cast and crew were milling and mumbling. I couldn't tell if they were going to respect Senator Brandon and disband, or continue the assault on Bilbo. Tinkie had withdrawn several steps and climbed on top of a chair. She had a primo view of the mayhem.

Brandon was still trying to gain control of the crowd, and I couldn't tell how it was going to play out. But right now I had the chance to talk to RoDa and took it. "If you know anything that would help us find Marlon, it might save the movie."

"I know," he said. "I've been to all the places we talked about. I honestly don't know what happened to him. And I'm afraid of what the true answer might be."

"Me, too," I said. "I can't help but believe he'd be here if he could."

"Marlon is a little spoiled, that's true. But he would never put the movie on the line like this. This was his dream. We've talked about it for the past five years. He's devoted his future to making this movie. And he is so close. He just needs to finish filming here in Greenwood. We have a lot of footage in the can already. Enough that I can start with the editing if we could only finish here."

I hadn't realized that Marlon had done so much work on the film already, which led me to believe even more strongly that his absence was not by his own hand. "What do you think happened to Marlon?" I asked his friend.

"I think someone took him."

"Someone like who?"

He shrugged. "Who stands to benefit if the film is cancelled?" he asked.

"Bilbo there. And Mary Dayle, who is now missing herself."

"Those are just two grudge holders. They're like so many

people who live in small worlds, unexposed to anything new because they're terrified that the little bit of power they hold might be taken away."

His assessment rang true, but it wouldn't help me find Marlon. "Kidnapping is a serious crime. Someone would have to have a lot more at stake than just hating change to abduct Marlon."

"Who else would benefit from production being halted? Not the city. Not the state. The Mississippi Film Commission is behind the movie and the documentary. They have a grant for Marlon, if we can find him."

"I know." I glanced at RoDa, wondering if he was playing an angle.

"This film is my future. I'd never do anything to jeopardize it. Most of the cast and crew feel the same way. Marlon is all about giving people an opportunity. He has some veteran actors and crew working, but also a lot of folks who are new to the business. This movie generates dreams for many of us. We can't let the old guard shut us down."

"Find Marlon," I said. "That's the only way to save this movie. Tinkie and I will see about getting Ana away from the sheriff."

"The thing with Mary Dayle, it was an accident. I saw it." RoDa clenched his fists. "Ana has to come back to work and we have to find Marlon."

"I'll do my best. Ask around. Someone had to see something."

RoDa leaned in toward me. "Did Marlon tell you about the threats?"

"No." I worked to keep the frustration out of my voice. "No one mentioned it to me."

"Not even Ana?"

"Nope."

"There was a group of guys in camo and black masks who showed up late one night and rode motorcycles around the set, threatening to damage the equipment and hurt us if we didn't pack up and leave. They were all talk, but it's troubling now that Marlon is missing."

I had heard rumors of disgruntled Greenville residents. Tinkie and I had asked around, but both Marlon and Ana had withheld the details from us. I figured it had something to do with the fact we worked for the company insuring the film. Had we made that report to the insurer, the cost of insurance could have gone up or the film might have been halted. "Oh, great. Do you know who they were?"

He whipped out his phone. "This is what they were wearing."

It was a ridiculous getup from a testosterone-and-comic-book-driven fantasy. They wore spandex camo, black masks that obscured their faces, and black cloaks with an insignia that looked like a blending of a Nazi symbol and a dead armadillo. *Johnny Boys* was the name on the cloak.

"Johnny Boys? Seriously?" I asked.

He laughed. "I know. They didn't do anything but threaten, but I thought you should know about it. For future reference, none of them need to be in spandex. Ugh."

He was right about that. "When did this happen?"

"Two days before Marlon disappeared. In fact, just before you got here. Marlon ran them off the set, but they said they'd be back. Maybe they took him to teach him a lesson."

"Maybe. I'll find out." And a few heads would roll in the process. Why in the world hadn't Ana or Sheriff Nelson told us about this episode? Or any of the cast and crew who knew of it? It was the best lead we had.

"I'll wait here to see if the divers find Mary Dayle," Tinkie said. "You go check out any incident reports made about the Johnny Boys and who they are."

"Are you sure?" I hated to leave Tinkie at the water's edge, helpless to do anything but wait.

"Go on. Get after it. If I see or hear anything, I'll be in touch."

"Thank you, Tinkie." I was off and running. At least there was something Delaney Detective Agency could actually check out instead of twisting in circles and chasing our tails.

20

When I pulled the car into the courthouse parking lot, I took a minute to check my appearance in the rearview mirror. My hair was a blowsy mess. I had to smile because Tinkie hadn't even reprimanded me on my slovenly appearance. She was as frazzled as I was.

When I returned the rearview mirror to its place, I cried out. A female form was in the back seat—breasts exposed and a crown of seaweed.

"What the hell, Jitty?" I glanced around to be sure no one else had seen the mostly naked woman in the back seat of an antique car.

"I am Salacia, goddess of the depths of the sea."

"I don't care if you're the Queen of Sheba, put some clothes on."

Salacia only laughed, a delightful sound that seemed to contain the susurration of water. "You're so provincial, Sarah Booth. And you like to think of yourself as a rebel."

"I'm not an exhibitionist, like you! Give it up and put a shirt on!"

Two blops of seaweed fell from her head and covered her breasts. "That'll do the trick," she said.

"No, it won't. Who the heck is 'Salacia' and what do you want from me?"

"I'm the bride of Neptune, the mother of Triton. Sea creatures do my bidding, but I must return to the salty sea."

Hope springs eternal in the heart of a goober. "Can you call that shark back down the river to the Gulf?"

Jitty laughed again, musical and calming. I thought of the ocean waves hurling themselves against the shore and slowly pulling back. "What if I can?" she asked. Her posture was regal, sitting in the back seat as if in front of a crowd of admirers.

"Please do it, before someone else gets hurt."

"It's not that simple, Sarah Booth. In the old days, the gods and goddesses interfered routinely in the affairs of man. We no longer have that power."

"I'm not asking you to interfere with humans, only with a shark. We need to move her back to the Gulf or someone will surely kill her. Can't you protect your creatures?" I thought playing on her power might motivate her to help. Wrong.

"The shark has a destiny all its own. Don't ever forget that sea creatures live by their specific natures, just like you and Tinkie. This shark might have initially been a pawn, but now she's a player with her own agenda."

"Did she come here to give birth?" I asked.

"The maternal instinct is alive in all creatures, even

sharks. The drive to protect one's young against all odds— it's universal. Maybe with one exception."

"What exception?" Jitty was seldom so chatty about her current incarnation, and I wondered how she knew so much about biological impulses since she'd been dead over a hundred years.

"You, Sarah Booth! I don't think you have a maternal bone in your body." With that, the goddess Salacia disappeared and my very own Jitty was sitting in the back seat wearing a flannel shirt and windbreaker. The dripping seaweed was gone, and in its place she had a poufy hairstyle reminiscent of the 1950s.

"Is that a beehive?" I asked before I thought.

"It's all the rage."

"You're in the wrong decade and the wrong place, Jitty. Get out of my car." I pointed to the passenger door. "Go now. You jump in here dripping water all over the interior of a classic car and insult me. Go. I have better things to do than listen to you maligning my abilities to be a good mother." And I did. I had to find the Johnny Boys and what beef they had with the movie people.

"Didn't mean to pinch your toes, Sarah Booth. It's just that you've been home almost two years. You've had several virile lovers and zero zygotes. I just assumed your body was rejecting motherhood."

I could feel my blood pressure rising to the top of my head. Any minute a blood vessel could burst. "You are infuriating! And mean. Get out now."

I seldom lost my cool with Jitty, but she'd gone too far.

"Hold on. I didn't mean to wind your crank."

"Of course you did. You say I wouldn't make a good mother; that's a lie."

"Prove it!" She cackled gleefully. "You're so good at mothering, prove it."

She had backed me into the exact corner she wanted to put me in. I'd followed into the trap like sheeple.

"I don't have to prove anything."

"Just like I don't have to tell you that I know how to get that shark back to the Gulf. As Salacia, sea creatures obey my command."

"Right. But you aren't Salacia any longer. You're just plain old Jitty, haint of Dahlia House."

"Oh, I can be that goddess whenever I wish." Jitty had her back up now.

"Prove it!" I taunted back at her.

Her reply was a whirlwind of iridescent water droplets. The back seat was empty.

I checked my watch. Less than thirty seconds had elapsed. Jitty might not be able to control sea creatures but she sure had a way of manipulating time.

I hurried into the sheriff's office, trying hard to forget the troubling conversation with Jitty. Was I not maternal material? She'd touched a nerve. My body was on high alert to the possibility I might not be a good mother. I wasn't certain I wanted a child, but I didn't want to be deficient in the skills necessary to raise a compassionate human being.

When I was in the office, I asked one of the deputies to clue me in about the Johnny Boys. He checked with the sheriff first, as all good deputies should, and then waved me into an interview room where we could talk without being overheard.

"Mostly those guys are wannabe bikers," the deputy said. "They don't have the creds or toughness to be real bikers, so they have this local group where they act like they have power and a street reputation. They roar around town and drink out at the Spiked Helmet, a bar that caters to pretend bikers and cowboys. You'd be surprised how many grown men live in a fantasy world."

"Did you know they'd been to the movie set?" I asked.

He shook his head. "No one ever filed a complaint. What did they do?"

"I'm not certain they did anything except show up and act tough, like you say. Maybe they only threatened Marlon, but it's worth checking in case they are involved in his disappearance."

"Thanks for the tip," the deputy said. "I'll get on that."

"Who runs the Johnny Boys?" I asked.

"Couple of locals. They like to strut like bad boys, but in the long run, the worst thing they've ever done is maybe tip a vending machine for the change."

"Why would they be opposed to a movie being shot here?"

He chuckled. "Maybe they got passed over for a part, or more likely someone local paid them to harass the cast and crew."

That sounded more than reasonable to me. "Who would do that?"

He looked at me and shook his head. "Sounds like a Lamar Bilbo move. He's another wannabe. The only thing they've got going for them is their pseudoheritage. It won't work for them much longer, and they know that. Maybe they just want to keep any outsiders away for fear of losing their grip."

What he said made perfect sense. "Can I have a list of the members?"

"If you promise you won't go poking around without the sheriff."

It was a promise I was reluctant to give, but I conceded, partially. "I'll tell Sheriff Nelson about it, and I promise not to go without him."

He went to the computer and printed the list. He handed it to me but held a corner. "You gave your word, remember that."

"I will." He'd put me in the hot seat, and I had to honor my promise. He let the corner go and I tucked it into my jeans' pocket before he could change his mind. In four seconds flat I was out the door.

Instead of a drink, I picked up two hot coffees from a local diner and headed back to the empty movie set. Tinkie was still there, watching the water as if Godzilla might rise from the deep. Worry etched lines in her face and I knew the same was true for me. I handed her a coffee and pulled out the list of names.

Together we went over them. I didn't know these locals, and they weren't the kind of people Tinkie would know from bank business or society gatherings. We needed local input.

I texted Sheriff Nelson to see how much longer they were going to be on the water. When he responded with an hour or two, Tinkie and I decided to go to Bluebeard's to ask the local barkeep about our list. He'd been helpful in the past.

We started toward the lot where we'd left the car when I noticed the door to Ana's trailer open. As in wide open. Instinctively we ducked behind another trailer and watched. I could see movement inside, but I couldn't determine what was happening. Ana was still at the courthouse. Nelson hadn't released her yet. Who else would have business in her trailer, which served as the office for the movie?

"It's Bilbo!" Tinkie whispered. "I recognize that hat he wears."

She was right. Lamar Bilbo stepped out of the trailer, closing the door behind him. In his hand he carried a sheaf of papers.

"He's robbing the place," she said.

"He's stealing something." I was torn between tackling him or following him. He might lead us to Marlon. Hope was renewed that the handsome actor was alive.

"Let's tail him." Tinkie made the decision.

"You got it." We pressed back against the trailer as he passed near us. He didn't even bother to look around. He was either confident or dumb as a post. A minute later I understood his confidence. Senator Brandon walked from the parking lot to greet him. The men huddled together. I couldn't tell if it was friendly or contentious. Bilbo shook the sheaf of papers in the air and Brandon made a grab for them and missed.

"Are they working together?" Tinkie asked.

"I can't tell. Maybe Bilbo is blackmailing Brandon. If he has Marlon, maybe he's making a devil's bargain with the senator."

It was all speculation. The two men could be discussing the movie or Mother's Day plans.

When they started to walk away together, Tinkie grabbed my arm. "We have to follow them, but we can't get caught. You really need a different vehicle, Sarah Booth. Something silver or gray and not flashy like that Roadster."

She was right, but her signature Cadillac was just as flashy and easy to spot. One of us needed to give up style for obscurity. I knew it would be me. "We work with what we have."

"We could call an Uber," Tinkie suggested.

"If we knew where we were going, it would be an idea.

As it is, we only need to follow and stay back. Maybe try to get a car or two between us." Tailing someone on two-lane country roads that were straight and without any verge was difficult. Often there wasn't a lot of other traffic.

"What if they take separate cars?" Tinkie asked.

"We'll follow Bilbo." We had to choose.

"Look!"

They headed to the senator's big, black Escalade. They got in and the senator drove off.

"What the hell is going on?" Tinkie asked.

"We're going to find out," I said.

Faster than a speeding bullet, Tinkie headed for the car. I was right on her heels. Before I could stop her, she got behind the wheel, which was fine by me. I had some research to do. I handed her the keys and we were off.

21

We'd been following the senator for twenty minutes when Tinkie said, "He's not headed home. Where are they going?"

"It appears they might be going to the woods. Maybe Senator Brandon is planning to shoot Bilbo. If so, we shouldn't interfere."

Tinkie laughed. "I agree. But why would Bilbo get in the car with someone he knew wanted to kill him?"

"Because he's Lamar Bilbo and he thinks his name will protect him from everything."

"If I were a Bilbo, I'd change my name," Tinkie said.

Now it was my turn to laugh. "Theodore Bilbo was governor of Mississippi twice, non-consecutive terms, and elected to the U.S. Senate in 1934." Thank goodness for Google and the cell phone.

"I remember that nugget of sordid history. He was supposed to have a campaign fundraiser at The Club," Tinkie said. "Our great-grandfathers put a stop to it."

"My great-grandfather belonged to The Club?" This was news to me. My parents, who didn't believe in exclusivity or elitism, had never been members of Sunflower County's fancy country club and golf course.

"He did. Your father and mother refused the invitation to join. It was quite the scandal in Zinnia when they gave their reasons. They were labeled socialists."

"Yeah, I heard that story." I continued pulling up information on the notorious Theodore Bilbo while Tinkie drove. Bilbo, the former governor and U.S. senator, was a member of the Ku Klux Klan and a rabid racist who was no stranger to corruption. New Cadillacs, swimming pools, construction—he acquired wealth and possessions through illegal dealing.

"Bilbo wasn't seated in 1947 after the election," I told Tinkie as I read. "Other senators stood up against him. He became very sick with mouth cancer. He died that summer, without ever taking his seat in the Senate. But he was paid the entire time."

"At least he was shut out of power." Tinkie was more pragmatic than I was. The pay-and-pension scheme of elected officials was a source of aggravation for me.

"Reading this, it's no wonder Lamar is worried that the movie is going to depict some families as villains." U.S. Senator Bilbo had been a one-man crime wave and a lot of other elected officials had helped and protected him from the consequences of his actions.

"Hold on," Tinkie said, turning off the main road onto a

gravel side road that led into the thick woods. She took the turn at a high speed, but the Roadster was so balanced it held the road. "Sorry, I saw them turn but I was so far back I almost drove past it."

"It's fine," I said. "I'm not even a little worried." Tinkie was a skilled and safe driver. She'd had a sports car in high school and had developed a reputation as a future candidate for the Indy 500.

She slowed on the gravel road. It was a fairly smooth ride, but there were places where the washboard felt like it was going to rattle the wheels off the car. A certain speed, which she quickly found, minimized the battering. The road led us deeper and deeper into the dense wood. The gravel gave out and the road turned into a two-track path. The weeds and foliage crept closer and closer to both sides of the road until Tinkie stopped. "I'm going to pull into this little turnoff," she said. "The river is only half a mile or so from here, if my geography calculations are right. We should walk the rest of the way."

"Good idea. We don't know what those men are up to, and it would be smart to slip up on them and spy." The fact the two men were hanging out together left me on edge about their motives. Maybe Brandon was trying to bribe Bilbo to back off from the movie business. It wouldn't be the first time a Bilbo went for cash.

Tinkie pulled the car into the side trail deep enough that it wasn't visible from the main track. If someone found and tampered with the car, it would be a long walk back to the road.

"Call Coleman and tell him where we are," Tinkie suggested.

"Why don't you call Oscar?" I teased her gently.

"Coleman is a lawman. Just call him." She got out of the car. Tinkie was on a roll. She wasn't going to wait for me.

I caught up with her on the path—after I got my gun out of the trunk of the car. We might not need it, but I sure didn't want to leave it lying around for Bilbo to snatch. He had a bad temper and not a lot of restraint, from what I could tell.

"So what does Lamar Bilbo do for a living?" I asked Tinkie. I might be the one to google the history of the Bilbo name, but Tinkie and Oscar's financial power in the Delta put them in the know.

"He sells heavy equipment."

"Like tractors and combines?"

"Like bulldozers and stuff like that."

"Then he likely sells to the county or state, supplying their roadwork equipment."

"Probably," she said. "Call Coleman and tell him where we are, and I'll call Harold and ask him to find out who Bilbo's best customers are."

I dialed Coleman's number and when he answered, he sounded far away. "Where are you?" I asked.

"On the river. We're still searching for Marlon, Mary Dayle, and the rest of Jules, but with the storm brewing up, we'll be heading in soon. Where are you?"

"Somewhere in the woods a little northeast of Greenville. We're tracking the senator and Lamar Bilbo. They left the movie set together."

"That's not suspicious at all," Coleman said sarcastically. "What's up?"

"We don't know yet. Tinkie and I are slipping up on them to spy."

"That may not be smart," Coleman said. "Bilbo is a hot-head, and the senator is used to exercising his privilege. Don't get hurt."

"My exact plan," I said. "See you soon. I just wanted you to know where we are in case we don't come home."

"That's not funny, Sarah Booth."

"It wasn't meant to be. I have a bad feeling about what we might find out here in the woods." Would we find Marlon's remains, buried out here where no one would reasonably look?

"I'm going in the water one more time before we quit. I'll see you soon."

The line went dead and Tinkie and I pushed our way through the undergrowth.

"I have a really bad feeling." I couldn't stop myself. I whispered my confession to Tinkie. I tried not to give voice to doubts and anxieties—call me superstitious but I thought it might make them come true. Today, though, Brandon and Bilbo had truly gotten under my skin.

"I know, but we can't stop now. All we're going to do is take a peek, find out where they're going, and ascertain if they're hiding Marlon out here in the boonies. I have to believe he's still alive."

"Why would Brandon be working with Bilbo?" I asked.

"It could be a million reasons. We'll investigate and get more information."

She was right, and my constant yammering wasn't help-ing us. I dropped behind her as she led the way, taking care to follow where she stepped and not to make a lot of noise. In a few minutes we came up on a cabin almost completely hidden in the woods. It was a hunting camp so camouflaged that I was willing to bet the hunters sat on the front porch and shot the deer over a baited field. Some hunters disliked actual hunting. They were all about trophy bragging.

"So this is the legendary Brandon hunting lodge," Tinkie said. "Forty years ago this place had a reputation for hard drinking and hot women. The men did a lot more than hunt when they came here."

"Drinking and whoring are a lot better than killing helpless animals," I said.

She nudged me in the ribs with her elbow. "You would say that. And I agree." She gripped my shoulder. Brandon and Bilbo walked out of the woods on the other side of the lodge and climbed the stairs. Brandon opened the door, and they went inside.

"Do you think Marlon is in there?" Tinkie sounded hopeful.

"We won't know unless we look."

"Do you think they'll shoot us if they see us?" she asked.

"I honestly don't know. Depends on what they're up to or hiding."

She touched my shoulder and took off running in a crouch. She made it to the side of the cabin and pressed against it, signaling me to follow. I obliged. Though we listened, we couldn't hear anything happening inside the lodge. I peeked in the window and saw an empty bedroom with several beds in it. We moved around the building, checking every window without any success. At last we came to a large kitchen and found Brandon and Bilbo sitting at a long table sipping bourbon. They didn't seem at odds, but they were both wary, watching each other. Waiting. But for what?

"This is weird," Tinkie said. "Do you think they're expecting someone else?"

That was about the only explanation I could come up with. My cell phone buzzed in my pocket and almost made me jump out of my skin. I checked it to discover Coleman had sent a text. The water search was over for the day. Nothing of importance had been found. No one had seen the shark since Mary Dayle disappeared. He asked if he should come find us.

"Not yet." I shot the text back. I'd have more time to type later.

"Duck! They're leaving." Tinkie hunkered down, as did I.

We were on the west side of the cabin, and we heard the front door close. The two men walked across the wide veranda, boots clomping on the cypress wood. They weren't talking, and they disappeared into the woods, heading back to their car, or so I presumed.

We waited five minutes. When they didn't return, we set to work.

"I think I can jimmy that window up," I said. "We have to make sure Marlon isn't in here."

"But we have to be quick. We hid the Roadster pretty good, but I don't want them to see it."

She was right about that. "Yes, hurry. We must do this now, though, unless we want to come back with a warrant."

I shook my head. "We'll never get a warrant. We don't have any evidence. The only wrongdoing would be us trespassing and spying."

Tinkie sighed as I went to a garden shed for a tool to lever the window up. It wasn't locked but the wood was swollen from the moisture in the air. It took some elbow grease, but we got it open. I boosted Tinkie in. She was smaller and lighter. In turn, she went to the front door and let me in.

Together we checked the interior of the cabin. The kitchen, except for the two glasses left on the big table, was squared away. The beds were neatly made. There was no trace of anyone having been there except for a stout arm-chair in the middle of a bedroom. Used duct tape and some rope were on the floor beside the chair.

"Do you think Marlon was here, tied up and detained?" Tinkie asked.

"I do." I went to the kitchen and got a plastic trash bag to put the rope and tape in. Sheriff Nelson could have it checked for DNA. At last we had a lead and possible evidence that Marlon had been abducted. We'd taken a baby step. Now we had to follow through.

22

As we made our escape, we hadn't seen the black Escalade. I could only think there was another road in and out of the lodge. I was just glad they hadn't seen us or the Roadster.

Tinkie drove slowly, watching ahead and behind us for any signs of the two men. "Do you really think Brandon is involved in the kidnapping of his grandson?" she asked. "Why would Senator Brandon do that?"

"It's impossible to say. Why would he want to wreck his grandson's career? Especially since the movie paints the Brandon family as noble and heroic for saving so many lives during the flood."

"Maybe Brandon was meeting with Bilbo to discuss paying a ransom to get Marlon back."

"That's a possibility." We didn't have enough evidence to make an informed guess, much less a legal charge.

"Where is Marlon now?" Tinkie asked. "If he was the person tied and taped to that chair, where did he go?"

"Do I look like the Wizard of Oz?" I parried, but with a chuckle. "I feel certain that except for the kidnappers, Marlon is the only person who can tell us what really happened."

"The good news is that I feel pretty sure he's alive."

Tinkie was always the optimist, but I shared her feeling. I believed Marlon had been abducted and detained at the lodge. Now he had been moved. If they went to the trouble to move him alive, then he would likely remain alive. "Maybe they just want to kill the movie. If Marlon is out of action for another few days, the cast and crew will disband and go home. The grant for the raft documentary will be withdrawn by the film commission. The movie will be dead and there won't be any bringing it back to life."

"Which may be the case. What would the senator have to gain by this?" Tinkie asked just before we hit a bump that knocked the breath out of both of us.

"Control of the family history. Punishment to Marlon because he left Greenville and the family. A payback to the son and daughter-in-law he detested."

"Old men do carry a lot of grudges," Tinkie said. "Old women, too."

I knew she was thinking of her mother, who still hadn't shown up to see her only grandchild. I was at the point of tracking Mrs. Bellcase down and giving her an earful.

At last we made it to the highway and started back to Greenville. "We need to figure out where Bilbo and Brandon are," she said. "They may lead us to Marlon."

"Let's make sure Ana is out of jail. I'm sure they won't hold her. But we can get her to follow one of them and I'll take the other. You need to go home to see Maylin."

"That isn't fair. I can't keep pushing all the work off on you."

"You aren't, and there's something you can do. Rent us a four-wheel-drive truck. I have a very funny feeling we're going to need it. The Roadster is too recognizable."

Tinkie's face lit up. "I've always wanted to drive one of those things with the giant tires. I'd need a stepladder to get in it."

"Not one of those!" I was horrified. Talk about sticking out like a sore thumb. "Something discreet. And rugged."

She sighed. "If you insist."

"Let me out at the courthouse, take the Roadster back to Zinnia and see that baby, and when Coleman is done, he can give me a ride home. You can pick me up in the morning in the rental truck."

"I don't like the idea of leaving you here without a set of wheels."

"I can also rent a car if I need to," I reminded her.

"If you insist." She pulled in front of the courthouse. The rescue squad happened to be walking across the lawn. They were gloom personified. I didn't need to ask to know they felt they'd wasted another day and that not a trace of Mary Dayle had been discovered.

I got out of the car. "I'll text if anything happens. I swear it."

"What about that list of bikers?" she asked. "Maybe they were hired to take Marlon to the cabin. And Bilbo took him from there."

"I'm going to have a chat with Sheriff Nelson and

Coleman about that. We'll take action on it tomorrow. I'm pretty sure Coleman is ready to go home."

"He looks tuckered out," she said. "Searching the lake for a body is disheartening work. That river water is like mud, filled with silt and debris. Visibility must be about ten feet."

"And there's always the shark." Jitty's appearance as Salacia came back to me. Sea creatures behave according to their nature. That was her message. But what was this shark's true nature? Was she ready to give birth to pups or was she simply hunting for human prey?

"See you in Zinnia," Tinkie said as she drove away in the Roadster. I walked across the lawn to the courthouse.

Sheriff Nelson invited Coleman and me into his private office. I handed over the tape and rope I'd found at the hunting cabin. Nelson didn't look hopeful, but he said he'd send them to the state lab to be tested. I also gave him the list of the Johnny Boys, and he looked it over. "Most of these guys are cowards and bullies," he said. "They like to pretend to be tough, but it's all a mental game. When it comes down to actually walking the walk, they tend to shut up and drift away."

"There's no one who might be willing to kidnap an actor?"

"Depends on who asked them and what they were paying," Nelson said. "Leroy King would do it for the right price. Maybe Vondie Jenkins. The others are just guys who like to ride motorcycles and pretend."

"Did you know they actually harassed the film crew before Marlon disappeared?"

Nelson stood up. "I didn't. No one reported it."

"Is Ana still here?" I asked.

"She's in an interrogation room."

"Ask her."

"Let's do that," he said. He opened the door and led us to a room where we could watch and hear the interrogation. He stepped into the room with Ana and closed the door.

"I'm not going to hold you here," he said. "You're free to go. But why didn't you tell me about the motorcyclists trying to intimidate you?"

Ana sighed. "I didn't want to stir up more trouble. They didn't do anything except make some noise and ride around the set. They acted like they were going to damage the equipment, but they didn't. I thought it was best to ignore it. So did Marlon. He said he knew some of the guys and he'd just as soon leave it. So I did."

Her response made perfect sense. Making trouble for the locals was a surefire way to get even more resistance to the movie. Marlon and Ana had called it correctly, as far as I could tell.

A deputy knocked on the door and entered the interrogation room and handed Nelson two photographs. He put them on the table in front of Ana. "Do you recognize these two men?"

"They've been around the set. That one," she pointed to one photo, "wanted to be an extra. The other one went on a rant about how Mississippi never got a fair shake in the media or films." She shrugged. "Neither of them threatened us."

It sounded like a dead end, but we would still check it out.

Coleman recognized the disappointment on my face and put his arm around me. "Let's head home if you're ready."

He was exhausted. The long days in the water, always on

alert for danger, had taken a toll on him. "Let's do it. We'll need to stop by Hilltop to get my car and the pets, but we won't stay. I just want to make a drink and sit in front of the fire with you."

"Agreed."

By the time we got to Hilltop I was almost nodding off. I sent Coleman on to Dahlia House while I got my keys and critters and gave Maylin a kiss on her cheek as she slept in Tinkie's arms.

With Sweetie Pie in the front seat and Pluto on the console, I was headed home—with two servings of delicious red beans and rice, compliments of Tinkie and Pauline.

Coleman had fed the horses by the time I got there. I made cocktails and Coleman lit the fire. It was warm for a fire, but the flames were a primal comfort. When we were snuggled up together, the flames leaping and the dry wood crackling, I heard him sigh.

"Do you think Mary Dayle is dead?" I asked.

"I don't know. That was just strange how she went in right at the edge of the lake and never surfaced. No struggling, no flailing, nothing. Just gone."

"The shark—"

"Was nowhere to be found," Coleman said. "I've been looking for her, hoping to lure her back into that cage and help her get back to the Gulf."

"Mary Dayle named her Betty." The name seemed a bit old-fashioned for a traveling shark. "Pregnant females try to find a place that's safe for the pups. Nothing in this river is big enough to bother them except for humans, so she may be hunting for a secluded place." I just couldn't let the day's events go. "How could Mary Dayle just disappear unless something ate her?"

"I don't know," Coleman said. "None of the disappearances makes any sense. But I will tell you that shark has a lot of people upset. I heard that locals are showing up with guns. Some of them are truly afraid of it, but others look at it as a trophy kill."

"That's not right."

"I know. But Sheriff Nelson can't be everywhere all at once. If we don't get that shark caught tomorrow, I'm afraid someone will take matters into their own hands and kill it."

"Can I help?"

"I wish there was something you could do, but we've done everything we know to do. Tomorrow is my last day on this. I told Nelson I have work to do here in Sunflower County. DeWayne and Budgie have been putting in twenty-hour days covering for me."

That was true. Coleman's deputies were loyal to a fault. They'd do whatever they could to help him and never complain.

"Enough about me. What happened with you and Tinkie?"

I gave him the rundown on the hunting lodge, Bilbo, and the senator.

"Something stinks to high heaven," he said.

"We're out of leads, Coleman. I don't know where else to look."

"On the way to Greenville in the morning, I'll stop by Muscogee Plantation and do a little recon work. I don't think Marlon is dead. Or Mary Dayle. Where they are or who took them, I don't know. But my gut tells me they aren't dead."

"But Jules Valiant is definitely dead," I said. I trusted Coleman's gut—and I sure wanted to about Marlon and

Mary Dayle, but he'd taught me to rely on evidence, not intuition.

"Yes, I'm afraid Jules is dead, but I don't think the shark killed him."

"But his foot!"

"It looks like a shark, but what if it's something else altogether? What if he was dead and the shark simply bit him?"

That was a question that brought up a lot of possibilities—possibilities that would take time to think through.

23

The pickup Tinkie rented was a gray Tundra with a back seat perfect for Sweetie Pie, Chablis, and Pluto. We decided to bring the animals along with us. "What's on the agenda for today?" she asked as we all loaded into the vehicle.

"Coleman told me last night that Sheriff Nelson worked with the Arkansas authorities, and they searched the rice plantation across the river. There was no indication Marlon had been there." It was disappointing news, but at least that lead was dead.

"Are they going to continue the river search?" Tinkie asked as we drove toward Greenville.

"Yes, everyone is still missing as far as anyone knows." Mary Dayle's disappearance was the strangest of all. There and then gone. And I knew she was an excellent swimmer.

It didn't make logical sense. "Let's run by the bookstore and see if we can find anything there."

"Like what?" Tinkie asked.

"I don't know. It's just a hunch, probably a waste of time. Any suggestions?"

Tinkie shook her head as she pressed the accelerator harder. "Sounds like the best plan. I got nothing. How do you search for people who disappeared in a river?"

"Sheriff Nelson and Coleman are doing all they can. I think Coleman is focused on getting that shark into the trap." Even saying the words made my gut clench.

"I'm glad the shark is Nelson's problem. We have enough on our plate."

We pulled up in the shady parking lot of the bookstore. The day was sunny and warm. The animals would be fine in the truck, though I would have preferred to take them inside. I was curious to discover who was running the store in Mary Dayle's absence.

Tinkie and I went inside and separated, walking around all the shelves of books. I found the section on Mississippi history. There were several books about the 1927 flood. I pulled one out and immediately became immersed in one woman's account of survival. She was a gripping storyteller.

"Callie O'Shay is a fine writer." The comment came from a young man who'd quietly slipped up beside me.

"She is."

"I'm Raymond Smith. I work here. If you need any help, just let me know." He took a step back, as if to return to the sales counter.

"Where is Mary Dayle?" I asked. "She was going to recommend some books to me."

"She won't be in today. She told me yesterday she'd be

gone for a few days." If he knew anything was amiss, he didn't show it.

"Darn. When will she be back?"

"She didn't say exactly. I just fill in here when she's busy. She has a lot going on. She said she'd call me when she got back in town."

So Mary Dayle had made arrangements for Raymond to mind her store. Had she known she was going to disappear? What the heck was going on in Greenville?

"The movie company asked me to do some research on the flood for them. Could you recommend some books?" I asked.

"You work for Marlon?"

"Yes." It was true, in a manner of speaking.

"I heard they had shut the movie down because Marlon couldn't be found." Raymond wasn't above a little gossip.

"Oh, no. There was an issue with permits, but all of that was straightened out. Ana McCants is directing right now, until Marlon returns."

Raymond pulled two big books from the shelves. "These will help with your research. Do you know when Marlon will be back?"

"I'm just a researcher. No one tells me the big news." I laughed. "So when will Mary Dayle be back?"

He pulled another book from the shelves and handed it to me. "She didn't say. I'm sure she'll call and let me know."

I didn't think they had telephones down in Davy Jones's locker, but I didn't say that. If Raymond was truly unaware of Mary Dayle's possible drowning, I wasn't going to tell him.

Tinkie appeared at my side. She took the books I held and studied them. "These are perfect," she said. "Oscar is very interested in the history of the flood. Since we've been in Greenville, he's been reading up about it. His family wasn't really affected by the flood, and neither was the Bellcase family," Tinkie said. "We were very lucky."

"You're both natives of Mississippi?" Raymond asked as he made his way back to the counter. "Could I take your names to tell Mary Dayle you were here?"

"Sure." I wrote down my name and phone number and Tinkie added hers. I didn't want to give him a detective agency business card. At least not right now. "Please ask her to call one of us when she returns."

"Will do."

"Did she say where she was going?" Tinkie asked.

Raymond turned a bland face to us. If he knew anything, he was a damn fine actor. "No, she didn't."

"I think Ana McCants might be looking for some locals to work for a few scenes," I said, watching him closely. "I think you're very good at acting."

"Thanks," he said. "I'm not interested in acting, but I'll run by during my lunch hour."

I paid for my books and we left.

"Where to now?" Tinkie was as antsy as I felt.

"Mary Dayle's house."

"What's up?"

"She knew she'd be away from work at the bookshop. It makes me wonder what else she knew."

Tinkie's blue eyes widened. "You think she knew she was going to disappear?"

"That's what I'm thinking. But we need proof."

"More important than proof is understanding why. What is her motive for this?"

Tinkie had an excellent point. Why would Lamar Bilbo's

chief conspirator want to disappear at this particular time? "Do you know where Mary Dayle lives?" I asked.

"I do. When her family had to sell all their land holdings, she bought an adorable cottage east of town. She has one of the most beautiful gardens in the state." Tinkie bit her bottom lip. "How are we going to get in?" she asked.

"Lie or break in. Whichever is the most expedient."

Tinkie laughed as she accelerated. "Never a dull moment with you, Sarah Booth."

"Just be thankful we brought the critters. They'll get us inside. I have supreme faith in Sweetie Pie and Chablis."

"Me-ow!" Pluto jumped into the front seat and put his paws on the dash.

"And you, too," Tinkie said, stoking his sleek black fur. "Of all the critters, you are the most devious, Pluto. And we love you for it."

Mary Dayle's home was exquisite. The driveway wound through flowering trees and shrubs that made spring in the South the showiest and most beautiful of seasons. Whatever else Mary Dayle had achieved, she had a green thumb for flowers. We passed a table and chairs set beneath an arbor of sweet-smelling Confederate jasmine. The vine, which was native to Vietnam, had zero to do with the U.S. Confederacy. The star-shaped flowers had bloomed early, and the fragrance filled the yard as we got out of the car.

"I need an arbor like that," Tinkie said. "That vine gives a lot of privacy. Beautiful and thick enough to keep out the rain."

Mary Dayle's yard had a billion hiding places in it, not just the arbor. Growing up, I'd often ridden my bicycle around Zinnia. My playmates and I would improvise chase games like cops and robbers all over town, hiding in yards and outbuildings. No one cared. Mary Dayle's yard would be a haven for imaginative children.

We parked in front of the house and I rang the doorbell. No one answered. "I wonder if she lives alone?" I asked Tinkie.

"I don't know for certain. As far as I know Mary Dayle never married, but she went away to college and then she worked in California and some islands in the Caribbean before she took the job in Gulfport. Since then, she seems to have been a loner."

"There are rumors all over town that she and Lamar Bilbo are lovers." We'd all heard them, but I couldn't see it. Mary Dayle was at least a hundred IQ points smarter than Lamar. But love was blind, as the old saying went. Anything was possible.

"I've heard the talk. I don't believe it," Tinkie said.

That didn't mean Mary Dayle didn't have a lover or someone like a maid who kept the house clean for her. We were going into the situation blind. If someone was in the house, we could get in real trouble. I rang the doorbell again.

When no one answered, Tinkie and I split up and began walking around the house, peeping in the windows. Not my finest moment, but I had to find a way in. My gut insisted.

The house had been designed with an interior patio, where Mary Dayle had created a paradise of exotic plants. A wrought iron gate secured the enclosure. I cupped my hands and Tinkie put her foot in. I boosted her up, and over the gate she went.

"I can get in a window. I'll open the front door."

For a grand dame of society, Tinkie was pretty good at breaking and entering. I hustled around the house to the front door, which opened five minutes later. Tinkie grinned.

"You rang?" she asked.

"No one is here?"

"No one. The house is eerily empty. What are we looking for?" She was clearly eager to get off the premises.

"If you wanted to disappear in a river, what would you need?"

"Diving tanks." Tinkie didn't hesitate. "You think Mary Dayle somehow managed to have air tanks waiting for her?"

"I think her disappearance is not what it seems. Either she's in the river dead, or she pulled off a great little bit of drama."

"Why would she pretend to drown?"

"Why would she take up with Lamar Bilbo?"

"Two questions that no one can answer. I'll take the garage and storage area; you take the bedrooms and laundry," Tinkie said. "Let's be fast and get out of here before we get caught. Are we sure there aren't cameras here?"

I hadn't even thought of cameras. Just another reason that technology was often my enemy. "I'll look around. You're right. Let's be fast."

I hauled boogie for the bedrooms. A cursory search gave me nothing useful. Mary Dayle was a neat freak, so it was easy to do a thorough search. There was nothing amiss in the bedrooms, baths, or laundry. I came upon a small office off the kitchen and found the mother lode. Things were neatly organized; there were folders for bills and other expenditures.

Tinkie joined me. "I didn't find anything outside or in

the garage," she said, picking up one of the files I wanted to examine. "Hey!"

I turned to face her and saw the excitement on her face.

"Look at this. It's a receipt for scuba tanks. She had her tanks checked and filled three days ago." She handed me the paper.

"Then where are the tanks?" I asked. "Did you see them?"

"Nope. They weren't in the garage or storage building. Bet I know where they are, though."

"Under the dock in Lake Ferguson." That was the only rational explanation. Mary Dayle had tucked the tanks away, got into an argument with Ana deliberately, provoked the incident where she was jerked into the water, and then faked her own drowning. But why?

24

I texted Coleman a message about the scuba tanks. When he didn't respond, I figured he was in the lake. I couldn't allow myself to think too much about the dangers, but I had to wonder what Mary Dayle had been thinking. She'd put herself in real danger, and for what? Hoping her mysterious disappearance would halt the movie again? That was foolish. Ana McCants and the film crew didn't care if she drowned.

Tinkie and I were both pensive as we left Mary Dayle's property. We made sure there was no sign we'd been there. Although the whole business with Mary Dayle was peculiar, we weren't any closer to finding Marlon. No matter how I tried to arrange the things we knew, I couldn't make anything snap into place.

"Let's go talk to the butler," Tinkie suggested when we were on the paved road.

"It couldn't hurt." Bianca had said that James was fond of Marlon. Maybe he could help.

Driving to Muscogee Plantation again, I had a chance to look around since I wasn't behind the wheel. The place was well maintained, but there was a shadow that lingered over the land. Senator Brandon had lost his only son, Jacob, and now his only grandchild, Marlon. It seemed that the time of the Brandons was drawing to a close.

"You look so sad," Tinkie said as we drove beneath the beautiful sign.

"I was thinking that the Brandon family has dominated Mississippi politics and leadership for a long time. If Marlon is dead, that's the end of the family. He was the last."

"I hadn't thought of that," Tinkie said. "That is sad."

"What will happen to all of this?" I waved a hand at the expanse of Delta soil and the big house that was coming into view. "Are there cousins or other relatives who might take it over?"

"I don't think so," Tinkie said. "All of Senator Brandon's siblings are dead. He had a sister who never married. Rumor was that her father never found a man good enough for her, so he kept her a spinster. Jacob was the senator's only child, and he died."

"The end of a dynasty." I checked the back seat of the truck, where the dogs and cat snoozed. I had a sudden dread feeling that Jitty was sitting back there, a smug look on her face. She'd be the very first one to tell me that Dahlia House would suffer the same fate if I didn't buckle down and breed.

"Now you look guilty," Tinkie observed as she pulled

up to the front of the big house. "Are you thinking about having a baby?"

"Yes." There was no point in lying to Tinkie. She knew me too well. "I'm thinking about the consequences of not having a child."

"It's odd how so many of us are the last of our families," she said. "Oscar has a sister, but she took her husband's name, so she isn't a Richmond. If I hadn't gotten pregnant, the Richmond name would disappear from the Delta. Maylin will keep her name no matter who she marries."

Tinkie was too much of a friend to point out that the Delaney name rested on my womb's ability to procreate. The Delaney women had suffered from a number of womb disorders over the generations, and I was pushing the envelope on a breedable age. I'd asked my mother once why I didn't have a brother or sister. She'd laughed at me and told me that when parents got a perfect child, they didn't need additional children. Of course the answer had satisfied— and delighted—me back then, but now, I wondered. Had she suffered health issues that I might have inherited?

"Do you think Marlon has any children running around out there? He's very handsome. And charming." Emulating Tinkie, I was searching for the silver lining.

"I doubt that Senator Brandon would acknowledge them."

Tinkie had a point. "I've never understood why anyone would deny their own blood. I mean a simple DNA test would confirm it." Why walk away from potential love and family? And who was Senator Brandon going to leave all of his wealth and holdings to?

"Let's ask the butler," Tinkie said, killing the engine and getting out of the truck. She whistled the dogs out and left the window down in case Pluto decided to take a stroll, too.

The animals would not leave the vicinity, but at least they could stretch their legs while we talked to James.

When we rang the bell, he answered. "The senator isn't here." He started to close the door.

"We're trying to find Marlon. Please help us." Tinkie pinned him with her China-blue gaze. "I know you care about him. Bianca told us. Please work with us."

James sighed and stepped out onto the porch. He closed the door. "I don't think Senator Brandon would want me to talk with you."

"Why not?"

"He's a very private man. This whole thing with Marlon and the movie has upset him, made him question . . . things."

"What things?" I asked.

"The important things in life. The past." He shrugged. "Many things. He doesn't show it, but he's worried about Marlon."

"No, he doesn't show it," Tinkie said. "Is the senator friends with Lamar Bilbo?"

James actually chuckled. "Friends? Now that's a stretch. Both families go back in the history of the state. I think that wielding power is a shared interest between them, but I wouldn't count that as a friendship."

"We talked to Bianca over in Vicksburg and she suggested we speak to you." It was only a small stretch of the truth.

James's face lit up. "She loved Marlon. She was his mother's best friend."

"She told us," Tinkie said. "She said you were very good to Marlon. You were family to him, even when the senator wouldn't be."

"The senator's heart can be stony." His jaw hardened. "He can be cruel. He blamed a child for something he couldn't help. And Jacob and Jackie loved their son. Marlon was special from the day he was born, and they knew it. The senator saw him as . . . inferior because of his mother."

"She fell down the stairs?" I asked.

"Yes."

"Was there any hint of foul play?" I pressed.

James turned away. "Not according to the sheriff."

I glanced at Tinkie. She'd caught it, too—that lack of conviction.

James opened the door and invited us inside. "Look, I can't believe the senator had anything to do with that young woman's death. She had been ill. She'd been in bed with a fever, and she was weak. She was a headstrong individual who insisted she was well enough to get out of bed. I was downstairs when it happened, and I heard her fall. The fall broke her neck."

"And where was the senator?"

"I found him standing at the top of the stairs, frozen. He literally couldn't move. He thought Jackie was beneath the Brandon status, but he would not have harmed her. In the end, her death cost him everything."

"How so?"

"If I'm going to talk about this, I need a drink," James said. "Would you care for something?"

We settled for iced tea and when we were served, we sat in the parlor. "Thank you for talking to us," I told the butler.

"I want to find Marlon. I can't believe he's dead. He's such a vital force." He considered for a moment. "I'll tell you everything I know in the hopes that you can figure out what happened to him."

We sipped our iced tea and let James talk without interruption. While he told us much of the same history Bianca had given us, I examined the parlor. Everything was pristine. The velvet drapes, a floral pattern, puddled perfectly on the floor in front of the walk-through windows that led to the gracious front porch. A baby grand piano gleamed in the sunlight. Even though the day was sunny, a fire burned in the grate. Bookcases, filled with expensive, leather-bound books, lined both sides of the fireplace. Many looked to be old.

What I assumed were family portraits hung on the walls. I recognized Senator Brandon. There were several males painted in the standard professional pose, one hand on a globe or book or desk. They bore a resemblance to one another, so I assumed it was the Brandon lineage. Brandon, his father, and his grandfather. There wasn't a painting of Jacob Brandon that I saw, or of Marlon. They had been left out.

"When was the last time Marlon was here?" Tinkie asked. Since she'd pulled James into the present time, I focused on what he was saying.

"He was here last year, briefly. And then a week or so ago he returned."

"And he spoke with Senator Brandon?" Tinkie asked.

"On the first occasion, yes. On the latter, no. The senator was out of town. I wondered if the timing of Marlon's visit was . . . deliberate."

I leaned forward. "You think he didn't want to speak with the senator? Then what did he want?"

James looked slightly uncomfortable. "He went into the library and stayed for several hours."

"What did the senator say about that?" I asked.

James cleared his throat. "I forgot to mention it to him. To be honest, I knew he would be angry with me for allowing it."

I let that sink in. In the pause, Tinkie put her glass on the coffee table. "I know Marlon and the senator got off to a bad start. Does the senator care for Marlon at all?"

James put his glass down on a mahogany side table. "The senator holds his emotions close. He isn't a demonstrative man, but Marlon is his only blood. That means something to him. He doesn't know how to be affectionate or loving. He drove Jacob away by his unwillingness to accept the woman Jacob loved. The events that transpired were tragic and cost the senator greatly. I would hope he wouldn't make the same mistake with Marlon now."

"But he sent him away when he was just a child, alone in the world without anyone except the senator." I wasn't about to forget that.

"It was a poor reaction from the senator. He put up walls to protect himself and in doing so, he took no note of who got hurt. I honestly think Jackie's death shocked him. He drank heavily for a while. He didn't manage the plantation holdings or his investments. Things were so bad some of his old friends from the Senate came to talk to him. He was in a real downward spiral."

"What pulled him out?" Tinkie asked—a question I wouldn't have thought to voice.

"I don't know," James said. "One day he just set the bottle aside, took a shower, shaved, put on a suit, and went downtown to the bank. It was like he decided he wanted to live."

"Did he contact Marlon?"

"I don't know that either," James said. "The senator doesn't confide in me. I'm merely staff."

James had been with the family for more than twenty years, but some people held clear class distinctions. The senator was one. To him, James would never be more than hired help.

"What was Marlon looking for?" I asked.

"History. He said he was putting the finishing touches on his script and needed to see some family papers."

"Do you know what papers?" The tea glass in my hand was sweating.

"The senator has a trove of historical papers about the state, Greenville, so many things. The Brandons have a long history here. They worked with the state to create the state prison at Parchman and protect some of the lakes and marshes from development. They consulted with the chemical companies to bring in that Roundup Ready corn. Some good, some bad."

"Was there anything specific Marlon said he was looking for?"

"He asked for some old photographs. I showed him where the senator keeps them in a climate-controlled situation. And he wanted any articles about the flood, about the construction of the levee system, where the breach happened, and all of that. He was looking for stuff for his movie. To make it exciting."

"Could we see what he looked at?" Tinkie asked before I could.

James picked up his glass and drained it. "I shouldn't allow that. Senator Brandon won't like it at all."

"We only want to help Marlon." I leaned even closer to him. "Please, James. We don't have any leads. Mary Dayle McCormick disappeared in the river yesterday. She fell off the dock and just never resurfaced."

"The water's not even deep there," James said. "Where'd she go?"

"We can't find a trace of her. Just like Marlon. Now she's

gone. They both vanished. We have only a foot belonging to Jules Valiant. This is serious. The movie is going to fall apart soon unless we find Marlon and he gets back to work. If someone has taken him or is maybe holding him prisoner, we have to find him before it is too late." I didn't tell him about the chair and bindings we'd found at the camp.

"Okay." He stood up. "Follow me."

After the huge bookshelves in the parlor, I was even more impressed with the library. The dark paneling, Turkish rugs, comfortable reading chairs, and several desks scattered over the large room made it the perfect place to read or study.

The library was so vast, though, we needed James to point us in the right direction. Tinkie told him so.

"In the filing cabinet there's material on the history of Greenville that the senator and his father gathered. Be sure you put them back exactly as you found them or else I'll be in serious trouble. I shouldn't be doing this, but I want to see that young man again. I'm willing to risk my position here to do that."

"I hope Marlon knows how much you love him," I said. "When we find him, we'll be sure and tell him."

James flushed. "Thank you." He crisply turned and left us, closing the library door to give us privacy. Tinkie and I fell on the file cabinet like locusts on a wheat field. We had no clue when the senator would be home, but we had to be gone long before that.

The files were organized in a way that even I could use them. I pulled out the folder on the Great Mississippi Flood of 1927. It was four inches thick and contained newspaper clippings, maps, geographical surveys, land holdings, waterways, and personal notes written by an unnamed source. It would take hours to go through this one file. And we didn't have hours.

Tinkie had taken a file marked financial holdings. Being the genius she was, she'd whipped out her cell phone and was photographing each page. I didn't have time for even that, but I plowed through the file and stopped on a story about a bank robbery in Greenville during the flood. I'd never heard a word about this, and in a land where story and legend were valued, it caught me by surprise.

"Tinkie, did you know the Greenville National Bank was robbed either before or during the flood? A security guard was shot."

"I never heard that." She photographed away. "I guess with all the death and destruction, a bank robbery just got lost. So many people died in the flood and there was so much destruction. Was anyone charged? Did the security guard live?"

That was true. "The guard was a young man named Bobby Davis. It only says he was shot in the robbery attempt." I read the entire article. It just seemed strange that in all the lore of the Great Flood, no one had ever mentioned a bank robbery.

"How much did the robbers get away with?" Tinkie asked.

"There isn't an exact amount, but the bank was flush with money. Estimate is close to a million."

"In today's money that would be what?"

"I don't do monetary conversations. That's your bailiwick."

"Over seventeen million," Tinkie said confidently. "That's quite a haul."

"It says here the robbers boated into the bank. They broke

an upstairs window and went in. They were able to open the vault before the bank totally flooded. They found the money and got out. The security guard shouldn't have been there, but he was waiting for a rescue boat to come for him. He'd sent all the other employees ahead but there wasn't room for him."

"That would make an excellent scene in the movie," Tinkie said, clicking her phone like an automaton.

We both stopped and looked at each other. I got out my phone and began photographing all I could find on the bank robbery and a number of other personal stories about the flood that someone had clipped from newspapers or written down.

"Maybe we could just take these files," Tinkie said when she checked her watch. "We should go."

"We can't. James would get in a peck of trouble."

"You're right. Just keep working. Ten more minutes and then we're out of here."

At the allotted time, as if he'd been listening outside the door, James opened it. "You should leave. The senator will be coming home soon."

We closed the files, careful that they were exactly as we'd found them and replaced them in the cabinet.

"Thank you, James."

"Did you find anything that will help?" he asked.

"Honestly, I don't know. We'll have to evaluate it." I hesitated. "May we come back if we need to?"

"Call first. If the senator is out of town, you may come. I hope you find Marlon before that's necessary."

"Thank you, James. So do we."

25

Because we had lots of material to read, and I needed to download the stuff onto a computer for easier access, we whistled up the dogs and cat and headed to Zinnia. Tinkie was eager for an afternoon at home with Maylin, and I was simply eager for an afternoon at home. Dahlia House was like a cocoon. I felt safe there, secure and competent.

Tinkie dropped me and the critters off, and I went to the office and started printing out the pages I'd copied. In the kitchen I started the process for a pot of homemade red beans and rice. I would never, ever confess it to Jitty, but I had begun to enjoy cooking. Coleman had a healthy appetite, and he was appreciative of whatever I whipped up. Some things were better than others, but he never complained.

Once the beans were in the automatic pressure cooker,

I went back to the Delaney Detective offices. I was pulled into the details of the flood as I read. A noise startled me. When I looked up I saw a strange shadow outside the beautiful glazed door Tinkie had insisted on installing. The shadow was ungainly. And a little creepy. I hadn't heard a car drive up and when I checked out the window, there was no vehicle in the driveway.

The shadow moved against the glazed door again.

Someone was definitely out there.

I reached for my phone and dialed Tinkie. Before the phone could ring there was a tap, tap, tap at the door.

"Who is it?" I asked.

"Candygram."

I turned the phone off. "What?"

"Candygram. Someone has sent you a candygram."

The voice was muffled.

"Who are you?"

"Candygram delivery."

"Who sent it?"

"Candygram delivery. There's a card. We're not allowed to read the card. That's for you to do."

My unease had given way to curiosity. I opened the door to find a giant shark standing on the front porch. The huge mouth had rows of teeth, and it opened wide to grab my head. Before I could do anything, it lunged at me.

I screamed, stumbled backward, and tripped over my chair. When I hit the floor, the shark was all over me, tickling my ribs and arm pits and laughing manically.

"Get off me!" I pushed back hard, only to realize my hands went straight through the shark.

"Jitty! Damn you! You scared the snot out of me!"

Jitty stood up and then sat on the edge of my desk. The

shark suit was superb. Her arms were fins. She pulled the head off to reveal her smiling face. "Gotcha!"

"You are going to pay for this. You are dead to me."

"What a shock, since I've been dead for decades," she said.

She was so smug and proud of herself that I finally had to laugh. I got off the floor and sat in my chair, glaring at her. "You are a trial. You are so bad, you could run an outlaw gang. You are so mean, you can probably spit nails."

"You are so whiny you could get your own reality TV show."

"Candygram?"

"You're worried about that big hunk of man flesh becoming chum. I thought I'd give you a laugh."

I finally exhaled a long breath. "You are going to be the death of me."

"Not before you breed," she said sassily. "Now let's talk about that."

Of all the things in the world I wanted to talk about, getting pregnant wasn't one of them. "Jitty, I have two people missing and one man dead. I don't have time for your redundant rants about a Delaney heir."

"When will you have time?"

"I don't know."

"Then I'll have to take it up with Coleman. If I try hard enough, I can make him see me."

That statement struck an ice pick of fear straight through my heart. If Jitty and Coleman teamed up against me . . . "You will not speak to him about pregnancy. Or anything else!"

She laughed. "You're too easy today, Sarah Booth."

I stood up. "Get out of my office right now."

"Or what?" She was smiling like a holy saint.

"Or I'll . . ." I lacked tools to use against her and she knew it. "I'll sign up for Doc to give me a tubal ligation."

"You wouldn't and he certainly wouldn't."

"Wanna push it?"

Jitty huffed, spun in a circle, and disappeared on a blast of sand that stung my face. She truly was going to be the death of me.

I turned back to the printer to read over the documents I'd stolen. The history of Greenville pulled me back into the past with a strong tug. I knew I shouldn't get too caught up in the 1920s, but it was hard not to. Fifteen minutes into reading the historical documents, I was living in a world that existed a hundred years before.

Back then the Mississippi River was an even more vital waterway because there were almost no paved roads and the railroads were spotty in the very rural South. The newspaper articles were fabulous, giving me a picture of life in the 1920s in a state that was twenty years behind most of the nation. Along with newspaper clippings and legal documents, there were handwritten notes in a faded black scrawl that gave me an insight into the business acumen of Jefferson Brandon, the first Brandon to settle in the state near the turn of the century. He came with money and increased his holdings whenever possible.

Over the years, the Brandon family acquired more and more land and opened small businesses in Greenville. Then around 1920, something happened. I couldn't find out the details, but the results were drastic. Land was sold, businesses closed. The Brandon family was on a steep downhill slide. And then came the flood of 1927.

The damage was extensive—the old photographs in the files were horrific as I searched the faces of men, women, and children on rooftops or on parts of the levee where they were stranded. Many had given up, beaten by exhaustion and loss of hope. I'd heard about the flood, but looking at the photographic evidence was heartbreaking. How did one recover from that kind of catastrophic loss? I'd been so fortunate. No war had ravaged the land around me during my tenure at Dahlia House. I'd avoided tornadoes, lightning strikes, wildfires, floods, and other natural disasters as well as the manmade disasters that plagued most of the world. I took things for granted that people born in other places would never experience, like peace and plenty to eat. If one truly studied history, one learned to be grateful.

I moved through the pages until I came to articles about the stock market crash in 1929. The Brandon family took some hits, but they also began reacquiring all the lands they'd had to sell earlier. They paid with cash at the tax sales. Their empire grew by leaps and bounds. Somewhere, they'd found an infusion of cash that gave them the position of one of the most prominent families in the South. Once the Great Depression was over, real monetary growth was synonymous with the Brandon name. When the senator was born, a child of the 1950s, he had a golden ticket to an Ivy League school to study law and the money to enter politics.

The Brandon history showed hard work and smarts. Senator Brandon had a right to be proud of his legacy—why wouldn't he want Marlon to portray that in a film?

Since I had the files already on my computer, I sent them over to Tinkie with my observations. She was the financial brain of Delaney Detective Agency. I thought of myself as the muscle. Tinkie was the marksman, and I was the sprint and tackle. We complemented each other perfectly.

Coleman returned home and I could tell by the way he walked into the house that something was up. I made a cocktail and handed it to him. "You might as well spill your secret," I said. "For a man who can pull confessions out of hardened criminals, you aren't very good at hiding the fact you know something I need to know."

"Mary Dayle is perfectly fine."

That wasn't what I expected him to say. "What?"

"She wasn't injured, and she didn't drown."

"How do you know?"

"I saw her."

"In town?"

"At the bottom of Lake Ferguson. She was looking for the shark."

"You're kidding me." Only I knew he wasn't. He looked too hangdog to be making this up.

"How long have you known she was safe?" I could feel the heat climbing into my cheeks. I was glad she was okay, but I'd been worried about her. Ana McCants had narrowly avoided being charged with involuntary manslaughter.

"I saw her this morning."

"She had scuba tanks under the dock, didn't she?" The heat in my cheeks kept building.

"How did you know?" Coleman asked.

"Because Tinkie and I broke into her home and found the paperwork for filling the tanks. Then there were no tanks around."

"I decided to wait to tell you when we were home to-gether. Maybe I should have told you before you committed B and E."

"Why did she do this? Just to get Ana in trouble?"

Coleman sighed. "If that had been the case, I would have arrested her even underwater. Or gotten Nelson to do so. No, she's trying to help the shark."

I said it to myself twice before I really grasped the meaning. "You have to be kidding me, right? She pretended to drown so she could flip around in the water to save the shark she brought here to gobble up the film crew?"

Coleman took a big swallow of his drink. "She didn't bring the shark."

"You know this or that's what she told you?"

"Both."

"You talked to her underwater?" I had no doubt my cheeks were fiery red. The fading sunlight gave the room a timeless sense, like being trapped inside a sepia-toned photograph.

"I saw Mary Dayle in the water, and I followed her across the lake to the opposite shore where we both went to land. She explained that she'd staged her disappearance so she could work to save the shark without Bilbo catching on. Her plan is to reappear downriver and claim she was struck in the head by a log or something and lost her memory for a few days."

"That sounds like the plot of a really bad soap opera." But I was impressed with her willingness to risk life and limb for the bull shark.

"I know. It's pretty dramatic and has a lot of unbelievable elements. But it's Bilbo. Other people—smarter people—may question this, but she's determined."

That said everything. "Okay. So did you catch the shark?"

"Tomorrow. And Mary Dayle arranged with a boat to pick up the cage and take it downriver to the Gulf to release the shark."

It wasn't going to be a pleasant journey for the shark, through New Orleans and all of that. But it could be done and the sooner the better. Unless the shark was pregnant. "Coleman, if the shark is pregnant you can't put her through that journey."

"She can't stay in the lake here or the river. Someone is going to kill her."

He was correct. The future of the shark looked bleak. "What did Mary Dayle suggest?"

"Transport to the Gulf."

"What is Mary Dayle going to get out of this?"

Coleman didn't answer immediately. "I don't know. I can't read Mary Dayle. She seems sincerely concerned about the shark, but totally unconcerned about Marlon Brandon and the movie."

"She isn't opposed to the movie?"

"She doesn't seem to have an opinion one way or the other. It's the shark. Only the shark, as far as I can tell."

"What are you going to do?"

"Catch the shark if we can and attempt to get her back to the Gulf. That's the only solution I see."

"Is Mary Dayle certain it's a female shark?"

"It's hard to tell. Mary Dayle isn't exactly forthcoming or consistent in her answers. But I do believe she wants to help the shark."

"I looked it up. They give birth at the end of summer, so around August, I guess," I said. "How long is their pregnancy?"

"Mary Dayle said ten or eleven months."

"I find it distressing that my boyfriend is talking gestation with another woman."

"Not something you want to be worried about," Coleman

said. He waved me over to his side. When I was snuggled against him, he sighed. "I'm not going to Greenville tomorrow. I need to do some of my work. What are you and Tinkie going to do?"

"Tinkie's going over some financial material. And I'm going to the library to see if I can find any books on the Great Flood. Did you ever hear of the robbery of the Greenville National Bank during the flood?"

Coleman laughed. "Someone had time to rob the bank when the town was going underwater?"

"Apparently. The robber or robbers shot a security guard."

"Did the guard live?"

"No, I don't think so," I said. "But I can check that out. I'm also going to pay a visit to Leroy King and Vondie Jenkins. They're with some motorcycle club."

"I should be with you when you do that."

I kissed his cheek. "I think not. Seriously, I don't think these guys are dangerous, just blowhards. Do you have any idea how much good energy is wasted by people trying to control others because they're afraid?"

"A lot of terrible things happen out of fear," Coleman agreed. "People who are afraid and greedy are capable of anything."

26

I lied to my partner the next morning and told her I was working on historical research. I weighed my options—tell Tinkie the truth and drag her into possible danger or fib and give her a day to be with her daughter. It wasn't an easy decision. Tinkie would be angry when I told her the truth, but she would also be safe.

I loaded up Sweetie Pie and Pluto and headed for the Agri-Co offices where Vondie Jenkins worked. Bracing him at work seemed far superior to confronting him at home at the end of the day.

The Agri-Co offices were northeast of Vicksburg, and I found the sprawling complex easily. The air was heavy with chemical smells when I got out of my car and walked to the offices. The day was cool. I'd parked in the shade, so I kept the windows up. I wouldn't leave Sweetie Pie and Pluto out there to smell the chemical-laden air any longer than I had to. Perhaps it was just unpleasant and not a health risk, but I didn't want to find out the hard way.

Vondie Jenkins was a fleet manager who supervised dozens of trucks that delivered fertilizer to farms in the Delta. While Billy Watson, the man who farmed my lands, was focused on using only organic compounds, many of the very large cotton, corn, and soybean farms relied on chemicals. Those same chemicals washed into the Mississippi River and created a dead zone in the Gulf of Mexico. It was a vicious cycle that no one seemed able to stop.

Vondie was behind a big desk with a bank of ringing telephones. The stress level of his job would drive me crazy. Someone always calling, complaining, wanting something. He seemed to handle it all with good cheer. I stood back from the open door of his office and observed him for several minutes, until he noticed me and signaled me into the room.

"What can I do you for?" he asked.

I laughed at his colloquial question and introduced myself. I handed him a business card and watched his eyebrows slam together.

"Private investigator?" He looked at me and hit a button that put all of this phone calls on silent. "What's this about?"

"*Hero at the Helm.*" I left it there.

"That movie they're making on the river?" he asked.

"That's it. You know Marlon Brandon, the senator's grandson, has gone missing."

"Him and that bookseller and another guy. But they found the first guy's foot is what I heard."

"You heard correctly." I had no interest in telling him Mary Dayle was also alive.

"You think that shark got all three of them?" he asked.

"The shark or maybe a predatory human." I let that sink in.

"Wait a minute. You think I had something to do with their disappearance?"

"When a motorcycle club buzzes a film site and threatens violence, yeah, I'd say that's pretty good grounds for thinking you might be connected to tragedy on the set."

Vondie stood up. He was a tall man, in good shape, but he seemed more the fatherly type than a biker. Khaki pants, a button-down shirt, and loafers weren't very intimidating. Even when he was annoyed his eyes had a twinkle. Which wasn't to say they probably couldn't shoot lightning forks if he was mad.

"We had a little fun with the movie people. You know how it is, those California types coming to Mississippi thinking we're all a bunch of yahoos. But we didn't threaten anyone, and we didn't hurt anyone. We just rode around a little bit and left."

"Who put you up to it?"

"What do you mean?" But the way his gaze slid to the left told me he knew exactly what I was asking and that I'd asked the right question.

"I don't believe the Johnny Boys give two hoots what those movie people do. Someone put you up to trying to intimidate them and halt production. Maybe you thought some of the cast and crew would feel in danger and leave."

"I don't have time for this." He started to pick up a phone but put it back. "We haven't done anything wrong."

"That's a matter of interpretation." I didn't want to press

too hard. What the motorcyclists had done was act out a little fantasy of pretending to be badass Hell's Angels and trying to scare off a movie company. But why? That was the heart of the situation. The Johnny Boys couldn't care less about the content of the movie. I'd be willing to bet they'd all buy tickets and go see it. Who really cared?

"How much did Lamar Bilbo pay you?" I asked.

When he didn't answer, I knew I was close to the truth. "I can talk to Sheriff Nelson and explain how you got pulled into doing that, but if Nelson finds out on his own that you were acting on behalf of someone else, he'll charge all of you with criminal mischief." I looked around at his office. "You've got a good job. You and Mr. King don't want this mess following you around, do you?"

He startled a little when I said King's name. That was all the info I had, but it was enough.

"I was told our little ride-by was a joke. It was never meant to be a threat or intimidation. It was supposed to give the movie people a jolt and then a laugh. You know, something to talk about when they called home."

I didn't know if I believed him, but if he gave up the person who arranged it, I didn't care.

"Who put you up to it?"

He looked down at his desk. "Lamar asked us. We did it as a favor. No one paid us."

"Did Bilbo say why?"

"He just said the movie people were too big for their britches and for us to have some fun with them. You know, teach them to respect the culture here. That was it. We just rode around them, gave a few yells and challenges, and then we left. That was the end of it."

"Will Leroy King tell the same story?" I asked.

"He should, since it's the truth. Leroy wants to act tough, but it's all a bluff. Go ask him."

"You know since Marlon has gone missing, there will be serious inquiries into everyone who has had anything to do with that movie set."

He nodded. "I've been on a couple of the searches for the actor. We really didn't mean any harm to him or anyone else. In fact, I don't even know if Marlon was there the night we rode by. That woman was there. Short little firecracker. She was ready to fight." He smiled at the memory of Ana McCants. I could see where she'd be a spitfire if she got angry enough, and obviously that impressed Vondie Jenkins. "Do you know if that McCants woman is single?"

"She is," I said. If he was willing to court her, maybe it would be good for both of them.

"Thanks. Tell her I'm sorry if I upset her. It really wasn't meant to be intimidating."

"That's something you should tell her yourself." I excused myself and headed out to the car. I still had time to visit Leroy King. It was probably overkill, but at least it was a chore I could mark off my list.

Leroy was retired, and I was hesitant to go to his place, but there wasn't another option. I pulled up in front of his neat brick home. He was in a back shed—I could see him—working on his bike. I let Sweetie Pie and Pluto out of the car, and together we walked around to confront him. When he saw me, he bristled.

"Vondie told you everything you're going to get from me."

I figured Jenkins would warn him I was on the way. "Good, then you won't mind repeating it just to be sure I got it straight."

"Get off my property." He looked at Pluto. "Scat! I hate cats!"

Where Vondie was neat and well-groomed, Leroy had gone the way of the wild. His beard was long, gray, and scraggly. He wore a black T-shirt with holes in it and worn jeans, a red kerchief holding back long gray hair.

"Why did Lamar Bilbo want you to buzz the movie set?"

"Those people come to town thinking they're all better than us. They sneer at the state of Mississippi. They put on airs and act like we're a bunch of uneducated yokels."

"Marlon Brandon is from Greenville. You know that. From all I've heard, he loves this state."

"Marlon wasn't there. Just all the others."

I wondered at the chip on Leroy's shoulder. A lot of Southerners carried that same chip, feeling that folks from outside the region looked down on them. Sometimes it was true, but no one on the movie set had given me that impression.

"Why did Bilbo want you to annoy the movie people?"

Leroy put his tools down and came toward me, his hands clenched at his sides. He gave Pluto a hard glare. "You need to leave and take that cat with you. I told you, I don't like cats and I don't like nosy gumshoes." He stomped a foot at me and lunged forward. "Scat! You and the cat!"

Pluto walked up to him and rubbed against his leg. When Leroy started to kick him, Pluto leaped up on his thigh with all claws extended. He grabbed hold and hung on as Leroy danced.

"Get him off! Get him off!" Leroy was like a kangaroo, hopping hither and yon. He tried to swipe at Pluto, but each time he did, the cat simply dug in deeper.

"Just so you know, he's had all his shots," I said as I

whistled up Sweetie Pie, who came bounding from around the back of Leroy's house. Pluto took a flying leap and joined me as I headed to the car. By the time Leroy stopped jumping around, we were pulling away. It hadn't been a productive visit, but it did make me smile. Sometimes justice came in the shape of a handsome black kitty.

I was stopped at a crossroads, torn between heading back to Zinnia and confessing to Tinkie what I'd done, or going to Greenville and seeing if Ana had heard anything from Marlon or anyone else.

I had the radio tuned to a blues station, and it was my luck that Robert Johnson's "Cross Road Blues" came on. Legend was that Robert Johnson had made a deal with the devil at a crossroads for musical talent. Johnson died a very young man, reputedly poisoned, which was, of course, viewed as the ultimate end of any deal with the devil.

Had Marlon made such a deal? Was this movie so important to him that he'd gotten involved with people who had harmed him? In all of our speculation about where Marlon might be, Tinkie and I hadn't thought about someone from his past out in Los Angeles being the culprit. At least it was another avenue to explore. One that Tinkie would be invaluable investigating.

While I was in the Greenville area, though, I thought I'd take another look at the hunting camp. I had Sweetie Pie with me. It would be interesting to see if she could find any trace of the missing actor.

Before I went to the cabin, I stopped at the B and B where Marlon had been staying. The owner remembered me and let me into Marlon's room to get a dirty sock—a scent for

Sweetie to trace. In no time at all, we were parked on the dirt path and walking toward the cabin. I really missed having Tinkie with me, but Sweetie Pie and Pluto were boon companions.

I pulled Marlon's sock from my jacket pocket and gave Sweetie Pie the scent. She took off with her nose to the ground.

I loved the song of her bay as she found a scent and disappeared down the trail. Sweetie Pie would go only so far, then return to me to make sure I was coming. If I could run as fast as my dog, I'd be an Olympic contender. Pluto, who disdained fast movement of any kind, except when he was in attack mode, sauntered behind me as I picked up my pace.

Pluto might not be in a hurry, but he was a cat. He had super cat powers and would find us.

When I saw the outline of the cabin through the underbrush, I slowed. Sweetie Pie had fallen silent, and I was winded. Leaning my hands on my thighs, I took a moment to catch my breath. I was staring at the cabin when I saw movement.

Someone slipped around the corner and disappeared.

I hadn't expected to encounter anyone, and my first thought was for Sweetie Pie. If the person was armed—a hunter or worse—my dog could be at risk. I didn't dare call out to her or the cat. Silence was the safest route for all of us. But I did pull out my cell phone to text Tinkie. She might be mad at me for leaving her behind, but she'd send the cavalry if I didn't show up.

The brief glimpse I'd caught of the interloper left me short on details. Tall, slender, wearing a navy or black jacket or sweatshirt. In the thick woods, the temperatures were lower, the wind chillier near the water. By my best guess, we weren't all that far from the river.

I held my place, hoping the person would walk back into sight so I could better evaluate my opponent—and I did view the person as someone who might harm me. Whether it was one of Bilbo's minions or someone from the senator's employment, I didn't want to give them the upper hand. If it was a local poacher hunting on the senator's property, I didn't want to confront them.

I caught a glimpse of movement about fifty yards from the cabin. The lone figure was hurrying away through the woods. He or she was on foot, which led me to believe it wasn't someone attempting to rob the cabin. I couldn't tell if the person carried anything small, like jewelry or ammo or something of value that they might have stolen. I let my breath out slowly, only realizing then that I'd been holding it.

I made my way to the back of the cabin and peered in a window. I saw no movement and nothing out of place. From the southwest, Sweetie Pie's melodious bay came to me. She'd struck a hot trail and it sounded like she was headed back to me.

Just as I was about to climb the steps to the front porch, Pluto joined me. He, too, had his head cocked as if he was listening to Sweetie Pie's song.

I was still standing on the steps when the front door of the hunting cabin creaked open. There was no sign of life, only the rasping of the hinge as the door swung inward. The hair on my neck stood on end.

"Jitty, if that's you I am going to kick your butt."

But there was no answer.

27

The interior of the cabin was dark, even though the sun was shining outside. Someone had closed most of the window blinds. Stepping into the front room of the cabin was like walking into a big closet. I reached out my hands to feel my way in, careful not to knock over a lamp or table. When I finally put my hands on a light switch, I flicked it up. Light flooded the empty room, revealing overturned chairs and a sofa that had been gutted, the stuffing pulled out and scattered. Something bad had happened, possibly a struggle of some kind. But definitely a search. Someone had been looking for something.

I didn't touch any of the furniture, though I noted much of it was expensive leather. The same disaster had struck the kitchen. Things were pulled out of cabinets, drawers dumped on the floor, spices broken open and scattered everywhere. The same was true in the bunkhouse-style bedrooms and the two bathrooms. Not even the laundry room had been spared. Whoever had searched had come in hard and fast.

I took some photos and sent them to Tinkie, assuring her I was fine and soon would be headed home. Since I'd sent the emergency text letting her know I was at the cabin, her only response had been, "Okay." I had some fences to mend today when I got back to Zinnia.

Sweetie Pie's bay of excitement came to me just as I was closing the cabin door. She was close and she was hot on something. I caught a flash of her red-tick hide barreling through the underbrush, but I didn't see who or what she was chasing. It might be a deer—she was, after all, a hound dog with a keen nose. But once set on a task, Sweetie Pie seldom deviated. Was it possible she was chasing Marlon? Was he the one who'd broken into his grandpa's hunting cabin to look for something? And what could that be?

A chill settled over me. There were layers to this case I hadn't considered. The fine hairs along my neck, standing on end, told me that danger was close by.

Sweetie Pie bayed again, giving the long, shrill scream of cornering her prey. She wouldn't harm anyone, but they might not know that. If the person she pursued had a gun . . . I didn't think any further. I hauled it for the woods with Pluto bounding in front of me. Pluto acted like he didn't care about anyone or anything, but he adored that hound dog. And he had more acute hearing than I did. He was homed in on Sweetie Pie's voice and making tracks.

I intercepted Sweetie Pie's run just as she leaped a fallen tree and knocked a person in a black hoodie to the ground.

She was on him in a flash, not growling, but tugging at his hoodie. The man—and it was a man—jumped up and tried to flee again, but Sweetie was having none of that. Pluto joined the fray, jumping on the man's head. That was never going to end well for him.

"Stand still and they'll stop," I called out to him.

He ignored me until Pluto sank his claws in deep. Then he screamed and sat down on the ground. Sweetie backed off and Pluto dropped beside her friend. I walked close. I didn't have a weapon, which was foolish, but if he tried anything the critters would retaliate quickly. Besides, if he'd been armed, he would have tried to defend himself already. As it was, blood was leaking down his face where Pluto had snagged him, and his clothes were torn and dirty.

"Who are you?"

He didn't look up, just kept staring at the ground.

I walked a little closer, still out of reach. "What's your name?"

When he didn't answer, I pulled out my phone.

"Who are you calling?"

"Sheriff Nelson. You're trespassing on private property, and I think you wrecked Senator Brandon's hunting cabin."

"I did. Don't call the sheriff." He finally looked up at me.

My sharp intake of breath let him know I recognized him. "RoDa." The young man was part of the cast and an alleged friend of Marlon. "You! Marlon helped you."

"And I'm trying to help him," RoDa said. "You must believe that. I tore up the cabin looking for evidence of where Marlon might be. We can't wait any longer to find him. The investors are threatening to stop funding the movie. Some of the cast and crew want to leave for Los Angeles so they can find work. Things are getting really serious."

"How did you know to come here?" I asked the actor.

"Something Marlon said before he disappeared."

"You might have told me and Tinkie. We've lost days." I was getting hotter and hotter.

"I didn't know if I could trust you or your partner. You were always talking to the senator and that Bilbo person. And you're from here. I couldn't be certain, and I couldn't risk it."

"What is this big thing you know?"

"Brandon had some information. Historical information. He said it was going to bust things wide open in Greenville."

"I've read the script. There is nothing antagonistic toward the citizens of Greenville in it." I was tired of this old saw.

RoDa got to his feet. "I don't think this was about the movie."

"Then what is it about?" I was debating whether I had to notify the sheriff or not. RoDa had done considerable damage to the senator's property. It seemed wise to report it, especially in light of the fact that RoDa seemed to know a lot more than he'd let on.

"I don't know," he said. "I was hoping to find something and maybe from there figure out where Marlon was being held."

"You think he's a prisoner?" I was interested now.

"I know he is. Or he's dead. He would never abandon this film. Never. He wrote the script, he put together the financial backing, he's put the last three years of his life into this movie. He cares about it. A lot. He would be on that set working if he wasn't being stopped by someone."

"Who?"

RoDa shook his head. "I wish I knew. I swear to you, I am acting as Marlon's friend. I told you he was trying to help me. Why would I do anything to interfere with that? I know he's in big trouble. I only want to help."

RoDa kept putting his hands in his pockets. And pulling them out. Nerves? Guilt? Black dirt clotted beneath his fingernails. It looked like he'd been digging in the soil with his hands. Was it possible he'd found something in the hunting lodge and when he realized Sweetie Pie was after him, he'd quickly buried it?

"Do you need a ride back to the movie set?" I asked. I was hoping he'd tell me how he'd gotten out to the hunting lodge. Had the senator or Bilbo brought him? I looked around for any signs of an accomplice.

"My car is that way." He pointed in the opposite direction I'd come from. "There's a road in that's better than the old road you probably came in on. Marlon told me about it."

"Okay." I put a hand on his shoulder. "I hope Sweetie Pie didn't scare you when she chased you down. She's just a hound dog with a super sniffer. I had hoped she'd hit a trail left by Marlon if he'd been out here recently."

"No problem," he said, taking a few steps back. He was eager to get away from me. I was eager to let him go—in the hopes that he'd leave me and seek out what he'd buried. I intended to track him, from a distance. Sweetie Pie and Pluto could help me with that. It struck me that Sweetie hadn't picked up on Marlon's trail at all. Maybe he'd never been at the lodge. I remembered the chair and bindings, though. The crime lab in Jackson still hadn't made a report on those but, clearly, someone had been detained. Of course it could have been a poacher caught on the property and taught a lesson, or it could have been one of the hunters playing pranks on another. I'd assumed it was Marlon because he was the person I knew was missing.

I gave RoDa a five-minute start before I whistled up Sweetie Pie and put her on his trail. Interestingly, she went to my pocket and pulled out Marlon's sock. She dropped it and bayed, then put her nose to the ground and followed RoDa. I picked up the sock, thinking. Was it possible RoDa was wearing Marlon's clothes, so that Sweetie Pie had caught that scent?

I had no answers, only more questions. I'd just started after my dog when a gunshot boomed. A bullet whisked past my head and smacked into a poplar tree. I dropped and rolled, not certain if the bullet had been meant for me or if some hunter was unaware there were people in the woods. I wanted to yell for them to stop shooting, but I couldn't. Otherwise RoDa would suspect I was trailing him. A second shot echoed, but no bullets struck close to me.

I hunkered down with Sweetie Pie and Pluto and waited a few minutes. When nothing else happened, I stood and followed Sweetie as she hit the trail. I'd put her on a leash, just to be safe. I didn't want her chasing someone with a gun. A lot of people thought nothing of shooting a dog or even a person.

Sweetie Pie tugged me forward and covered a quarter of a mile fast. Then Sweetie Pie stopped. Blood splattered the fallen leaves on the trail. Someone or something had been shot. Now I picked up the pace with Sweetie. Every fifty or so feet, we found more blood. If the wounded person or animal didn't get help, they would die.

28

The blood stopped at a cleared space where a vehicle had been parked. Evidence indicated RoDa had been shot but he'd made it back to his vehicle and left. Whatever he'd buried in the woods, he likely hadn't recovered. The critters and I started the walk back to the hunting lodge and, ultimately, my vehicle.

Without the compulsion to find RoDa and spy on his actions, we took our time on the walk back. I kept a sharp eye out for the shooter, but I felt safe. RoDa had been the target, not me. I sent a text to Sheriff Nelson and told him of the shooting and the break-in at the senator's hunting lodge—I was obligated to do that. He'd been generous with information for Tinkie and me and I had no idea what role RoDa played in Marlon's disappearance. I texted Coleman and Tinkie and let them know I was fine and heading home. Both of them would be annoyed with me, but I'd survive it.

I sent a second text to Tinkie to ask her to check into Robert Davis, aka RoDa. I mentioned that the name sounded like an alias. The farther I walked, the more I felt I'd been played. Who was Robert Davis? I should have been on top of this sooner. I tried hard not to beat myself up, but this entire case seemed like I'd missed opportunities at every turn. The whole Mary Dayle disappearance made me mad at myself. I'd swallowed that hook, line, and sinker and wasted a day trying to find her. She was hiding out somewhere, and likely Coleman knew the location. That was another loose tooth I needed to pull.

My phone buzzed. I paused to read Tinkie's text. She urged me to find Ana McCants and get the scoop on Robert Davis. He wasn't listed as a Mississippi resident, no matter what he claimed. Dammit! I'd been played by the actor. I picked up my pace. I'd likely find him in a local emergency room or urgent care. If he'd truly been shot, he'd need medical attention.

Once I got my hands on him, he'd squeal like Porky Pig at a barbecue. I'd make sure of that.

I used my phone to pull up all the urgent care offices in the Greenville area, figuring that RoDa would avoid the hospital emergency room for fear they'd report his gunshot to the sheriff. The doc-in-the-box clinics were supposed to do that, too, but I doubted the scrutiny would be as intense. My hunch paid off at the third clinic I visited. I caught RoDa limping across the parking lot. When I pulled up beside him, he didn't even attempt to run. He got in the passenger seat that Sweetie Pie grudgingly vacated before I told her to.

"I'm sorry," he said.

"How badly are you hurt?"

"Not nearly as much as they wanted to hurt me." He patted his left leg. "Flesh wound. The bullet went all the way through. Lucky it wasn't a hollow point or some military ammo."

He was lucky. Plenty of untrained people had assault-style weapons and ammo that tore flesh apart. Getting shot with "normal" weapons and ammunition was no fun, but some of the firepower available now could have torn his leg off. "Who are you?" I asked. "Don't lie. I'll find out anyway and I'll just be really mad."

"I didn't lie. I'm an actor and a friend of Marlon's."

"There is no Robert Davis of your age and occupation living in the state."

"You're right." He sighed. "My birth name is Lucifer Davis. That's not a lie. My mother was stoned most of the time and thought it would be funny. It's not."

I had to agree with him. No one should stick a child with a name that would invite torment, though I myself had named a gorgeous black horse Lucifer. What had his parents been thinking?

"My mom was a good person, she just stayed loaded all the time. Her sense of humor was . . . different. She did the best she could, with her background and the addictions she had to tamp down. She came from an abusive home. She left at sixteen, got pregnant with me, and tried to provide a home for us. By the time I was ten, I was working odd jobs just to be sure we had bread and milk in the house. She died when I was fifteen. Overdose. I suspect it was deliberate. She had only self-loathing, no matter how much I loved her. I've been on my own since then. There was no one to stop me, so I changed my name to Robert. It was a name that attracted zero negative attention."

"But you never legally changed your name."

"No, it seemed like a lot of hassle for little benefit."

"What about your Social Security card and all of that?" I was a little sympathetic and honestly curious.

"It was easy enough to pull off. I just made up a name, an address, a backstory, all of it. I gave myself the life I wanted to have. Small-town boy who had stars in his eyes for Hollywood. I moved around a lot and found work in New Orleans on several film sets. Then I met Marlon at a bar in Vicksburg and we hit it off. I told him the truth and he just laughed. Said I had balls to pull something like that off. And he loved the idea of RoDa. He said I could be an icon. His support has meant everything to me, and you have to believe that I would never hurt him. No one else had ever believed in me."

"What did you bury in the woods?" I cut a glance at him to let him know I wouldn't be fooled again.

"I found a key to a safety deposit box in the hunting lodge. Then I realized someone was on my trail. You. And that dog with a keen sniffer." He reached into the back seat and gave Sweetie Pie some scratches behind her ears. "I stopped long enough to bury it because I didn't want you or the cops to search me. I figured you'd turn me in for trespassing and destruction of property."

"Did you leave any fingerprints in the lodge?"

"No. I was careful." He sighed. "I was so hopeful I'd find Marlon there."

"You think his grandfather is holding him hostage?"

"A lot of people use that cabin. The senator learned

long ago that he could have plenty of riches as long as he shared with the people who funded his campaigns. Politics. Scratch my back and I'll scratch yours. Marlon said the prominent men in the Delta had wild parties and orgies there. You know, bringing in hookers and drugs and such. Marlon hates hunting as much as I do."

I wasn't shocked. The hunting club sex parties were all too common, but there was little privacy in the design of the lodge.

"Hell, I'd say only twenty percent of the time guys are at the lodge are spent in the woods. The don't want the bother of hauling and cleaning a deer. They're there for the sex and drinking, playing cards, and shooting the breeze with their buddies."

That was perfectly all right with me. If their wives didn't object, I had no opinion.

"RoDa, I'm not buying your story completely. I want that key."

"It looked like it would open a safety deposit box, but I can't guarantee it."

A red flag warning went up in my brain. RoDa was a very good liar. But at least if I had the key, he couldn't use it. "Let's go."

"Are you sure the person who shot me is gone?"

I'd forgotten he was shot. At least he wasn't a whiny baby. "Tell me where it is and wait here."

"How do you know I won't run away?"

"A, you're shot. B, if you try that Pluto will scalp you. I believe you've met Pluto's claws. He's a temperamental cat and believes violence is the answer to any problem."

RoDa leaned back. Blood pooled around his sneaker. More than a little. I took off my sweatshirt and fashioned a tourniquet with a sleeve and a stick. "Release it slightly every couple of minutes but try not to bleed to death while I'm gone. I hope your directions are accurate and easy to follow. Then you're going to the hospital." He wasn't in danger of dying, but it didn't hurt to make him wonder.

"Don't you feel guilty leaving me here?" he asked.

His question surprised me because I did. "Yes. But not as guilty as I'd feel if I lost a chance to find Marlon."

He actually laughed, then gave me the directions I needed to find the buried key. I hurried toward the spot he'd indicated with Sweetie Pie leading the way.

29

Sweetie Pie found the key easily enough. RoDa had a good knowledge of local flora and fauna. His description of the hiding place was detailed. I found the "strange" holly bush—half of it was dead as RoDa had described—that made me certain we were in the right spot. Sweetie's keen nose led me straight to it. As much as I wanted to look for evidence of the shooter, I knew he was gone. Sweetie would have sussed him out and taken him down.

Key in hand, I headed back. I half expected RoDa to be gone when I got there, but he was sitting with Pluto in his lap stroking the cat. All had been forgiven, even though RoDa might need hair transplants in the future. Pluto was tough on the scalp.

He gave a weak smile of relief. "Thank you. I'm not certain I can walk now."

Sweetie and Pluto jumped into the back seat. "I'm taking you straight to the hospital," I told him.

"Yes, I think that's best."

All of the fight was gone from him. I dialed Sheriff Nelson and asked him to meet us. "Someone was in the woods trying to kill me and one of the film crew, Robert Davis."

"I'll meet you there."

"I wish you hadn't done that," RoDa said.

"I have to. There's no getting around it. And besides, someone was trying to kill you. And me. We have to find out who that was."

"What if I already know?"

"Do you know? Tell me!"

"I need medical attention first."

I wanted to slam on the brakes, but RoDa was growing weaker, and I didn't want to jostle him. I drove as quickly as I could over the bad roads. When I hit the pavement, I put the pedal to the floorboard and the truck purred up to ninety without a complaint.

"What happened to that great Mercedes?" he asked. "The truck is nice, but not like that antique. I'd love to have that car."

"These roads are too hard on it. It was my mother's." I found it strange that I felt comfortable talking to him about my private past.

"I have a set of earrings that belonged to my mother. I considered getting my ears pierced so I could wear them. They're only little golden circles. Probably fake, but she loved them so."

"Help us find Marlon and I'll get my childhood doctor to pierce your ears for you."

"You don't think it's silly?"

"Not when it's something your mother loved." His affection for his mother, though she hadn't protected him, touched me.

"Do you know where the safety deposit box is?" I was holding the key in my hand, feeling the long shaft and the two prongs that opened what looked to be an ancient lock. It reminded me of the keys to the church basement room in the Baptist church where the choir robes were stored. Tammy Odom and I had stolen the key from the Baptist minister's desk when we were visitors in the church one Sunday. We meant to return the key and had no intention of stealing anything. We thought they had an immersion pool for baptisms in the basement and we were dying to see it.

Boy, I'd gotten the worst spanking ever for that prank, but I'd protected Tammy. She hid in the choir robe closet, and I didn't rat her out. I took all the blame. Since she was Black, I feared she'd be in worse trouble than me.

My birthday gift that year was a book on religious practices. Thanks a ton. I wanted a skateboard.

"You're very quiet," RoDa said as we pulled into the hospital parking lot.

"Lot on my mind."

I stopped at the emergency entrance. RoDa got out and waited for me.

"You aren't going to follow me in? What if I run away?"

"It's your leg that would have to be amputated." I had no idea if his wound was that serious, but he'd been bleeding steadily and needed attention. "I have to talk to Nelson and Coleman Peters. I'm going to tell them everything."

"I expect nothing less," he said as he limped up the ramp and went through the double doors.

I would talk to the lawmen, but Ana McCants was my first stop. I had a bad feeling she wasn't playing straight with me. Possibly hadn't been since I first arrived in town.

Ana was on the set, explaining to the cast and crew what she needed. I stood back as she called out, "Action!" The scene unfolded, and I found I was caught up in what was happening. They only filmed for a few minutes, but it was a compelling scene about a family that lost everything in the flood. The actors brought real emotion to the set. If the rest of the movie was this good, Marlon would have a barn burner on his hands when it was finished. If he was around to enjoy it. When the filming finished, I pulled Ana aside.

"You lied to me about Robert Davis."

She didn't deny it, which was in her favor. Her gaze never flinched.

"Why?" I asked.

"He was searching for Marlon. I thought if he was left alone, he might have more luck than anyone else. They are friends. That's not a lie. Marlon shared things with him. Stuff even I don't know. Family stuff. RoDa is from here, though he has never lived anywhere long. He had an understanding of the Brandon family and the culture that I don't always get."

"No one on this set has been honest with me," I said. I was angry and didn't bother to hide it. "I've been spinning my wheels for days based on false assumptions and bad leads. I can't continue working on the case. I'm going to notify the insurance company to find someone else."

"No!" Ana grabbed my wrist. "Please don't. I'm sorry. We're all sorry."

"RoDa is at the local hospital being treated for a gunshot wound. Someone was in the woods and shot at us. He was hit so he was probably the target, but we both could have been killed."

"Is he okay?" She seemed genuinely concerned.

"No, he isn't okay but he's going to live. Who hates you, Marlon, or this film enough to attempt to murder RoDa or me?"

"What? Maybe it was an accident. A poacher hunting out of season." She looked genuinely shocked.

"No, it was deliberate. They weren't shooting blanks or rubber bullets. They hit RoDa in the leg. It could as easily have been his brain or heart." Anger and fear made me more aggressive than I normally was. The reality that I'd almost been shot and that RoDa could easily be dead had finally sunk in.

"No one that I know would shoot anyone. We didn't bring any guns from California. The film doesn't have any guns in it. Someone local has to be behind this." She brushed tears off her cheeks. "You know, it's okay if you want to quit. I'm exhausted from this, from fighting and trying to keep this movie afloat when it looks like Marlon will never come back. I'm just burning good money after bad. This is going to ruin my reputation in the business. I'm ready to head home to Los Angeles."

Ana's defeated attitude caught me by surprise. I could see where she'd be discouraged, but I hadn't expected her to fold so instantly. "You don't have a clue who might have done this?"

"I swear I don't." She waved me toward the trailer where her office was.

I wanted to ask her about the key I still held, but I didn't. After Tinkie and Coleman had examined it, I'd go further afield for an answer to whatever bank the safety deposit box might be in. Right now, I was playing my cards close to my vest.

We talked for ten minutes, and I learned nothing new. In truth, I had no big revelations to drop on Ana. I left the movie set and went to the sheriff's office where I filed a report about the shooting. A deputy left immediately and went to the hospital to find RoDa, but unsurprisingly, he radioed back that the actor had been treated and had left. The wound was not serious, but RoDa had been warned to stay in bed to heal. Even I knew that wasn't going to happen.

I left Greenville and headed to Hilltop. I had to make amends with Tinkie and also get her help with the key. I talked the case over with Sweetie Pie and Pluto. If they had any insight, they kept it to themselves.

When I stopped in front of Hilltop, the animals bounded out of the car. I hurried inside. She met me with a frosty greeting, but when I told her about RoDa and the gunshot, she forgave me. I hustled her toward the door. "Let's go."

"What's the rush?" she asked. "You didn't even give Maylin a kiss."

"When we return." I checked my watch.

"Where are we going?" Tinkie planted her feet and demanded.

"To buy a vehicle for me. It's time. Having that rental has spoiled me to the joy of a rugged vehicle that no one really notices."

"Have you researched what kind of vehicle you want?" she asked.

Everything was so damned complicated. I could remember the days when you drove to a car lot, looked over what was available, and picked one out. You might dicker over the price or loan or accessories, but generally there weren't all that many choices. Now it was like a ginormous life decision and some of the SUVs and trucks cost as much as a starter home.

Tinkie saw the frustration. "Ask Coleman. Get him to go with you. He'll get a better deal." She held up her hand. "It isn't fair, but that's how life works still. You have a man who knows mechanics, so take advantage of it. What's the rush?"

"I just about beat the wheels off the Roadster, and I don't want to tear up your new car either. The rental has been nice, but that's burning money. I promised myself that I would take care of this."

Tinkie grinned. "Then tomorrow will be soon enough. You can just borrow Harold's new truck for this case. It's loaded."

My partner was a master manipulator, and she knew it.

30

Once Tinkie got me inside her house and seated at her breakfast nook in the kitchen, I showed her the key. "Car shopping is going to have to wait," she said, picking up the key and examining it.

"Why?"

"This opens a safety deposit box. Probably in the First National Bank of Greenville."

"Why would RoDa have a safety-deposit box key in Greenville?"

"Because it isn't his." Tinkie rolled her eyes. "Why would he have a key?"

"Because he stole it from the hunting lodge."

"Bingo!"

Relief flooded me, and then humor. I started laughing

and almost couldn't stop. "RoDa stole the key from the hunting lodge because, if he really is Marlon's friend, Marlon sent him for it. Either that or he's our prime suspect."

"You are on fire!" Tinkie slapped my shoulder a little too hard.

I checked the time. It was too late to go back to Greenville today—the bank would close before we got there—but first thing in the morning, we'd be at Greenville National and see what we could find out.

"Let's stay home," Tinkie said. "I've had such a wonderful day with Maylin. I hadn't realized how much I missed her until I had her all day long. She has learned new things, new habits. She likes English peas now!"

The joy in Tinkie's face was a tonic for me. "Really? She hated them last week."

"I know. Everything changes so quickly with a baby. Their perception, abilities, just everything."

"Pretty soon she'll be working with us to solve cases."

"You know she will!"

When it was time to go, I called Sweetie Pie and Pluto. They came bounding out the front door and jumped into the vehicle. I'd take it back to the rental place. Of course, when I got a new vehicle, I'd have to take them with me to be sure they approved of my selection.

Coleman was no longer working all day on the search and rescue for Marlon, but he stayed in close touch with Sheriff Nelson. The search was all but dead. There'd been no sign of the actor, and while Coleman and Nelson knew Mary Dayle was alive and safe, they were keeping the information under their hats. The shark had disappeared. Without any sightings, the furor had died down. Even Lamar Bilbo had fallen off the radar, though I expected he was up to any dirty tricks he could engineer. The pace of the sleepy river town seemed to have fallen back to normal.

Coleman grilled some fresh Gulf shrimp he'd found at a local fish market, and I made a pitcher of Salty Dogs. We sat on the front porch with our plates and enjoyed the ending of a beautiful spring day.

Coleman updated me on what Nelson was doing, but there wasn't a lot to tell. I showed him the key. "This is great," he said. "Whatever is in that safety deposit box may answer a lot of questions."

We discussed a new vehicle, and since we weren't selling the Roadster or trading it in, Coleman volunteered to handle the purchase for me—a chore I was double happy to hand over to him. How remarkable to express a need and have someone offer to fulfill it.

I had total faith in him. The Roadster was the car of my heart. After that, I didn't care as long as it was reliable and rugged. Coleman had the superior knowledge and would make the wiser choice. Once he had the vehicle spotted, Tinkie would drive me to pick it up.

With the vehicle situation under control and all the news shared, I refilled our glasses. We settled on the steps so we could sit close to each other in the fading twilight. When the first star appeared, Coleman drew me close against him. "Make a wish, Sarah Booth."

I considered for a moment. "I wish our future to be as happy and content as this moment. What do you wish for?"

He kissed my neck. "I have everything I could ever want right here, with you."

Life is filled with good times and hard times, but moments

of bliss are too often fleeting. I felt joy as I kissed him. "This is a perfect evening. One I'll always remember."

"These times are precious. I know you have good memories with your parents and Aunt Loulane, happenings in college, and when you first moved to New York so full of hope and expectations."

"True," I said. "And you. We had fun in high school, though I would never have predicted we'd end up sitting on a porch drinking Salty Dogs and mooning over each other."

"No one could have predicted that," he agreed. "You make my life complete, Sarah Booth."

I took the compliment with a long kiss that foretold of what was to come when we went inside. Whatever the future held, I would always have this memory with Coleman. And many more, I hoped.

He took my hand and helped me up. Together we went into the house and locked the front door. These few hours were ours alone, and I had no intention of squandering a moment.

31

We were at the Greenville National Bank when they opened at nine o'clock in the morning. The key had a faint number etched in it. 1024. We asked to see that deposit box, and to my surprise no one balked at our request. When the young bank officer took us into the vault, I was surprised by the size of the box. It was big. Tinkie squeezed my hand. This could be a real payout of information that would lead us to Marlon, or it could be bloody gloves or love letters. We had no way of knowing until we opened the box.

When the bank employee showed us the box, Tinkie inserted the key while the employee did the same in a second lock. They turned the keys together and the box was freed. As the deposit box was slid out and placed on a small table,

I heaved a sigh of relief. I hadn't been certain the key would work, and I'd feared we'd be challenged by the bank since we were clearly not Marlon Brandon or anyone related.

Tinkie held my gaze as she lifted the lid. A pile of papers, photographs, and maps were revealed.

"No diamonds or gold," Tinkie said. She didn't sound disappointed as she lifted the stash of fragile old papers from the box. I'd brought several plastic storage baggies and we gently put them inside. It took three big bags, but we packed everything.

"We can only hope this gives us a solid lead. Now let's take this stuff out of here fast. We can bring it back and return it once we've made copies."

It was a good plan. And I knew exactly where to find a copier so we could return all of this before we left town.

"Where are we going?" Tinkie asked.

"The sheriff's office. I think Nelson will allow us to make some copies."

"Good thinking."

As I predicted, we were shown the copier and left alone in the room to work. Nelson owed Coleman a lot for his help with the search, even though no rescue had been made. Tinkie didn't mind making the copies, and she'd found something that held her interest. In the meantime, I wanted a moment to talk with Nelson about Mary Dayle and her crazy decision to pretend to drown. I slipped away to Sheriff Nelson's office. He was behind his desk drinking a cup of strong, black coffee.

"You were there when Robert Davis was shot?" he asked.

It wasn't exactly the direction I wanted the conversation to go, but I understood his annoyance. "I was, and I reported it."

"After you gave the young man time to get treated and flee."

"Look, Sheriff Nelson, I did everything by the book. How would I know he'd take off? Heck, it normally takes at least twelve hours to be seen in an ER. I had no idea he'd split."

That was a lie, but I was sticking to it.

"Who shot him?"

"I didn't see. They almost got me, too."

"And what were you doing in those woods?" he asked.

"It's Senator Brandon's hunting camp. I was looking for the senator and I also hoped Marlon might be holed up there." Another lie. I knew he wasn't there. "But I want to formally report a break-in at the hunting lodge. That's why I'm here." I pulled out my phone and handed it to him and showed him the photos I'd taken. He looked through them.

"Any idea what they were hunting for or who might have done it?"

"No, I got there and found the lodge had been burgled so I left. Sweetie Pie struck a trail, and I went after her. That's when the gunshots came, and after that I saw blood on the ground. I followed it and found Robert Davis wounded. He's allegedly a friend of Marlon's."

"Allegedly?" He cocked an eyebrow.

"I don't really believe anyone anymore. He claims to be Marlon's good friend. He may be truthful, but until I have evidence, he's *allegedly* a friend of Marlon's."

Sheriff Nelson studied me for a long moment. "I'm trying to figure out why you helped him if you view him as a suspect."

"When you have an answer, please tell me." I gave a wry grin. "So, are you charging Mary Dayle with anything?"

"There should be a charge for pretending to drown, but so far I haven't found a law that covers it."

"What about the cost of the search and rescue teams? Can you bill her for that?"

"We were already out looking for Marlon and, to be honest, Mary Dayle has really helped a lot with trying to corral that shark. Mary Dayle and Coleman. They make an excellent team."

I couldn't tell if he was gigging me or if he was serious. She was a smart, attractive woman, if a little off the rails. I only smiled big, because I knew Coleman wasn't going to chase women behind my back, nor would I chase men.

It was interesting that Mary Dayle was going to get away with her stunt scot-free, but it honestly had nothing to do with me or my case. Except for the link to Lamar Bilbo, who remained my prime suspect in whatever happened to Marlon. For that reason, I pursued the line of questioning. "Why did Mary Dayle pretend to drown?" I asked. "I can't see how that benefits her in any way."

"I suspect it has more to do with her personal relationship with Lamar. He won't know she's helping to relocate the shark."

"Which will help the movie, if Marlon ever returns to finish it?" I could follow that line of thinking.

"Exactly. By the time Mary Dayle returns, unharmed, Bilbo will have either won on stopping the film or given up."

"Is it worth all of that to have a relationship with Lamar Bilbo?" I didn't see it.

Nelson laughed. "I can't see his physical charms, but the family has money and influence. I never took Mary Dayle for that kind of woman. In fact, I would say that she disdained the old Delta society ways. But I don't know her well. I'm just glad she volunteered to help us."

"About that." I was still annoyed by the fright she'd given us when she fell in the lake and disappeared. "Why is she doing this?"

Nelson leaned back in his chair. "I suspect she still feels guilty about how her assistant died. They euthanized the shark. Maybe this is her way of making up for it."

"What's the latest with Bilbo?"

"He's been up here at least five times a day and says he'll pay for a private search party. I've discouraged him but he's determined. From the way I read things, Mary Dayle needs to reappear fast. Bilbo is getting really itchy."

"I second that." And I wanted to be a fly on the wall when she explained her miraculous resurrection to Lamar Bilbo. Either the man was a gullible fool, or she was a master spin doctor. Or both. She had a lot of folks in town worried and concerned about her and, boy, were they going to be pissed off when she strolled into town uninjured and very much alive. That wasn't my problem, though, and I was thankful.

"Have you given up searching for Marlon?" I asked.

"We've looked everywhere I know to look, Sarah Booth. There wasn't a trace of Marlon on either side of the lake or anywhere downriver. No sightings have been reported. No one knows a damn thing about where that young man has gone. If he actually did leave of his own volition, he left a lot of people holding the bag for him."

"Do you believe he's alive?"

"There's no evidence that he's dead."

It wasn't an answer, but it was a statement of fact. "I hope he's unharmed."

"Me, too. But the reality of that hope is that if he is alive, then someone is likely holding him prisoner."

"Oh, I've thought of that."

"Any leads?" Nelson asked.

"We'll take a look at those old documents and see what we can find," I said. "Maybe we'll hit on something."

"Let me know if you do," Nelson said.

I nodded. My hand was on the doorknob when it twisted and Tinkie poked her head in the room. "We're ready to go," she said, assessing the room carefully.

"Thanks for the use of the copier," I told the sheriff, and we were off, back to the bank. We returned all the documents to the safety deposit box and hustled toward Zinnia. We needed time to assess the papers.

"Did anything jump out at you?" I asked as I drove.

"Yes. Did you tell Nelson about the safety deposit box?"

"I did not. If we find something, we can tell him then. I was afraid he'd try to confiscate the documents."

"Good thinking!" Tinkie patted my shoulder. "I want to dig in right now, but we have to organize this."

"What all is there?"

"A family pedigree, historical documents, birth and death certificates for at least a dozen Brandons, letters written between family members. But the one thing that I really want to investigate is a loan pledge signed by Great-grandpa Brandon. He didn't have enough money to pay his taxes. Then the flood came, and he was flush."

"Interesting." Where could a cotton farmer get a grubstake for anything during the stock market bust? Banks were folding left and right. Who would make a loan big enough to make a farmer "flush"?

I'd dropped the critters off at Hilltop when I picked up

Tinkie. When I got out of the car, I folded some money and put it in my pocket. The nanny had kept my critters for this whole case. I'd slip her some cash to compensate. She loved Sweetie Pie and Pluto, but even so, I wanted to show her how much I appreciated it. I was just glad that Poe the raven hadn't followed me over to Tinkie's place. I loved the bird, but he had gotten playful with me, dropping sticks in my hair, and sometimes flying at me in a dive that made me think he'd break his silly neck. When I got home, I'd make a point of looking for him. He generally stayed close, and I let him in the house whenever he pecked at a window. He was a tidy bird, I was happy to discover.

The minute we were in the house, Tinkie made a beeline for Maylin and I had a moment to pay Pauline. I took the bags of copied documents and headed for the office we had set up at Hilltop. I carefully began to lay out the material into sorted stacks. Tinkie joined me with two steaming cups of coffee, and we set to work.

While she went over the loan document, I traced the Brandon family tree and began mapping out land purchases. The Brandon empire, up until the 1900s, was epic. They'd owned a lot of land in Mississippi from the Gulf Coast to Memphis. The Spanish flu came and that began the decline of the family's fortune. By 1927, when the Great Flood came, they'd lost all but a few hundred acres in the Greenville area. After the flood and the infusion of a million dollars, which would be about $17 million in today's dollars, according to Tinkie, they had cash to buy land. Who had that kind of money to loan in hard times?

Tinkie would find out for sure.

32

After the flood, and all during the Depression, the Brandon family bought land around their original holding at Muscogee. Today they owned about four thousand acres of the most fertile soil around. The Brandons had parlayed that one-million-dollar loan into a vast fortune.

"Have you found who they borrowed the money from?" I asked Tinkie.

"It's weird. There's the document, signed by the elder Brandon, for the one million, but I can't find any information about who he owed. The money just appeared."

"Do you think he ever paid it back?"

"I don't think a creditor would walk away from that much money without a big stink. There were never any charges that I've found. It's like his fairy godmother appeared to give him a wagonload of money. I'll see if Harold can get us access to the bank records for some of the prominent families of Greenville in the 1920s."

"Is that likely?" I asked.

Tinkie shrugged. "Not from the bank. They'd never give those records to anyone. But Harold may have resources we don't know about. You know his family goes way back in Delta history even though he wasn't raised here in Sunflower County."

I did know that about Harold, and I could only hope his old family ties reached back into the Brandon family. I found out my hopes were fulfilled when Tinkie called Harold. She put him on speaker.

"My great-great-grandfather helped found the bank in Greenville," he said. "I'll see what I can do."

"When was it founded?"

"I believe in the 1840s. Maybe the 1850s. It was a hub bank for the planters and cotton brokers. The Greenville port was huge. Tons of cotton came down the interior rivers to Greenville to be shipped out on boats bound for New Orleans and the European market. The Port of Greenville would have rivaled Natchez—home to over half the millionaires in the U.S. in the 1850s. That Greenville bank would have been flush with cash every day of the year."

That still didn't explain how the money ended up in the hands of the Brandon family. Tinkie and I were missing the paperwork that showed the clear path. It was possible we'd never find the facts for something so buried in history. An equally important question—did any of this matter at all? I didn't know.

I'd uncovered numerous documents about the Brandon family tree. I'd need some help fully understanding the ins and outs of fourth cousins, confusing antecedents, and their connections. It was a bit mind-boggling to find the tentacles of the Brandon family extended into local, state, and national politics. The Brandon family had immigrated from Wales to America. The most valuable thing they brought with them was a good education and knowledge of how the financial world worked. That and the belief that land was never a bad investment.

I pushed a stack of papers away from me. "I'm frustrated."

Before Tinkie could respond, my phone rang. Coleman was calling. I answered and put it on speaker. "What's up?"

"You need to hurry to Greenville. Now."

"What's wrong?"

"The shark is back, and a child is missing."

My gut clenched. "A child? They think the shark got a kid? I thought it had left."

"We were hoping it had headed back downriver, but it's still here. Someone saw the dorsal fin about ten minutes ago. Nelson called me. I'm headed out to help him if I can. He says a citizens group is forming to kill the shark."

"And Mary Dayle?" She was the expert, after all.

"I hope she'll help. I really do. This can't keep happening."

I'd much prefer Mary Dayle to be in the water with the shark than Coleman. But I didn't say that. "We're on the way."

"I'm on my way, too," Coleman said.

"Are you at the sheriff's office? Want us to pick you up?" I wanted an excuse to stay close to him.

"No, I'm in Yazoo City. I had something to take care of. I'm on the way to Greenville now, though."

I was curious about Coleman's errand, but I didn't ask. We were all in a big rush and I'd have time to talk with him this evening. I hung up the phone and grabbed my keys. "You ready?"

Tinkie literally looked green. "I don't know if I can do this, Sarah Booth. A child eaten by a shark? I just don't know."

Since her pregnancy and Maylin's arrival, Tinkie was super sensitive and extremely compassionate. I understood. It was too easy to mentally put a loved one in a tragic situation. "You keep working on the financial aspect and I'll handle this. I don't know what I can do to help, but I'll be there."

"I wonder where the shark attack occurred."

I should have asked Coleman that, but I could get the info when I got to Greenville. "I'll text you. Take care of things here."

"I'm sorry, Sarah Booth. I feel like I'm not really a full partner. I'm a slacker."

"Hogwash. You're working; I'm working. We don't have to do everything together like conjoined twins."

Her laughter was my reward.

"Would you take care of the critters? I sure don't want them around the river if the shark is attacking close to shore." I forced the words out in a normal voice. Dread almost choked me, but I wouldn't let on to Tinkie. She felt bad enough about pushing this chore off on me.

"Will do. I'll cook something delicious for dinner for all of us." She grinned and I knew my face must have shown shock and horror. Tinkie was a terrible cook. Dangerous, even. She'd made biscuits once that I swear could have been used as devices of destruction if we'd had a cannon to shoot them out of. "Okay, I'll get Pauline to cook something, and I'll watch the baby and critters."

"A much better plan." And then I was out the door.

By the time I got back to the sheriff's office, the search and rescue team had already gone to the lake to get supplies and start a new search. I hurried to the lake and hesitated at the water's edge. A woman with a child clinging to her leg stood watching an older toddler play in the sand.

"They found the missing child," Coleman said. "He's absolutely fine. He just wandered away and everyone panicked. He was never in the water, just exploring."

"Thank goodness." I was relieved.

Coleman gave me a kiss. "Keep your eyes open, Sarah Booth," he said. "I mean it. The town is out for blood regarding the shark. Mary Dayle is supposed to meet us here. She's given up hiding her role in saving the shark from Bilbo. We have to act fast or it will be too late."

"I should talk to the boy's mother. Just in case she saw anything."

"Her name is Becky Graham. Nice family, the sheriff says."

Coleman drew my attention back to him. He sounded so serious, so concerned, that my heart dropped. He held out his hand. "Take these."

I turned my hand palm up. He dropped keys into my hand. I looked at them. They were for a car. "What is this?"

"Your new vehicle." He nodded toward a gray Solterra SUV crossover. "Gray and discreet, as you wanted. A higher profile than the Roadster to handle the bad roads you love to drive on. And it's all electric. I'd hoped to surprise you, just not at the lake."

"Thank you."

"Tinkie told me what you'd like."

"It will be wonderful." Anything as long as I didn't have to study, compare, or calculate.

"I left the Roadster at the dealership getting it all checked out."

I put a hand on Coleman's cheek. "Thank you." He knew how I loved that car.

Before he could respond, I heard a female voice behind me. "I'm here." I turned to find Mary Dayle, carrying her own tanks and headed toward the boat. "We'll get that shark today," she said. "I know we will."

"Gotta go," Coleman said.

I watched Mary Dayle, Nelson, and Coleman load the boat and head off on the lake.

When the rescue searchers were out on the water, I walked over to Becky Graham and introduced myself. She was relieved to have her son safely back and a little embarrassed that she'd jumped the gun on his disappearance and a shark attack.

"He's really cute," I said, watching him roll a ball at the edge of the water.

"He's seven. A good boy. Really good. His name is Larry."

"Tell me about Larry."

Her pride won out over her shyness, and she talked about her son and how well he did in school, sports, and social activities. "He's just a good all-round kid."

"Did you see anyone or anything unusual around here?" I asked.

"No. But then again I wasn't looking."

"Would you mind if I talked to Larry?" I was curious where he'd disappeared to or what might have prompted him to go off exploring on his own.

"Go right ahead."

I walked to the edge of the lake and knelt down to be on Larry's level. "You had an adventure," I said.

"I'm okay," he said. "Tell Mama don't be mad. The man said it was okay to go with him."

"What man, Larry? What did he look like?"

"The movie man."

I brought my phone out of my jeans pocket and opened the photos. "This man?" I had a photo of Marlon in my phone, and I showed the boy.

He nodded. "Maybe."

"That's a big help, Larry. A really big help. That man has been missing, too, and we need to find him. Where did the movie man go?"

He pointed into the woods. "He was supposed to play with me, but he got scared of something and ran away. He told me to stay back, but I followed him. I wanted to play."

Was it really Marlon? "He was scared?" I asked, hoping Larry could give me a few more details.

Larry reached into his pocket and brought out three cat's-eye marbles. "These are mine. He gave them to me."

"Did he say his name?" I asked. "Was it Marlon?"

Larry shook his head. "No, not that."

"Was he limping?" I had another thought.

Larry nodded. "I don't know. He didn't say his leg hurt."

"Hey, Larry, was it this guy?" I had a photo of Robert Davis that I'd taken from a poster. He and Marlon both were tall, dark, and good-looking. I showed him RoDa, then flipped the phone back to Marlon. "Or this guy?"

Larry studied both photos. "I don't know."

The disappointment was bitter, but I pasted on a smile. "Thank you, Larry." I'd jumped the gun when the child said movie man. "Do you remember anything about this movie man?"

"He said to give you this. He said a nice lady would come talk to me." Larry pulled a piece of paper from his pocket and handed it to me. "He taught me this." He dropped to the ground and drew a circle in a bare patch of dirt. He put two marbles in the center. He used the green cat's-eye as his shooter. He was a second grader, but he had good aim with a marble.

I unfolded the slip of paper. "Muscogee." The word was printed in black ink. I didn't know what to make of the message. Was RoDa or Marlon sending me to the Brandon estate because I would find something there? Or was this clue merely part of a setup?

"Thanks, Larry." I tousled his hair, then turned to his mother. "He's a fine young man. You keep him safe."

"I'll do that. Thank you." Taking the younger child's hand, she headed back to the parking lot and her vehicle.

She had nothing to thank me for. Not really. I just couldn't figure out what Marlon or RoDa was doing near the water and taking up with a child. Not very smart. I'd point that out to both of them when I finally ran them to ground.

I was tempted to go back to the sheriff's office to wait for Coleman, but I didn't. I was going to Muscogee. Against my better judgment. For a moment I walked along the shore, watching the boat traffic. The Mississippi was low, but still navigable. I found myself moving down the lake shoreline until I stopped at an isolated place where a tree had fallen. It was the perfect place to sit and think.

Had RoDa or Marlon attempted to lure Larry into the woods? Still, if one of them was using Larry as a messenger, they were flirting with fire. Even a hint of abduction involving a kid was unacceptable. And what did the message mean? Muscogee was the name of the Brandon estate but also a Native American tribe that once roamed the Delta area. Was that the clue? I felt a stir of excitement.

I whipped out my phone, prepared to call the local library for information on the Muscogee tribe that had lived on the banks of the Mississippi River. I paused when I heard singing. I didn't recognize the song, but the minor key and the melody were so beautiful, I stopped everything I was doing so I could listen. The song sounded familiar, but I couldn't catch the words. Without thinking about it, I walked closer to the water's edge. The singing seemed to be coming from beneath the water, which was impossible.

My body reacted to it before my mind could make a decision. The song promised many things: love, comfort, belonging, acceptance. All I had to do was find the source. I walked to the water's edge. A dark shadow moving close to the shore stopped me. The shark. The dorsal fin broke the surface forty yards from the shore. The shark dove again, and the fin disappeared. The surface of the lake returned to calm and stillness, almost as if the deadly creature was only in my imagination.

A little shaken, I was ready to head inland, and fast. I needed some time to figure out what had happened to me in that brief moment of delusion. Had I imagined the song, too?

No. The melody floated to me again, this time from the opposite direction, from inland. I fell under the spell of the singer. The song was a compulsion. I had to hear more clearly. It called and beckoned to me. I had no choice but to follow, to find whoever sang with such a beautiful voice.

I thought the song was coming from behind some storage buildings, but the wind shifted, and I realized it was coming from a stand of tall trees. I went there in a daze. Who was singing? When at last I tracked down the source of the song, I stopped, my feet going backward even when I didn't want to. The singing creature was horrific. She was beautiful, a woman with flowing locks of blond hair and skin as milky as a newborn. But she stood on chicken legs.

"Holy sh—" I was ready to run, but my feet seemed stuck to the ground. This couldn't be happening. At last I understood the power of the song and the creature that sang it. "You're a siren."

The woman turned to confront me. "Yes. I am. And you've answered my call."

"I'm not a sailor." The music stopped and my senses were returning. I knew exactly what was going on and who was to blame. "You have sway only over sailors. It's in the literature."

"Do you believe everything you read?" the siren asked.

"Only when it's a fact. You have no influence over me; I'm a landlubber. Besides, I know who you are. Jitty, cut it out." She'd almost gotten one over on me, but I'd awakened to her game. The truth was, though, she had an incredible voice. Jitty could sing, dance, twirl a fire baton, recite Shakespeare, and drive me crazy. Jitty had many talents, and new ones popped up every day.

"I have a message for you," she said.

My hopes rose on a tidal wave. "From my parents?" Jitty was sometimes the go-between for the Great Beyond and my parents to me.

"Muscogee," Jitty said softly.

"What?"

"Muscogee," she said. "That's all you need to know."

"But what does it mean?"

Instead of answering me, Jitty walked on her chicken legs toward the water. She stepped in and kept going until she disappeared. She was no help at all.

33

I wanted to go back to Zinnia but it wasn't in the cards. Instead, I drove my brand-new Solterra to Muscogee Plantation. On the way I called Tinkie, in awe of the fact that my telephone call went through the car radio so I could talk hands-free. There were all kinds of bells and whistles on the car. Since I'd been driving an antique for the past two years and prior to that using public transportation in New York, I'd missed the technology revolution in automobiles.

The sun was shining brightly, so warm I could almost feel the earth awakening and ready to get to work growing things. While I was talking to Tinkie, I pulled over in the shade of a tree. I told her about the new car, the kid who hadn't been eaten by the deadly fish, and the written message I'd received from the man I presumed to be either Marlon or RoDa. I didn't mention that Jitty had delivered the same message. Muscogee.

"Where are you, Sarah Booth?" Tinkie asked.

"I'm on the road to the Brandon estate. I'm going to call the library and ask about the Muscogee tribe before I tackle the senator. I'm not sure if Muscogee applies to the Brandon plantation or the Native American tribe. I need to have as many facts as I can line up."

"That sounds like a good plan. Harold is coming over to help me with this financial information. I've tried to figure it out until my eyes are crossed. The figures don't make sense to me."

"Harold is coming to help you. Hah! He's really stopping by to see Maylin." I knew my friends too well. Harold was as smitten by the baby as anyone. In fact, between his ongoing romance with the sexy writer Janet Malone and his fixation on Maylin, I hadn't seen him in several weeks. "What's wrong with the financial information you have?"

"It just doesn't add up. There's money that appears, a large sum of it."

"Campaign contributions?" Lots of elected officials made a hundred times their annual salary by taking gifts and payola from lobbyists. It was illegal but the forensic accounting necessary to find such fraud was in short supply at the IRS these days.

"No, this money came in before Senator Brandon was elected. This might even predate the flood."

"Maybe an inheritance?"

"It could be, but there should be documentation. It could also be a land sale or an investment into one of the dozens of corporations the Brandon family has operated over the decades. But again, there should be documentation—a paper trail of who gave the money."

Tinkie got very annoyed at sloppy accounting, which was why I'd never allow her to help me with my private tax returns. Her hair would catch on fire at my lackadaisical bookkeeping. When I needed help I went to Harold, who might disapprove but he never gave me the stink-eye or lectured me. Maybe this year Coleman would take over the tax duties. A delicious hope but not likely to happen. I didn't think I had enough tools in my arsenal to bribe or blackmail him into that.

"Let me know what Harold says. I'm going to call the local library before I step foot on the Brandon property."

"Good thinking, Sarah Booth."

"Give me two hours to check in. If I don't . . ."

"We'll come looking for you. Thanks for letting me know. And remember, play it safe."

Words to live by.

Elton McCoy, the reference librarian at the Washington County Public Library, was a pleasant-sounding gentleman with a wealth of knowledge and a set of impressive research skills. When I asked him about the Muscogee people, he had plenty to say.

"The Muscogee wasn't one tribe. They incorporated smaller tribes like the indigenous peoples of Alabama into their structure," Elton said. "They were very sophisticated with a mico or chief appointed for life and a council to debate and decide issues of import. They roamed the Southeast from the Mississippi River to the Atlantic."

"I thought most of the indigenous peoples were removed

and sent on the Trail of Tears," I said, trying hard to remember the smidgen of Native American history that had been included in my textbooks. For the most part the story of the original settlers had been ignored in school teachings.

"Some natives managed to escape capture and hide. Of those, many were affiliated with the Muscogee Creek Confederacy. The majority of them ended up in Georgia, but we believe they were all descendants of the Mound Builders, who created the mounds at Winterville. The Mound Builders predated all the Choctaw tribes."

I knew a bit about the Winterville Mounds. One of my cases had concluded there. The site of the very impressive mounds wasn't far from Greenville proper. "Is anyone excavating the mounds now?"

"No, that's all over and done," the librarian said. "For a while this spring, a team from the University of Mississippi was here doing a comparison and contrast with Winterville and the mounds in Georgia. I don't know what conclusions they reached, but they left Greenville the first of this week. Wonderful group of young people. They were all very interested in the movie being filmed."

College kids would be interested in a major movie on location. Most people would. "The Brandon plantation is named after the Muscogee tribe. Is there a connection there?"

"Now that depends on who you ask," Elton said.

"I'm asking you." I was keenly interested now because it sounded like Elton was going to dish the dirt on someone.

"There are rumors that the Brandon family brought several Native American slaves to Mississippi to work the fields. It was illegal to enslave indigenous peoples, but a lot of things were illegal, and folks still did them. Anyway, the story is that Jefferson Brandon, the Brandon who brought his family to Greenville, fell in love with a beautiful young Muscogee woman. When she became pregnant with his child, he freed her and allowed her to return to her people."

Muscogee. The name of the Brandon plantation made a lot more sense if this were true. The potential link to a lost love left me with a lot to think about. Did Marlon know any of this? Had he planned to hint at some illicit connection in his film? It hadn't been in the script, but the script had changed. Was this the big reveal everyone was so stirred up about? And, more importantly, did anyone really care about a checkered family pedigree now?

"What happened to the baby?" I asked Elton.

"There's no record of a baby," he said. "I've researched it out of personal curiosity. I never found a clue that the baby was ever born."

"What about the woman that Jefferson fell in love with?"

"No record of her, either. Unless the Brandons have some private store of papers and documentation. That is possible. A lot of the original settler families kept their own records, either at home or in a church. The family Bible was a record of births, deaths, marriages. Some of the family recordkeeping is very detailed and, depending on who was making the written record, deliciously catty."

I could only imagine. "Thank you, Elton. I owe you a drink."

"Call me when you have time. I'm particularly fond of Mojitos."

"I can make that happen."

We hung up and I called Tinkie back and relayed the information about a possible member of the Muscogee tribe in the Brandon lineage.

"That would be fascinating," Tinkie said. "It could have ruined the family at one point in time. Especially if this impacts the senator. There were laws against interracial marriage, and community standards against illegitimate babies. That child would have likely had a terrible life."

"Bloodline purity is not of any interest to me, but what I'm wondering is, what if the word 'Muscogee' was left with that young boy as a clue of where to find answers? Clues to figure out where Marlon is?"

"That would be fabulous. What are you going to do? Go to the estate and confront the senator with what we've found?"

"Definitely. I'll see if I can flush out a reaction from the senator. That'll tell us plenty."

"Marlon isn't the only person in his family who can act. Remember that," Tinkie said. "The senator is very controlled and an excellent poker player, according to Harold. Our friend says the senator has nerves of steel."

"And Harold has often told me that I can get on the nerves of the most implacable humans on the planet."

Tinkie laughed loud and long. "It's true. You could worry the warts off a frog, Sarah Booth."

"I love you, too." I eased the car down the long drive. The suspension system of my new ride handled the ruts and potholes. Coleman had done big, and I was eager to thank him. The fact he'd taken the initiative meant the world to me.

34

When the big house came into view, I slowed again, idling on the drive before I pulled up in front of the porch. What secrets did Muscogee hold? Was there something here—evidence or clues—that I had overlooked earlier because I didn't know what I was looking for? As I was about to exit the car, I noticed two men standing in front of a big window. They were arguing aggressively. Brandon and Bilbo. What did those two have going on? Were they partners or enemies?

Hoping that neither would recognize my new vehicle—if they noticed me outside at all—I backed out of the drive, turned around, and left. No point in confronting the senator after he'd been fighting with Bilbo. Harold's assessment that Brandon was a good poker player didn't hold water. Even from a distance of thirty yards or so and through a window pane, I'd seen the heat in his face and the fury in his words as he'd stabbed the air with his finger while talking to Bilbo. He was anything but cool, calm, and collected.

When I came to the paved road, I stopped for a moment. Why was the road into Muscogee in such terrible shape? The county road graders would probably take care of it for the senator at no charge. It was how the good-old-boy network worked. But Bilbo probably sold the county the heavy equipment they used. Had he pulled some strings to make the senator suffer? It was an interesting thought.

Undecided where to go next, I idled by the side of the road. Finally, I took a left and headed back to Greenville. Other than asking the senator about his family's history, I didn't know how I'd find out about the Muscogee woman. There had been some paperwork about the Brandon family tree in the papers that we'd stolen from the safe deposit box. I shot Tinkie a text and asked her to take a look at the Brandon lineage.

With no firm destination, I drove to the bookstore. To my surprise, Mary Dayle was behind the counter. She waited on two people before she waved me over to the counter.

"I thought you were shark hunting?"

"They called off the search until later today. What do you want?" she asked.

"A history lesson."

"I don't like the sound of that." She checked her watch. "I'm supposed to meet the sheriff in an hour. The missing Graham child was found safe. That likely saved the shark."

"Why aren't you working on the capture of the big fish?" I asked.

"I intend to. A little later, when it is near their feeding

time. So if I can help you find a book, you better ask now. I have to go soon."

I nodded. "I'll be quick. What does the Brandon family have to do with the Muscogee tribe?"

"That's a question for the senator to answer. Not my business."

She knew something! She hid it, but I'd caught a glimpse in her eyes. I changed the direction of my questions. "Did you bring the shark upriver and set it loose here?"

She blew out a breath. "You won't believe me, but I'll answer. No. I would never do that to a shark. Or any other living creature. The shark can adjust to living in fresh water, but the humans are never going to allow it. That shark is on death row, just waiting for the right hunter with the right gun to kill her. She doesn't deserve this for simply being what she was born to be."

"That matters to you?"

"Yes, it does. These creatures are not ours to toy with and destroy. I believe that totally."

"Do you know where Marlon is?"

She held my gaze. "I don't believe he's dead. I think Bilbo has him. You won't believe this either, but I was hanging out with Bilbo to try to find out what he was up to. He's been plotting against the movie ever since he heard about it. He's pulled some dirty tricks on the Brandon family, and I believe he's behind all of this trouble. I could have told you, or the sheriff, but if word had gotten back to Bilbo, I would have been totally ineffective. I played the cards I had."

"Dirty tricks?" I was curious.

"He was bragging about how he threatened the county supervisors that if they took care of the road to Muscogee, he would up the price of the heavy equipment he sells and leases to the county. I'm sure you've noticed that the road to Muscogee is a series of potholes, bogs, and ruts."

"I had noticed that."

"The means to an end, Sarah Booth. I'm sure you've done the same."

"I haven't." It was true. I'd never dated someone for gain.

"Well goody, goody for you." She laughed. "There are times in life when you do things you never imagined. Bilbo is loathsome. Yet I needed to get close to him to see what he was up to. And just so you know, I wasn't *that* close. More than a lover, Bilbo needs an audience. That was the role I fulfilled."

Rather than debate the ethics of the tactics she'd employed, I went straight for the nut. "And what is Lamar Bilbo up to?"

"Oh, you wouldn't date him, but you'll be glad to have any information I weaseled out of him while dating him with an agenda."

I shrugged. "Well, yeah."

She laughed out loud. "You're a hypocrite, Sarah Booth."

"And you're a liar." That wasn't exactly the proper description, but I couldn't think of a better word.

"Well, we're both just badass Bs, aren't we?"

"We are." And I found that I enjoyed the banter with Mary Dayle. She had a sense of humor about herself and a little devil sitting on her shoulder. She no longer cared what people thought about her. An admirable position to be in, and a rare one for a member of the upper crust in a small Delta town.

"I'll tell you what I found from Bilbo," she said, waving me into an armchair in the front window of the store. She took a seat in the other chair. "Lamar hasn't had an original thought in his head, ever. He's easily led and manipulated. He's fighting the movie and all progress in Greenville that comes from outside sources, but the question is why. Why is he so opposed to those things? The growth, I get. The Bilbos and Brandons have held power in the state for decades. They fear that anyone new moving in will build more power than they have."

"Power to do what?" I asked.

"There's always money to be made for a person in a position of power. Senator, mayor, sheriff, police chief—lots of opportunities for gifts and kickbacks. Any road building or facility building project is just a gravy train for corrupt officials."

"The movie won't change any of that, and I'm pretty sure Ana and Marlon would cross some palms with silver to catch a break."

"The movie people are dangerous because they think differently than the locals. The entire structure put in place by corrupt officials requires that the population stay asleep. The movie brought excitement, new ideas. New hope. Those holding power are afraid it will upset the status quo."

She had a point I'd never have come to on my own. Mississippi was a poor state. One of the poorest in the union. But there was plenty of money for a criminal to feather his or her own nest. It was the age-old problem of greed.

"You've made your point. But who is pulling Bilbo's strings?"

She shook her head. "I don't know. For all that Bilbo has never read a book in his life, he's a cunning man. I've searched his vehicles, but he would never leave me alone in his house long enough for me to really look around. Ugh. The dinners I ate there, hoping he'd pass out or at least run an errand. Not a chance. He doesn't trust anyone. I was making headway, but that's all over. By pretending to be dead and trying to save the shark, I've lost his confidence. He knows I'm not trustworthy, and he'll be more wary than ever now."

She had lost her "in" with him for sure. Pretending to drown while helping the enemy was going to cost her. I had an urge to confess that Tinkie and I had checked out her house, but I bit my tongue. No point in going there. And also no point in telling her that if she called Bilbo to come talk to her, I'd break into his house to see what I could find. I didn't need her permission, only her unwitting cooperation.

"Call Lamar."

She stared at me. "Why would I do that?"

"To distract him. Keep him off balance. I can't figure out which angle you're playing, Mary Dayle. Are you for the movie or against it?"

"I'm for the shark. How about that? I can say that with total honesty. I'll do whatever I can to protect the shark and get it back into open water."

"I need to know which side you're backing." I didn't trust her. I wanted to, but I didn't.

"I'm sorry, I didn't get the court order where I had to tell you squat."

One thing about Mary Dayle, she felt no need to win hearts and minds. "If we're working toward the same goal it will be easier. For both of us." I tried to sound reasonable and persuasive.

"Look, I did what I had to do in an effort to slow Bilbo's roll. I've given Marlon a lot of help and advice about the history of the town. I've given the sheriff and your fellow all the help I could in trying to capture the shark."

"I understand. Coleman really wants to save the shark, too. He's determined. And I'm glad that kid wasn't really missing this morning. That would have been the kiss of death for the shark."

"I'm glad the kid wasn't hurt, but the shark's days are numbered." She checked her watch. "Which is why I have to meet those men who are willing to help me catch her."

"Before I go, I want to ask one more time. What's the connection between the Muscogee community and the Brandon family? If you know, please tell me."

All emotion drained from her face. "You need to be careful, Sarah Booth. Marlon was asking me the same thing right before he disappeared."

35

I checked in at the sheriff's office only to learn that the divers and rescue team were still out on the water. Since Larry Graham had been found safe and sound, the attention had turned to wrangling the shark into the submerged cage. They'd found a boat and captain who could take the shark back to the Gulf. Mary Dayle was going to rejoin the team just before dusk. No one would tell me how she was going to lure or drive the shark into the cage, but everyone seemed pumped that she could do it. I hoped so, for the sake of the shark.

I stopped by the tax assessor's office and looked up the property owned by Senator Brandon. Even though the family had sold off some holdings, they still owned at least four thousand acres in Mississippi. I dropped by the county agent's office, which was also in the courthouse. Bamboo and hemp were the big topics for agriculture. Senator Brandon was one of the first landowners preparing to convert to both crops, the agent told me. Interesting. I understood crop rotation was the best way to care for the soil, but both bamboo and hemp, as commercial crops, were unproven in many regards. The senator was a risk-taker.

I moved on to the chancery clerk's office. I was an outsider, but also a child of the Delta. I told a few jokes, got the workers laughing, and accepted the offer of a cup of coffee. I didn't ask questions. No one would tell a nosy outsider squat. But I listened to the divorce cases that were hot news and leafed through the minutes of the county supervisor meetings. I was looking to find any discussion of the Muscogee road, but mostly I was doing busywork so I could eavesdrop.

Lawyers came and went, leaving files and chatting up the staff. I listened to talk about contentious divorces, land disputes, charity events, and sports. Always sports. When talk turned to the movie, I eased in a little closer. The consensus in the office was that the film would somehow get finished. Two local lawyers had been cast, and they talked about the excitement. One lawyer was holding forth. "As soon as Marlon returns and the weather breaks, they'll finish the filming. Ninety-five percent of it is in the can."

I had no idea the movie was that close to completion. I wondered where the lawyers were getting their facts.

"Can I get anything else for you?" One of the clerks was standing in front of me.

"I'm good. Thank you."

I was drawing too much attention to myself, so I walked over to the two lawyers. "When will Marlon be back on set?"

One lawyer was a good-looking young man. His smile was quick and friendly. "I heard he'd gone to some hospital for treatment of a medical condition. He's supposedly fine and on his way to finish the filming. And a good thing. They need those action scenes of him on the boat and rescuing people. My friend and I get to play Greenville merchants who help rescue the people stranded on the levee. It's exciting."

"Judge Freeman is going to fine you both if you're late for court again," the clerk said, teasing them. "He won't take the fact that you're movie stars into consideration if you disrupt his court schedule."

"If we're movie stars, no one will fine us," the other lawyer said.

I returned the reference books I'd been exploring and prepared to leave. I had to go back to Muscogee. I didn't want to, not by myself, but it was the only move left to me. It had to be done. I could only hope the senator was there. I had questions only he could answer. I had a sudden inspiration.

On the way to Muscogee, I called Sheriff Nelson's office. Neither Coleman nor Nelson was there, but I left a detailed message telling them where I was and what I was doing. The dispatcher who took the message swore she'd deliver it as soon as they came back from trying to wrangle the shark.

Nothing left to do but drive to Muscogee.

Twenty minutes later I pulled up to the house, got out, and rang the bell. Brandon himself opened the door. He took no notice of my vehicle, so I hoped he hadn't seen me on my earlier stop. "Do you have news of Marlon?" he asked.

"I was hoping you had something for me."

He scoffed. "My grandson has vanished. The movie he put his personal fortune and life into is going down the drain. The persons hired to find him are wandering around Greenville like lost souls. Sorry, I don't have anything good to add."

His contemptuous attitude pissed me off, but there was no point in accelerating the ill will. "Tell me about the Muscogee woman who bore a child for Jefferson Brandon."

He stepped back and I slipped into the foyer. "Who told you that?" he asked.

"You can try to hide and delete history, but you can't. Not really. The truth always resurrects and comes after you. So who was this woman?"

"I don't have to tell you anything."

"No, you don't, but if you want Marlon back, you'd better be straight with me."

"How can something like that from the past play a role in what's going on with Marlon today?"

"I don't know, but I need the truth to find out. Your grandson may be in terrible danger. He may be hurt and waiting for rescue." The more I talked, the angrier I became. I was done with games. The entire Brandon family seemed to feel they were free to manipulate everyone and all the facts. "Was Marlon including any of that history in his movie? I didn't see it in the script."

"I don't think so, and to be honest, I don't care. It was a long time ago, well before my time."

"Why all the big secrets?"

"Jefferson Brandon was a man who felt no law applied to him except the ones he chose to obey. Times were different, and Jefferson had great ambitions for his family. The woman, Tsianna, didn't fit into those ambitions, no matter how much he loved her."

"What a skunk." The words slipped out before I could stop them.

"Yes, he was a skunk. But he did return her to her people. That's in his favor. And this information isn't relevant. It's not even near the time period of the Great Flood. Since the child never returned to the Brandons, it's not an issue. So far, I don't see you've accomplished much in the way of finding my grandson. Now I'd like you to leave."

I had one more thing to say. "If there's any chance something from the past has come back to haunt you, maybe you should address it before it catches up with you."

The senator had drained the last bit of energy from my bones. I couldn't get home fast enough.

36

The next morning, after some restoring cuddles with Coleman, I called Cece. My friend and journalist had resources I never would, and she was always good to help me and Tinkie with our cases, just as we took photos and videos for her newspaper work.

"Sarah Booth, *dahlink,* I thought you had died," Cece drawled. "You must be in the first stages of putrefaction. Good thing you called because I don't want you coming in here stinking my office up."

I had to laugh. Cece Dee Falcon was often over the top. It had been over a week since I'd talked to her, though, and that was out of character. We chatted almost every day at least once. "I've been in Greenville, working on this missing movie star case. I'm home now but about to head out."

"Yes, I was hoping for more photos, tips, leads, smashing headlines, and delicious gossip. You and Tinkie have failed me utterly."

"You and everyone else."

"What's wrong?" Cece was instantly concerned.

"No leads, no clues, no sign of Marlon. The shark is still in the river. The plug is going to be pulled on this movie. It's all just been a waste. I have no clue where Marlon might be."

"Perk up, Sarah Booth. I have some news that will get you over your pique."

"What?" I was eager to get in a better mood.

"Lamar Bilbo will be honored by a civic organization today."

"Civic? More like white knights, I'd guess."

"You'd be correct, but the good news is that he'll be tied up in a ceremony today. Which makes it a perfect time for us to search his house and see what we can find."

"Are you suggesting we break and enter Lamar Bilbo's home?"

"I am indeed."

"Thank heavens. I'm ready for some action."

"Head out and I'll meet you at the CVS parking lot on Elmer Road in Greenville," Cece said. "I'm at the paper now, but I'm all but finished. We should have time to get to Bilbo's place and search it completely. Just to give us that extra edge, Millie is catering the shindig and she'll make sure Bilbo stays late."

"Thank heavens for friends." I was all in. I called Tinkie and told her the plan, and she said she'd flag a ride with Cece and be there ASAP. The three musketeers were about to ride again.

I picked the girls up at the Greenville CVS parking lot.

On the way to Bilbo's home, I filled them in on all I'd learned about the Brandon family past.

"I've always wondered why Jefferson Brandon named the farm Muscogee," Cece said.

"I don't know." It was an honest answer.

"Let's focus on that scoundrel Bilbo," Cece said. "I have a feeling he's at the bottom of all the troubles."

I'd never given much thought to Lamar Bilbo or where he lived. Cece knew everything. His home was on the outskirts of town, set on twenty acres and invisible from the road. All of that worked in our favor. I parked down the road a little from his house and we walked back, cutting through his yard, dodging among the landscaped plants. The grounds were beautiful. I hadn't anticipated that Bilbo would care about natural beauty.

"Does he have servants?" Tinkie asked.

"I don't think so," Cece said, "but Tinkie, you should knock on the door. You're the social Queen Bee. Make up a story if an employee answers."

"Easy for you to say," Tinkie said, but it was clear she relished her role.

While Cece and I hid in the shrubs, Tinkie rang the bell. When there was no answer, she rang and knocked. Repeatedly. "There's no one here," she called to us. "We're in luck."

We swarmed the house, Cece and I going in opposite directions. Tinkie pulled out her lock picks and started on the front door. One of us would find a way into the house that would leave no trace.

"I got it!" Tinkie called out. I had to give her credit. She'd picked that lock in under three minutes. She opened the front door and we slipped inside.

"What are we looking for?" Cece sensibly asked.

"Evidence that Marlon has been here. Anything related to Marlon. Ransom notes. Family scandals. Anything useful."

"Oh, something that should be easy to spot," Cece said sarcastically. "Anything that implicates Bilbo or gives us a lead. I'm desperate."

"Split up and get busy," I said as I headed for Bilbo's office. Cece took the kitchen and Tinkie, the bedrooms.

I rifled through Bilbo's desk. The man hadn't hit a lick at a snake in the last five years that I could tell. Mostly his appointment book was filled with gab sessions with his buddies. I did find where he'd taken a meeting with the bikers, the Johnny Boys. It wasn't evidence that he'd hired them to harass the movie company, but it was a connection.

"Hey, someone is coming up to the door," Tinkie whispered from the hallway.

I froze in place as the doorbell rang. "Who is it?"

Cece had the best view out a window. "Handsome guy, slight limp. Young, dark hair."

"Yeah, we met him on the movie set." Tinkie was now peeping out the window.

I suspected who it was, and I slipped to the window to take a gander. RoDa had reappeared and now stood on the porch, holding an envelope in his hand. Marlon's good friend, Robert Davis, was consorting with the enemy.

"Do you think he'll leave the envelope?" Cece asked.

"Maybe." We could hope. "Just stay quiet." We were all three holding our breath and watching RoDa as he fidgeted at the front door. Finally, he bent down and stuck the envelope under the welcome mat. He didn't linger. He took off.

As soon as we were sure he was gone, I opened the door

and retrieved the fat envelope. I tore it open and hundred-dollar bills fluttered to the floor.

"It's a payoff," Tinkie said. "But for what?"

"Maybe for the release of Marlon." I sighed. I had no clue what RoDa's real motives were. "Or it could be payment for keeping Marlon away from the set."

"The only thing to do is to split up and track Mr. RoDa. I need my car," Cece said. "One of us needs to sit on Bilbo, and another needs to follow RoDa and see where he goes."

"Put the money back under the mat," Tinkie said. "If it's to release Marlon, we can't interfere."

"Tinkie, would you wait here to see if anyone shows up to retrieve the money?" I asked. "I'll take Cece to get her car, and then I'll follow RoDa, if I can find him. Cece will come get you."

"You'd better hurry," Cece said. "I'll wait in the yard. I don't want to be in here if he comes home. I know Millie said she'd call, but Bilbo is a slippery eel."

"Thanks!" I was out the door with Cece right beside me. We were only a few minutes from where she'd left her car, so I dropped her off and headed to the movie set, hoping to pick up RoDa's trail. I was in luck. He was in an intense conversation with Ana McCants. I would have killed for one of those parabolic listening devices all the spies had in movies. As it was, I just had to sink down in my seat and make sure no one on the set recognized me as I waited for RoDa to make a move.

Patience was not one of my virtues, but I was digging my new stealth vehicle. Because it was electric it didn't make noise, plus it looked like hundreds of other SUVs, and it had clearance for bumpy roads.

Slouching in my seat, I watched RoDa via the rearview

mirror. It looked like he and Ana were at each other's throats. I wondered why. And I also wondered if RoDa knew the sheriff wanted to question him. He'd left the hospital before the deputies could pick him up. Right now, he needed to be free so I could follow him.

It didn't take long before he came limping up the hill to his vehicle. When he left the set, I was discreetly behind him.

37

RoDa headed northeast, and I figured he was going back to the hunting lodge in the woods. Perhaps he was returning to look for the key he'd buried. He would be disappointed in that pursuit. Or maybe he was meeting someone. Marlon? Bilbo? The senator? Only time would tell. I kept a good distance in between, but it was hard to tail him. The long, straight Delta farm roads held little traffic. The fallow fields offered no cover. It was a wide-open vista that stretched for miles.

I was completely unprepared when RoDa slammed on his brakes, skidded to a stop, and did a U-turn in the middle of the road. He was coming right at me. Had he realized I was tailing him? I pushed sunglasses on my face and slunk lower in the seat, but I kept a steady foot on the gas pedal and refused to look his way when we passed each other.

To my utter relief, he kept driving. He appeared to be going back to town. I came to a crossroads and turned left, driving until I saw a windrow in a field. Trees gave me cover to turn around, and I blasted back toward town. I had to catch up to him, but not at a speed that would give me away. Just as he entered Greenville City limits, I caught sight of his car.

He continued through town and then south, angling toward the river. My gut clenched. There were so many things I didn't want to find in the river. Nonetheless, I followed. RoDa continued into an area I didn't know at all, twisting through woods and brakes until he pulled down a two-lane track. There was no way I could follow him without being spotted. I pulled farther down the trail and parked. I could smell the river. The leaves danced on the wind that blew off the water. RoDa couldn't go far on foot with a bum leg, and there was no way to get across the river.

I could either run him to ground or hide out and wait. I set off on foot, but not before I got my gun out of the back of the car. Coleman had thoughtfully transferred all of my "tools" from the trunk of the Mercedes to my new ride. I had binoculars—a gift from Coleman—and my gun, both tucked into what looked like a camera bag.

I set off through the undergrowth. My cell phone was in my pocket, on vibrate, and I felt it shiver just as I came to the slope that angled down to the river. I paused to read the text from Tinkie. She and Cece were still at Bilbo's. So far, no action. I texted my location, as best I could, and said I was following RoDa. I had learned the hard way to be sure and check in with folks in case something went wrong and I disappeared. The cavalry couldn't ride to the rescue without a location.

My new car had a GPS system, and I wondered if Coleman could track that as I walked. I'd never thought to ask because such things hadn't been invented when the Roadster was new. This could be a blessing and a curse. Even though my mind was spinning, my ears were working double-time. I heard the crackle of a stick. I stopped and listened. Another snap. Someone was just ahead, tramping through the dead limbs and scrub.

I caught movement and ducked behind a cypress tree. RoDa was moving toward the river. I could see the water; we were in a bend of the river. The bustle of Greenville would be hidden from us, and us from the town. But what in the hell was RoDa up to? I couldn't decide if he was one of the good guys or the bad.

I crept forward. His voice stopped me. He was talking on the phone. I was almost close enough to hear what he was saying. Taking a chance, I inched closer.

"I can't do that."

There was a pause as the person on the other end of the call talked.

RoDa's voice was filled with stress. "I can't. I won't. You can't make me."

It would seem the other conversant disagreed. I could hear an angry male voice.

"I've done everything you asked. I planted the information. I did everything you told me, and I got shot for my trouble. Now I'm done. I won't do this."

Again, the angry male voice. I just couldn't hear clearly enough to know who he was or what he was asking of RoDa.

"I'm done. You can shove it where the sun don't shine." RoDa punched his phone off.

He walked down to the river. I prepared to confront him, to tell him I'd help him if he'd help me with Marlon. I knew he was involved, I just didn't know how. And I couldn't tell who he'd been talking to.

Just as I stood up to move, a shot rang out. RoDa tumbled into the river. He came up, shouting for help and struggling.

It was then I saw the dorsal fin. It broke the water about two hundred feet from shore. It turned and headed straight for RoDa. I had no choice. I dropped my phone and the bag with my tools and ran for the river. I didn't hesitate. I did a flat, racing dive into the water and swam for RoDa. The cold water almost knocked the breath out of me, but I swam with all I had. He wasn't far from the bank, but the water was deep and the current strong. Fear that we'd both be swept downriver gripped me, but I fought on.

I grabbed his shirt and he spun, trying to climb on me. It was an impulse for anyone who was drowning. I went underwater, escaped his grip, and came up behind him. When I surfaced, a lot of the fight had gone out of him. The water around him churned, tinged with blood. Oh, this was not good.

"Stop struggling!" I managed to yell. "Stop."

He was panicked but he was also weakened by the gunshot. I was able to get an arm across his body and I swam for shore. He was on his back, and I was dragging him with everything I had in me.

I dared a glance at the shark and my heart almost stopped. It was trailing us, fast! The shore was only twenty feet away, but I didn't know if I could make it, or if I could even get on the land. If the river bottom was sloped, I stood a chance.

If it was a steep drop-off, I wasn't strong enough to drag RoDa to safety.

My feet propellered in the water, and I could almost feel the shark's teeth clamp down on my legs—but it was only my imagination and fear. At last I felt the bottom of the river beneath my feet. We'd been swept farther downstream in the current, and I wasn't certain where I was. RoDa was bleeding profusely from a gunshot wound in his left shoulder. I felt a lump where I held him. Thank goodness he'd drifted into unconsciousness or he would have been screaming with pain.

Just as I hauled him up on the sand the shark came out of the water, mouth open. She snapped on air and disappeared. I pulled RoDa the rest of the way out of the water and then collapsed beside him on the muddy bank. I checked his shoulder, where the bullet had entered the back and come out the front. Luckily there were no broken bones. Other than that, I couldn't tell how seriously he was injured. The bleeding was slow, but steady. He needed help.

I didn't know how I would get him back to my car or get help for him. My phone was upriver on the bank where we'd gone in. The only thing to do was leave him and walk back for my gun and phone.

Not much point in telling him I'd be back—he wasn't aware I was leaving. I set off along the bank, hoping we hadn't drifted too far. I hadn't been paying attention to the riverbank because I'd been focused on avoiding shark teeth. I kept my focus on the ground in front of me. Every time I looked at the river, I saw the maw of the shark rising out of the water, teeth snapping the air so fiercely, droplets of water flew everywhere. The episode was burned into my brain. The one thing a Delta girl never anticipated was having shark PTSD.

When the riverbank firmed up, I notched my speed up to a jog. I was limp from the struggle of the swim, but now wasn't the time to stop. RoDa, and possibly Marlon, depended on me to carry on. At last I came to the bend in the river and saw my bag on the ground, my phone beside it. I dialed Coleman first—to let him know I was okay and also that someone had shot RoDa, again. He would tell Sheriff Nelson and the deputies would be here double-quick. As it was, I moved to the tree line and tucked into a nook in a large willow tree. The shooter might still be watching. It was probable that the shooter had fled once RoDa went into the water, but I had no way to be certain and I didn't want to be a target.

I texted Tinkie to let her know what had happened. She blasted right back with exclamations and an offer to come to my rescue, but I delayed that. She and Cece were more valuable sitting on Bilbo's house.

I urged them to keep a sharp eye to see if Bilbo arrived with a gun—or had one in his vehicle. I suspected him to be the shooter. When RoDa had given the man on the telephone guff, he'd been shot. The two things had to be connected.

It was also interesting that RoDa had admitted that all the information on the Muscogee woman—the whole dreaded Brandon family secret—was a plant. One that I'd been led to and then led around by the nose with. Which made me wonder if the whole thing was a lie. And why would RoDa participate in setting me up to sniff after a lie since he claimed to be Marlon's friend?

I could hear Aunt Loulane saying "'Oh what a tangled web we weave when first we practice to deceive.'" Deadly true. RoDa had almost lost his life, twice. So if he was working for Bilbo during the first instance, who had shot him at the lodge? And if he had riled Bilbo in the second incident, had Bilbo been the shooter? There were just too many questions.

RoDa was going to tell me the truth, if he lived. I had to get back to him now to do what I could. His gunshot wound wasn't fatal, but it was possible he could bleed out. I picked up my things and hurried downriver as fast as I could go. When I came to the place where I'd left RoDa, I stopped. He was gone. Completely vanished—except for a second set of drag marks that led to the water.

There was no sign of the actor, only a small puddle of blood in the sand. I had a terrible feeling. Had the shooter come back and tossed him into the river for the shark to finish off? Dread made my heart thud. A wounded man just couldn't vanish from the bank of a river in a wilderness area.

I searched everywhere, carefully, looking for clues. If RoDa was still bleeding, I couldn't find any spatters in the sand. And no footprints leading away from the area where I'd left him. Someone had taken a leafy branch and swept the area clean. When I got up into the trees, there were too many leaves and limbs for footprints to show. I did find several snapped limbs, which indicated someone had gone through that way.

I pulled out my phone and texted Coleman. "Are there any tracking dogs available in Washington County?" The state penitentiary kept bloodhounds, which local sheriffs often borrowed. But it took time.

"I'll call the prison and ask," Coleman said. "Good suggestion."

"I wish Sweetie Pie was here."

"I'll ask Harold to bring her and Chablis," Coleman texted back. "It may take him awhile to get clear of the bank,
but I'm sure he'll bring them."

That was the best outcome I could hope for. If anyone
could track RoDa and the person who'd moved or taken
his body—or dumped him—it would be my lovely hound.

38

Coleman was the first to appear on the spit of sand where I waited. I'd watched the river, but there was no sign of RoDa or the shark. I fought against the possibility that he might be lunch for a predator, already in the digestive system of the big fish. It seemed RoDa had betrayed me, but he didn't deserve to be shark bait. At least not yet.

Coleman saw me and rushed toward me. His first action was to pull me into his arms. "Thank goodness you're okay. Where's RoDa?"

His gaze swept the bank and then the river that rushed past the bend.

"I haven't found him yet."

"He was shot in the shoulder and his leg?"

"Yes, he was shot, but once I took a good look, there

didn't appear to be any bone damage. Still, the pain must be excruciating. And the leg wound—getting in that river isn't going to help him heal at all."

"Have you searched in the woods?" His gaze followed the drag marks to the river.

"I did. There's no sign of him along the perimeter. Someone swept away the tracks in the damp sand with a brush broom. It would seem he's been taken into the woods. What about Sweetie Pie?"

"Harold said he would bring her as soon as he could. Text him where you are. Do you think RoDa could walk?" Coleman asked.

"He was out cold. I don't know if he could move once he came to. He would definitely need help."

Coleman pulled out his phone and called Sheriff Nelson. "Be sure your deputies are heavily armed," he said. "Robert Davis has disappeared. No sign of him. The shooter or someone had to have taken him. He's vanished. He may be in the river, but he didn't crawl there on his own. We need some men to fan out and search the woods. If he's on his own, he couldn't have gone far. If he isn't in the river, we need to find him and the person who tried to kill him."

"Coleman, the shark almost got me and RoDa when I went in to save him. It was really close. Has Mary Dayle had any success figuring out how to trap her? You can't let her be killed. She's just doing what sharks do."

Even though she'd almost eaten my legs, I didn't hold it against her. She was only behaving as her nature demanded. I did want her captured and removed, though. This was no place for her or the humans who would come in contact with her.

Coleman sighed. "Sarah Booth, your ability to complicate

things never fails to amaze me. Finding RoDa and Marlon is the priority, but yes, I will do my best to see Betty gets a chance to go back to the Gulf."

"Thank you," I said, kissing him quickly. "I love you, too." I was saved by the arrival of Sheriff Nelson and a dozen men. Nelson and Coleman went to work dispersing the men through the woods to search. I walked back to the bank where RoDa had been shot and had originally gone into the river.

Deputies were searching that area, too, but I knew the direction the shot had come from. Coleman's deputy, Budgie, would be able to calculate the angle of the shot using geometry or some other higher power math skill. I did the best I could eyeballing it. I walked into the woods, careful not to disturb any potential evidence.

My cell phone buzzed, and I checked the message. "Call me," Tinkie texted.

I did. "What's up?" I asked.

"Bilbo is home," she said. "Cece and I are hiding in the wisteria arbor, and we have a great view into his office. He is tearing the place apart looking for something. We found a rifle in his truck, but we didn't check to see if it had been fired. So many men carry them in the gun rack in the back window."

"Was he after the money?" I guessed.

"Maybe." Tinkie said. "We did move it out from under the mat."

"Take the envelope it was in and put it in the yard where it flutters in front of him. That should—"

"Great idea!" She hung up. So much for warning her to be safe.

I noticed a scrap of something dangling on a huckleberry bush. I moved closer. I didn't have gloves, so I didn't touch it, but I recognized what it was. A bookmark advertising a thriller, *Crime Always Pays*. I'd seen the book on the counter at McCormick Book Inn. It was a hot seller by a beloved Mississippi crime author. Mary Dayle had been putting the bookmarks in any books she sold.

I looked closer. The bookmark was new. It was caught on a buck vine in the huckleberry bush. The hair on the back of my neck stood on end. I texted Coleman. "Where is Mary Dayle?"

"When we came off the water, she said she was going to her store. I'm about two minutes from you. I'll be right there."

Mary Dale had had plenty of time to follow RoDa and take a potshot at him. I had underestimated the bookseller and her link with Bilbo. I wouldn't make that mistake again. She was on my radar and as soon as I finished here, I'd corner her and wring out the truth.

The bookmark rustled in a gentle wind. It was hanging by a thread of the tassel. Any moment it could be gone, blown into the river. I used my car keys to pinch it without touching it. Thank goodness Coleman had arrived. "Coleman?"

"Yes."

"I need an evidence bag." I couldn't hide it from him. Nor did I want to.

He held a bag open, and I deposited the bookmark. Fingerprints might tell an interesting story, although the report from the Jackson lab on the bindings I'd found at the hunting lodge had been inconclusive.

He keyed his radio. "Sheriff Nelson, I need you to pick up Mary Dayle McCormick right now. Can you send some men to the bookstore?"

"Just got a report that someone tried to burn the bookstore down. The fire department was able to put out the flames with very little damage, but Mary Dayle wasn't on the premises or at home."

I listened with growing alarm. What had Mary Dayle done? "Sheriff Nelson," I grabbed Coleman's hand that held the radio, "pick up Lamar Bilbo, too, please."

"On what charges?" Nelson asked.

"Make something up. Just get him to the courthouse and hold him until we find RoDa."

"She's right," Coleman said. "If Bilbo and Mary Dayle are working together, they may kill the young man. If he was working with them and balked, as Sarah Booth overheard, they will finish him off. If they haven't already."

"We know RoDa was working with Bilbo," I told Nelson. "He left a large amount of money at Bilbo's house. Like a payoff or something."

"How do you know that?" Nelson asked.

I looked at Coleman.

"You don't want to know, Nelson. Trust me. Just believe what she's telling you. Robert could be in danger."

"I'll send some deputies out to search for him. I'll have to pull them off the search in the woods."

"We've covered the area and come up with not much."

"Is Sarah Booth okay?" Nelson asked.

"Better than she has any right to be." Coleman gave me a pointed look. "And we still have that shark to deal with. Sarah Booth is determined to save it. I'd hoped Mary Dayle could work some magic for us, but I'm not sure she's playing for our team," Coleman said.

I agreed with his assessment but kept my lips zipped.

"I'll send some men to pick up both McCormick and Bilbo. They can cool their heels at the courthouse until we get back into the office. They're not going to be happy."

"Yeah, life sucks and then you die." I couldn't hold back any longer. Like I cared if Bilbo and Mary Dayle were happy.

I could hear Nelson chuckling. "Good luck with that one, Coleman."

"I'll need it," he said and put the radio away.

In the distance I heard Nelson calling his men together. A lot of things had happened in Greenville, yet we were no closer to finding Marlon than we'd been from the first day. I stepped away to text Tinkie and tell her to grab Cece and get away from Bilbo's house. The deputies were on the way there to arrest him. "Let's meet at Bluebeard's when I'm done here."

It was a plan that met my partner's approval.

We searched the woods high and low without any evidence that RoDa or anyone else had been there. He'd vanished as completely as Marlon had. I'd hoped that RoDa might lead me to a very much alive Marlon. Now I wasn't certain I'd find either of them alive. I was just lucky that I hadn't ended up down a shark's gullet.

I texted Harold, who was tied up at the bank, but he assured me he would meet me when he could. I drove back to Greenville and met Cece and Tinkie at the bar. They'd caught sight of Bilbo being arrested—and showing his pa-tootie. He tried to fight the deputies, but he wasn't much of a boxer. No one was injured and none of us were surprised.

I didn't want to scare them, but I told them about the shark and how close it had come to getting RoDa and me. Cece and Tinkie agreed with Sheriff Nelson. It was time to eliminate the risk. Jules was already dead. We had no evidence the shark had killed Jules, only bitten his foot off.

But something had to be done. Betty was an animal acting only in a natural way, but if the sheriff didn't take action, area residents would. The shark could not escape its fate.

I told the girls about the bookmark I'd found in the woods, and we decided to pay a visit to the bookstore even though Mary Dayle was allegedly being held for questioning at the courthouse.

We were in Cece's car—she'd insisted on driving us—and I was glad to have a moment in the back seat to think about what, if anything, useful I'd discovered today. We were passing under the tree-shaded road to the bookstore when up ahead a shiny black sportscar tore out of the bookstore parking lot. Tinkie braked hard to avoid hitting it. Since I wasn't driving, I got a good look at the driver. Mary Dayle. She was on the run.

A sheriff's car was right on her heels. Tinkie avoided that vehicle, too. Then we fell in behind them.

"She's going to the river," I said. "It's the shark. She's heard they're going to kill it."

"What does she think she's going to do to change that?" Cece asked.

The worst possible answer came to me. As soon as Tinkie stopped the car near the public dock, I jumped out and ran toward the river. I saw Mary Dayle at the dock's end. She was tightening the straps of a scuba tank. I yelled her name, and she grinned, gave a thumbs-up, pulled her diving mask over her face, and stepped off the pier. Only a few bubbles marked the area where she'd disappeared.

Not fifty yards away, the dorsal fin of the shark split the water.

39

I texted Coleman, who called me back. "I'm on the way with Nelson and two other divers. Where did she go in?"

I told him everything I'd seen. "What do you think she's trying to do?"

"Save the shark." Coleman sounded angry. "We've tried everything. Somehow she thinks she can do this without our help. Without anyone. Gotta go. We're on scene now."

A patrol car arrived, and Coleman got out. He had scuba tanks and a mask, too.

"No!" I ran to him. "You can't go in there. It was her choice."

Coleman looked at two other divers. They handed him a spear gun. "I have to, Sarah Booth. She doesn't stand a chance without a weapon." He handed me his phone.

"I should have let them kill the shark earlier. Then we wouldn't be in this predicament."

"Everyone wanted to save Betty. Mary Dayle more than anyone. You can't blame yourself because she wouldn't wait for help or wouldn't work with you."

He sighed and I knew he heard my words but hadn't yet accepted the truth in them. Coleman was a fixer, and he held himself to high standards. "I have to go." He kissed me and then slipped into his scuba gear just in time for a deputy to arrive at the dock with a boat. A moment later, the divers were headed out on the river. With the boat they might be able to get ahead of Mary Dayle before she found the shark. Luckily, I had work to do myself or the waiting would drive me insane.

Even though Sheriff Nelson and his men had searched the woods by the river, my gut told me to go back there again. The bookmark indicated Mary Dayle—or one of her customers—had been in the area recently. Why? It was possible we'd missed something in the first search. I held on to that as I rounded up Tinkie and Cece.

"I have to get back to the newspaper," Cece said.

"And you should check in with Maylin," I told Tinkie. "I'll wait here for Coleman."

Tinkie and Cece exchanged looks. "You're going to wait?"

My reputation for impatience was well known by my friends. "Yes, I will wait. I don't know how to scuba dive."

"Thank god for small blessings," Cece said. "You promise you'll stay out of the water?"

"Yes." I had no intention of diving into the river with a shark and three men with spear guns. I'd felt the snap of those huge jaws on my body once today—and even though it was only my imagination, it was enough. There was another issue. In the murky water, mistakes could be made. I didn't want to be a pin cushion for a spear. I hoped they could save the shark, I really did, but that was out of my hands. I was no closer to finding Marlon or even the more recently missing RoDa. I didn't even know if RoDa was still alive. Two gunshots. Someone really wanted him dead. He should have been straight with me when I had a chance of protecting him.

Tinkie dropped me off at my car while they both headed back to Zinnia. I drove down to the movie set, looking for Ana, but she was nowhere to be found. The cast and crew were setting up for new scenes, and I talked with a young woman who said she was a script consultant.

After one too many questions, she backed away from me. "I'm sorry, I have to go. I need to change out some pages and get the new script to the actors."

"New script? Someone is changing the story?"

She looked startled. "Yes. Ana gave me these new pages to distribute right now." She edged away as if I might grab her and keep her from doing her job.

"That's wonderful!" I enthused. "May I have a copy, too? Ana gave me the entire script. I'm working for the insurance company, and it would be good for me to be up to speed."

She looked doubtful, so I reached and took a packet of pages from her hand. "Thank you so much. I'll tell Ana how helpful you've been."

She turned abruptly and left. She had enough good sense to know she probably shouldn't have shared the script. I hated to do that to her, but I had the best of reasons. Was Marlon alive and changing the script? Had Ana been playing me all along? Someone would pay if that were the case.

I glanced over the pages. The shots were basic exterior setting shots with some interaction of local actors. Nothing of great significance that I could see. The issue was who had authorized the changes. I needed to talk to Ana. To be thorough, I went to her trailer and knocked. There was a commotion in the trailer, but no one came to the door. I knocked again, louder. "Ana! It's Sarah Booth."

Again it sounded as if furniture were being moved, but no one came to the door. I tried the knob—the trailer wasn't locked. I eased the door open slowly. The drapes were pulled over the windows, and the inky interior made it too dark to see anything. "Ana!" I was a little concerned someone might have harmed her. "Ana, are you okay?"

A body came hurtling out of the darkness and plowed into me so hard I flew backward into a bookcase. My head struck a shelf and I saw stars. My assailant ran out of the trailer. By the time I caught my breath and got my feet under me, there was no sign of the human bulldozer. All I could say was that it had been a sturdy male. I examined the rest of the trailer to be sure Ana wasn't hurt or restrained. There wasn't a sign of her.

I walked out of the trailer and sat on the steps to let my head clear and wait for Ana and Harold. The minutes ticked by and there was no sign of the producer or Harold and my hound dog. The film crew milled about, looking constantly for a sign they could begin their work. I had a bad feeling. After twenty minutes, I felt fine and went to the car. I was going to search the riverbank again. And the hunting lodge. This was like a game of Whac-A-Mole. Only today, I was going to be the prizewinner.

I considered filing an assault report with the sheriff's office, but I decided it could wait. I had an itch to get into the woods. Instead, I texted Harold my location and said I would wait for my dog.

"Turn around and look behind you," he texted back.

To my everlasting gratitude, Harold had parked his pick-up behind me, and Sweetie Pie was in the front seat. "I didn't stop for Chablis," he said as he came to my vehicle. "I didn't want to take the time. Sweetie Pie can handle it."

"Thank you, Harold. Really, you're the best." I gave him a quick hug and opened the door so Sweetie Pie could jump into my car.

"Nice ride," Harold said. "Coleman chose wisely."

"He sure did."

"I'd offer to go with you, but I have a meeting with the bank board, and I have to be there."

I took note of the worry on Harold's face. "Everything okay?"

"Yes. For right now. The economy is just wacky and it's hard to keep our investment plans ahead of it."

Harold took his role seriously, and I admired that. "I'm fine. Coleman is in town if I need help. I swear I'll call him. And the sheriff here is also helpful. No worries."

"Promise you won't risk yourself?" Harold asked.

"I promise." I had no intention of risking my life or that of my dog. "I owe you, Harold. I'll make it up to you."

"You always show up to help Roscoe when he gets in trouble."

Harold's little Muttley was constantly getting into mischief. He tore open trash bags, stole lingerie or shoes, peed on people's feet, and had a predilection for predicting the stock market. Maybe Harold should consult him. I kept that piece of advice to myself.

Harold headed home and Sweetie Pie and I took off for destination hunting lodge. I'd check there first to give the deputies time to clear out of the woods near the river where

RoDa had disappeared. Besides, my gut was prompting me to see what Sweetie Pie would find around that cabin this time.

I was glad we'd avoided rain as I turned off the paved road onto dirt. In the Delta, dirt roads were generally passable, except if it rained and the soil was more gumbo than sand. Then even powerful trucks could get stuck. Today, all was good. The threatened storms that were always a part of April had held off this year. A mass of clouds often hovered on the horizon, but so far, none had moved across the land. It was almost as if the storms were waiting for Marlon to return so he could film his scenes. A nice fanciful thought, but not productive.

Sweetie Pie was whining at the window by the time I arrived. Instead of going down the road I normally followed, I went the other way—the route the senator, Bilbo, and RoDa had used. It was a slightly better road. I watched for tire tracks. I didn't want to stumble on the senator if he was using the lodge. There was no evidence anyone had taken this path before me.

The day was sunny and cool, perfect for an exploration of the woods. No bloodsucking insects were out yet, and that was a good thing. I parked a little distance from the cabin and Sweetie Pie and I set out on foot. I wanted to give her a chance to smell what was around. She'd helped me look for Marlon, to no avail. Now her delicate sniffer might pick up RoDa, the senator, Bilbo, or whoever else might be in the woods. I could only hope Sweetie Pie would give me enough warning that I would be prepared.

We followed along a creek, more of a branch, really, until Sweetie gave a bay of joy and struck out through the woods. She had caught the scent of something. Human or animal, I couldn't say. I removed the gun from my purse and made sure it was loaded and ready. Just in case.

Sweetie called to me from the other side of a rise. I wished I spoke dog. She was telling me something, but I couldn't be sure what. I trudged up the small hill and stopped, using the binoculars to scan the area. I caught sight of my dog on top of the rise, trailing something. Nose to the ground, she coursed back and forth, finally stopping to bay loudly. When I called her name, she looked at me and took off.

She was after something. It was my job to follow.

Running through the scrub trees and tangle of under-growth wasn't easy, but Sweetie Pie was counting on me. She called back to me, knowing I was following. I started to call out but thought better of it. If she was on some-one's trail, I didn't want to alert them that I was also in the woods. I hoped to take them by surprise.

I topped the rise and descended the gentle incline, fol-lowing my dog. She wasn't in sight, but I heard her. She'd run something to ground. I could tell by the excitement in her voice. I put on a burst of speed and slid down the little hill and set out running again. When I entered a thicket of buck vine and briars, I slowed. Someone had been this way. I could see where the plants and dead leaves had been disturbed.

I tripped on a tree root and took a tumble. The ground was soft and cushioned with dead leaves. I wasn't injured, but I had the wind knocked out of me. While I caught my breath, I heard what sounded like moaning. I slowly got to my feet and carefully inched closer to the sound. Someone was moving about in the woods. A man stood motionless some fifty feet ahead of me. To my amazement, he dropped to the ground as if he were exhausted. I crept closer.

40

The tangle of dense foliage gave way to a small clearing. I couldn't believe what I saw. Marlon was sitting on the ground. He looked like hell. He was bruised from a beating, and he looked as if he'd been starved. He sat with his arm around my hound, and he talked to her softly.

"If Grandpa is the one who set you after me, this is where I'll die. But he won't take me alive again."

Sweetie Pie licked his face.

"Dogs don't understand duplicity or cruelty," he said, stroking her ears. "Remember that."

"Marlon?" I spoke softly. Even so, I startled him. He whipped around, bunching his legs under him as if he meant to sprint off again.

"It's me, Sarah Booth. Are you okay?"

"No." He didn't sugarcoat it. "I'm starving and dehydrated. That bastard kept me in the old cistern at Muscogee. I escaped the other day and caught a ride with a fisherman here. Grandfather didn't feel food or water were really crucial."

"I've been hunting everywhere for you. All of us have."

"What do you want?" He was rightfully suspicious. If his own grandfather had betrayed him in this fashion, he had every right to be wary.

"We've all been worried sick. Ana has kept the film going, but just barely. Lamar Bilbo has worked to shut it down, but Ana fought back. We helped as much as we could, but you're desperately needed on set. Everyone is waiting on you. People are beginning to lose hope."

"And what role did the senator play in trying to close the film?"

"I don't know. As far as I know, he was helping you."

Marlon's laugh was bitter. "Helping me into bankruptcy, if not worse."

"What's going on between you two?"

"He found out what I was up to."

"And that is what?" My voice held a little snap in it. I was tired and feeling more than a little put upon. Marlon had been missing for days, and half the county had been searching for him one way or the other. I didn't even want to think about the rescue teams that had scoured the river and lake, the scuba divers, the members of his crew who'd been sick with worry.

"Are you familiar with the Brandon history?" he asked in a flip tone that made me want to smack him.

"You're rich, entitled, and a jackass. What else do I need to know?"

To my surprise he laughed, and the stiffness in his face and manner disappeared. "I'm sorry, that did sound rather pretentious."

"Yes, it did. What should I know about your family?"

"My parents were good people. Maybe the only two good people in the entire family. My grandfather is a snake, and his father was a thief and murderer. I meant to expose that in my film."

"So this isn't about the poor people stranded on the levee?"

"No, I was never interested in telling that story. It's been told before. I used the terrible behavior of some people during the flood as a ruse to torment my grandfather. The Brandons weren't exactly the rescuers as they pretended to be. The story I want to tell, along with the flooding, is about robbery and murder. I wanted to zero in on my great-grandfather. He was an influential man in the Mississippi Delta—a lawyer and a community leader. Well, he was a thief. All of the Brandon money comes from one ill-gotten gain. Great-grandfather Brandon brought his boat to Greenville to help flood victims, but that's not what he did. He robbed the First National Bank of Greenville, stole a pile of money, killed a security guard, and then parlayed that money into great wealth because he was able to buy up land at tax sales after the flood. Farmers lost a year of their crop and many of them were forced into bankruptcy. They sold lands they'd cleared with their hands and a mule. Losing that land broke a lot of men. But heck, Old Pawpaw never met a desperate person he couldn't fleece."

Bitter didn't begin to describe Marlon's attitude toward his family. And it made perfect sense. His grandfather, the senator, had looked down on Marlon's mother, had considered her unworthy to have the Brandon name. It was possible he'd played a role in her death, deliberate or otherwise. I could see why Marlon would be furious. But he'd hid it well enough when I first arrived on the set. He'd seemed like a well-adjusted man who was forging his own destiny. Now, I had to wonder how far gone he was, plotting revenge against his family while risking the livelihood and future of his cast and crew.

"You concocted all of this to punish your grandfather?" My voice rose with each word.

"He deserves everything I can dish out. I have reason to believe he killed my mother, and he couldn't get rid of me fast enough."

"He kept you in the cistern on the plantation?"

"Part of the time. I was in the hunting lodge initially. I was grabbed off the levee, knocked unconscious, and woke to find myself tied to a chair in the lodge. When you were hired, he knew someone would search the hunting property, so he moved me to the cistern."

Tinkie and I had searched the property, but we hadn't looked in the cistern. Who would put a relative in such a damp and dangerous place? "How did you escape?"

"James heard me calling out."

"The butler saved you?"

"And not for the first time. James has given me more love and support than anyone else. James was there for me when my folks died and I was shipped off to a military school. He would spend the holidays with me in the car, driving me around the state to see things so I wouldn't have to be alone with Grandfather in that house. I was just lucky he was outside near the cistern picking dewberries and he heard me calling out."

"When did he free you?"

"Time runs together. I really don't know. I wouldn't let James help me anymore—he had risked his livelihood for me already—and I took off. I came here looking for the senator. It's time I faced him and told him the truth of my movie. I'm going to set the record straight for all the murder and corruption that the Brandon family really stands for."

I understood his impulse, but I also knew it wasn't going to accomplish what he hoped. "You realize someone is dead. This isn't just revenge talk. Jules, part of your crew, is dead."

He nodded. "It's terrible. You know who's responsible, right?"

"I have suspicions."

"Lamar Bilbo. He paid to have that shark brought here and dumped."

That Mary Dayle! She'd been working with Bilbo all along. "Mary Dayle helped him, didn't she?"

He looked confused. "Bring the shark here? Absolutely not. She's only trying to save the shark. Once she learned about the plan to bring it here and turn it loose, she's done everything she could to stop it and then to help catch the shark."

"What? She's run all over town telling everyone the movie is going to blacken the reputation of the wealthy families of Washington County. She's part of the problem. She incited folks to speak out against the movie."

"I know. I asked her to do it. She was one of my weapons in keeping Grandfather at bay."

"Why do this?" Why would he stomp an anthill?

"Lamar and the senator were going to work against me. I asked Mary Dayle to align herself with Bilbo so she could watch him. He's such an arrogant narcissist, he really thought she was interested in him romantically. He was a goose ready for the plucking."

Marlon had a string of phrases I hadn't heard since Aunt Loulane died. And he had an air of self-righteousness that made me want to bop him on the head. "You've put all of your friends and crew through a nightmare, Marlon. Folks have been searching for you in the water and on land. Your friends have worried themselves sick. And you act like you've done nothing wrong. One of your loyal supporters has been shot twice and is now missing. Robert Davis, remember him?

"Robert's missing?"

"He's badly wounded and now he's disappeared. Was this part of your plan?"

"No. Not at all." He considered for a moment. "There's a viper in my cast or crew. Someone has been feeding intel to Grandpa. He knew everything we were going to do before we did it."

"But he didn't know about the bank robbery and murder you were planning to reveal, did he?"

"No. That was the one thing I kept from him and everyone else. I didn't tell another living soul. I'd saved filming those scenes for last."

"If you don't get back to the set, the film is done for."

"I have to find RoDa now that I know he's missing."

"He knew you were alive, too?" I was hot under the collar.

"No. He didn't. Not until I escaped. I had to trust someone because I didn't have a vehicle or anything. Grandfather was foolish to leave me a phone. Once I got it charged at the lodge and found myself a place to hide in the woods, I called Robert. I wasn't certain I could trust him, but I had no one else."

"He left a key for me to find to a safety deposit box at the bank."

"Yes. I was hoping you'd confront Grandpa about it and get him all worked up about that family history. He's so sensitive about losing his privilege as a Brandon."

"What did the senator hope to gain by bringing a shark into the river here? I mean I know Bilbo brought it, but the senator had to have been aware."

"Oh, he knew. He wanted to start a panic. He was hoping the shark would chase the actors and crew away."

"That didn't work out so well for him."

Marlon laughed. "No. It didn't." The humor left his face. "It was a tragedy about Jules. He was a great guy and he fell in love with the Mississippi River."

"What happened to the gaffer?" I still didn't know how he'd gone from the dock into the river.

"Jules was eager to work on the raft. I urged him to wait for me. I'd had dinner with a couple of local men who wanted to invest in the movie, and I was walking along the water when I saw him on the raft trying to set the mast. He was hardheaded and wouldn't wait for me."

I had the picture in my mind. "What happened?"

"I don't know for certain. I didn't hear a shot or anything, but suddenly he just toppled into the water. I ran as hard as I could, but I was too late. There wasn't any sign of him in the water. I searched. I dove in and looked around, but the water isn't clear. I didn't have diving tanks. I tried until I was exhausted. He was just gone."

"You think he was shot?"

He nodded slowly. "I do. And I believe the shooter may have thought he was killing me. I normally worked on the raft at the end of the day. It was dark and Jules was working under a light. They couldn't clearly see who was on the raft."

"You saw your employee fall into the river, and you didn't notify anyone?" I was angry.

"At first, I honestly thought Jules was playing a prank. That he saw me coming to the raft and meant to torment me. On the set, we all really like each other. We played tricks. Not mature, I know, but it happened. It wasn't until the next day that I realized he wasn't on site. He'd disappeared. The crew had been swimming all around the raft for days, and it never occurred to me that he could be in real danger. I should have been more concerned, but I honestly thought he was playing—you know, where we would search and search and he'd pop up somewhere."

"But he didn't pop up."

"No, he didn't." Marlon sounded sincerely remorseful. "I told Ana at noon the next day when he didn't show up to work. She called the sheriff and the insurance company; they hired you. To my way of thinking, I was handling it through the local authorities. And I was still suspicious Jules was having a laugh. He was a great guy who loved to pull a prank."

"If only that had been the case. So what happened to you?"

"It was the next evening. I'd had dinner with some local ladies, and I was on my way to the river when the senator called me over to his car and offered to help me. I was desperate to believe him, to think that at last he saw who and what I was. That was my mistake. Trusting my own grandfather."

"Did he threaten you?"

"No, he's smarter than that. He seduced me by pretending to be interested in what I was doing. I should have known he didn't care. I'm just pathetic enough to have wanted him to be interested in my work. He tricked me into getting into the car, and when I did, Bilbo popped up in the back seat and chloroformed me. They held me captive until James found me and let me out."

"Marlon, surely you know that a movie about a bank robbery a hundred years ago isn't going to fix the past."

He began to pace. "I do know that, but—" He turned away for a long moment before he continued. "If only he'd given me his approval, just once. Now Jules is dead and RoDa is missing." He put a hand on my shoulder. "We have to find Robert. We do. Will you help me?"

"Yes. After we talk to the sheriff. Whatever his involvement, he's suffered for it. And you might be worried about Mary Dayle. She went into the river to try to catch that shark. My fiancé and two other divers are in the water, too."

"Now that I'm free, I can help them," he said. "We have to find Mary Dayle. Let's head to the river."

"What about reporting your grandfather for kidnapping?"

"After we find Mary Dayle and RoDa. I'm afraid Bilbo may have them."

"Not at his house. We checked."

Marlon paused. "Thank you. Would you give me a ride into town?"

"How did you get out here?" I asked.

"I hitched a ride. James would have brought me, but he's clinging to his job. I understand. He freed me and helped me escape. I couldn't ask more."

"Why didn't you just go to town? You could have gone to the courthouse and been completely safe. The senator couldn't get you there."

"I honestly didn't know who to trust. I took a risk with RoDa and told him about the lodge and how the senator used it for all sorts of nefarious activities for prominent men whose help he hoped to win. I shared a lot with Robert, and if he's in trouble now because of me, then I have to fix it."

I understood Marlon's guilt, and it softened my attitude toward him, but I was still annoyed. "Why didn't you call Ana or me when you got free?"

"To be honest, I didn't know who to trust. I'd been romantically involved with Ana in the past. We mutually ended it, but sometimes, I thought maybe . . ." He sighed. "I don't know. I was so focused on what I wanted to accomplish. Someone on the set was feeding information to Bilbo and the senator. Then the whole shark thing. I just wasn't certain who was out to get the movie and me. And I also had to protect James. I should have done a lot of things differently."

Plausible—and annoying. "We can sort all this later. Let's go."

On the walk to the car, we were quiet. I had a lot of new information to plug into the puzzle, and Marlon seemed lost in his own thoughts. At the car, I checked my phone. No cell reception here. As soon as we got to town, I would call the insurance company and let them know Marlon was safe. My job was almost done.

41

At Marlon's insistence, I drove straight to the river where Mary Dayle had gone in. The sheriff's boat was offshore about two hundred feet. Marlon stood beside me, judging what to do.

"Has anyone seen Mary Dayle since she went in?"

I checked my phone. "No. They would have texted me."

"Do they have an extra scuba tank?"

"I don't know. I don't think it's a good idea for you to get involved in this. The divers have their hands full as it is."

"I could help." Marlon shielded the sun from his eyes with his hand. "Do you know anyone who can get me a tank and take me out there?"

"I'll text Coleman." I did, knowing he probably wouldn't respond. And certainly not in a way to enable Marlon to put himself in danger. To my surprise he came back with "Meet us at the dock."

"Jump in the car. We're going to the movie set. Coleman will talk to you there." When we pulled up at the set, I was surprised at the emptiness of the area. It looked as if Marlon's long absence had finally resulted in the cast and crew departing. I saw the young woman who'd given me the script pages. "Where is everyone?"

"The senator hired a bus to take them to the Memphis airport," she said. "They packed up in a real hurry to start back to Los Angeles." She squinted into my car. "Who's in the car? Is that—Marlon!" She dropped her clipboard and ran to my car. I took a moment to watch the reunion. Marlon might be a scoundrel, but this member of his crew loved him. Her relief was tangible.

Marlon got out of the car and came toward me with the script consultant at his side. "I need scuba tanks," Marlon said.

"There're some on the riverboat," the young woman said. "We had them for the storm scenes, which we never got to film. Now everyone has gone home."

"What?" Marlon looked genuinely shocked. "Clarice, you're saying the cast and crew have left?"

"They're on a bus to the Memphis airport. They've gone. Your grandfather herded them onto the bus like they were cattle. He told them if they wanted their final paycheck, they'd better step on it."

"Ana, too?" he asked.

"I don't know. I didn't see her when the others were loading. I live near Greenville, so I didn't leave. I said I would wait here for the equipment company to come pick up all the stuff we rented."

"Thank you, Clarice, but could you call them and cancel the order to pick up the equipment? We have a film to finish!"

"You bet I can," she said, giving him and then me an impromptu hug. "Let's finish this movie."

I was game for that, but I didn't know if Marlon would go along. He strode to the dock where the raft and the riverboat were tied up. In a moment he'd boarded the beautiful old paddle wheeler. Five minutes later he hopped back on the dock with scuba tanks, fins, and a mask.

He was half starved and in bad physical shape. I had to stop him from this madness. "You don't know where to look for Mary Dayle. You should wait until the sheriff comes over here. Just let the professionals do the work."

"I can't wait." Marlon strapped the tanks on. "Is there any type of weapon on the riverboat?"

Clarice shook her head. "Not that I've ever seen. It's used mainly for parties and tours, so not much need for violence."

"I can't wait for someone to locate a spear gun." Marlon walked to the edge of the dock. "I have to do this, Sarah Booth. If it doesn't work out, I still did what I knew to be right."

Yeah, that would etch nicely on his grave marker—he died righteous. "What can you do without a weapon? You aren't thinking."

"The senator told me they were trying to trap the shark. I didn't know if he was lying about any of it, but with enough of us in the water, maybe we can divert the thing and catch it."

"They've been trying that for days. Nada. The fish is smart. Do yourself and the rescuers a favor and stay out of their way."

"I can't." He looked into the river as if he saw a reflection of his fate.

From the set, I heard a female voice call out. "Marlon, what are you doing?" Ana McCants was running toward us. Behind her were Clarice and two other crew members. The two guys assessed the scene and began moving their cameras to follow the action.

"I'll be back, Ana. Thank you for holding things together."

"Where in the hell have you been?" She'd dropped back to a race walk and was steaming toward us like a ship of war. Her face told the depth of her anger at Marlon.

"He was held hostage by his grandfather," I told her, trying to mitigate her fury. "He couldn't help it."

Ana ignored me. "Marlon, come back to the shore. Now."

"I have to do this," he called to her. "Bilbo brought that shark here to kill the movie. I have to help Mary Dayle."

"Your responsibility is to help me and your investors. Don't be an idiot. Now that you're here, we're only days away from completing the movie."

"Everyone is gone." Marlon waved at the empty set.

"I'll call the cast and crew back." She checked her watch. "They won't make the airport for another two hours. We can get them back. You just get away from the water."

"No. I can't abandon Mary Dayle. Not after—"

He froze, staring at Ana. It took me a moment to realize she held a gun. And she was only ten yards away from us. "What are you doing?" I asked her.

"What's necessary. Marlon, come up here. If you jump in the water, I'll kill Sarah Booth. And anyone else I have to."

"What's going on?" I couldn't figure Ana's angle. Sure, she didn't want Marlon in the water with a shark, but shooting him—or me—was a better idea?

"Ana, what are you doing?" Marlon asked. He was obviously as confused as I was.

"Come up here now. Off the dock."

Marlon cast a glance at the raft, which was almost complete and bobbed beside the dock. Ana shifted the gun from Marlon to me. "I'll kill her."

Marlon took a step toward Ana. "You're part of this. You're working with the senator."

"I never intended for you to know." She smiled, revealing the depth of her betrayal. "Your disappearance should have shut down the movie. You would have been returned, and we would have gone back to Hollywood together. We'd find another project and your grandfather would have helped us get funding. But you couldn't listen to reason. You couldn't hear the future he offered both of us. I'm sorry, but I can't be the tagalong for your career any longer. I deserve to have this for myself and the senator has promised to open all the right doors for me."

"You shot Jules, didn't you?" Marlon asked. He was amazingly composed, standing on the dock ready to dive into the water. "Why? Why would you do that?"

"I thought it was you. I only wounded him, but he fell in the water. The blood drew the shark. It would have been the perfect ending for an action actor like yourself, Marlon. I meant to give you your due—a celebrated death while working."

I exhaled softly. She still had the gun trained on me. When I turned to look at Marlon, I saw the dorsal fin of the shark. It wasn't far from the dock. "Marlon, come back to shore, please," I said. "Let's sit down and talk about this."

"Talking time is done. Remember all those conversations when you told me about your grandfather and how he'd

betrayed you," Ana said. "And then you dumped *me*. This
is all on you, Marlon. Every bit of it. Now get up here. I'm
going to finish this off. I have an airline ticket to a nice
South American country that doesn't honor extradition.
Your grandfather thought of everything."

"Until you get there for your ticket and the cops pick you
up," Marlon said. He laughed. "This is delicious, Ana. You're
about to get the royal Brandon treatment. Scapegoating and
betrayal. Just like he did my mother and father, because they
didn't measure up to his exacting standards. You know I
suspect he killed my mother. You won't get a fair shake. After all, you're the murderer here. Grandfather hasn't killed
anyone. Your big reward is going to be a ticket to the state's
executioner."

Ana's mouth hardened into a tight line. "Shut up. You're
just trying to scare me."

"Am I?" Marlon took another step forward. "Or am I
just telling you what you know already? No honor among
thieves, Ana. Something you shouldn't forget."

"I have a deal with the senator."

Marlon laughed out loud. He was pushing her too hard.
I could see her finger on the trigger of the gun. It was tightening, almost subconsciously, as he prodded her into hotter
anger.

"Enough of all this. What's done is done. What we need
to talk about is what's going to happen next. What we *want*
to happen next." I tried to turn down the temperature.

"Shut up." Ana lifted the muzzle of the gun. I was looking straight down the barrel.

"She isn't in this, Ana. It's you and me and the senator."

"She's a meddling hussy." Ana's anger shifted to me, and
I closed my eyes, expecting the bullet any second.

"Don't do it, Ana." Marlon sounded scared for the first time. "Don't take another innocent life." He started toward her.

"No one is ever innocent." She swung the gun barrel back at him. "Just wait right there, Mr. Hero. That's what this movie was all about. You being the hero. Showing everyone that the senator had benefited from criminal actions. That was more important to you than making the best movie or taking care of your responsibilities."

"I wanted to do all of that," Marlon said. "You know I did. I thought that was what you wanted, too. Remember, this movie was going to be your ticket to bigger things."

"You never cared about my dreams."

Emotions were hitting Ana hard, and I was more concerned than ever. She was volatile. Anything could make her pull the trigger.

"I always cared, Ana."

"Then why did you end things with me?"

"You needed to know me. The whole me. I owed it to you to understand how screwed up I am about relationships. My grandfather probably killed my mother and did nothing to help my father recover from her loss. I have trouble trusting anyone. I wanted you to understand that. Filming the movie here was your chance to see all of this. To see the depths of depravity in my family. If you still wanted to be close to me, I intended on proposing once the movie was concluded and you'd had a chance to make up your mind."

I didn't know if he was feeding her a line of bull crap, but it was having the desired effect. The barrel of the gun tilted lower.

"You should have told me this," she said.

"I didn't want to trap or obligate you. That's the currency

the senator deals in. Obligations, favors returned for favors given. No one has intrinsic value except for what they can do for him. I didn't want you to experience any of that with me. I wanted you to see it all and make the best decision for you."

"You really should have told me." The gun came up abruptly and her finger was on the trigger. I watched it in slo-mo, like a movie. There was nothing I could do. I tried to leap toward her, but my body didn't respond quickly enough.

A shot rang out and Ana jerked forward. The gun discharged, but into the ground. She stumbled forward, a disbelieving look on her face while red blossomed on her right shoulder. I looked beyond her and saw a very bedraggled RoDa stepping out from behind a pile of pallets. He stumbled and almost fell. I reversed direction and went toward him while Marlon rushed to Ana's side. He kicked the gun far from her reach and knelt beside her, applying pressure to the wound on her shoulder.

"Call an ambulance," he said to Clarice, who'd been frozen in place for the whole thing.

"Can you watch over her?" Marlon asked me.

"Why?"

"I want to help with Mary Dayle. I have to. Please."

Ana wasn't going to shoot anyone else. "Go on," I said. "Just go. If you get eaten by the shark it will be a relief to me."

He laughed. "Not the most sporting of comments, but I understand." And then he was hurrying to the end of the dock. Before I could say anything else, he was in the water. I searched for the shark fin, but I didn't see it. Maybe the sound of the shots had driven the predator back into deeper water.

I knelt beside Ana and applied pressure to her wound as

RoDa, with Clarice's help, slowly made his way to me. "I hope she lives," he said.

"You saved my life," I told him. "Thank you."

"Marlon's okay." He grinned. "I really thought they'd find him and kill him. I'm glad he's good."

"If the shark doesn't get him."

"If he outfoxed the senator and Ana, that shark doesn't stand a chance."

RoDa had a point. The sound of the ambulance gave me a sense of hopefulness. It was a little premature, but maybe not. When the EMTs rushed up, I stood and backed away as they checked over Ana and loaded her for transport. "RoDa, you go with them."

He was about to topple over. "I'd like to disagree, but I think I should go."

I put a hand on his arm. "Thank you. I'll be by the hospital later. Just let them patch you up and make sure those wounds don't get infected."

"Will do."

I backed away from the group and eased toward my car. I was glad I hadn't brought Sweetie Pie to the set with me, but she was probably sick of being stuck in the car. I'd rectify that immediately. But first I stopped beside Clarice. "Call the rental company. Tell them not to come. Call the cast and crew and get them back here. This movie is going to be finished."

"I'm on it." Clarice looked as happy as I felt.

42

While I was driving to the sheriff's office, I called Tinkie and filled her in. She was elated and promised to relay the information to Cece.

"Sarah Booth, if they start filming again, don't forget photos for Cece. She's counting on you."

"And I won't let her down. Thanks for the reminder."

Before I parked at the courthouse, I went by a fast-food joint and got Sweetie Pie some chicken tenders and me a sweet tea. I didn't need the sugar, but I was parched and exhausted. A little pick-me-up was in order.

By the time I parked at the courthouse, Sweetie and I were both feeling better. Sheriff Nelson didn't object to Sweetie in his office, so we walked in together. I was in luck. The dispatcher told me Nelson and the divers were on their way to land.

"Did they catch the shark?" I asked.

The dispatcher shrugged, but her expression was elated. I sank into a chair. I was ready for more good news.

When Nelson arrived, Coleman was right behind him. Mary Dayle and Marlon brought up the rear. All were safe. I rushed to Coleman and hugged him as tightly as I could.

Nelson called his deputies and staff together, motioning me to join the group. When I did, he picked up Mary Dayle's arm and held it up. "Champion Shark Catcher! I hereby bestow the title." He turned to the rest of us. "The shark is in the cage and the charter is returning her to the Gulf. The journey is already underway. Betty, as Mary Dayle has named her, will have plenty of time to find a secure place to have her babies. This was the best ending anyone could hope for."

We applauded as Mary Dayle celebrated by accepting a fresh cup of coffee from the dispatcher. It was almost rude to spoil the moment with the truth about Ana McCants, RoDa, and Jules, but I did, ending with the return of Marlon Brandon—obvious to all since he was sitting in front of them—and the resuming of filming of the movie.

"Where's your partner?" Nelson asked as everyone bombarded me with questions.

"Right here." I called Tinkie and put her on speaker. She was thrilled—and reminded me, "Go to the set and get some photos, Sarah Booth. Remember, you owe Cece."

"Will do," I assured her. "I'm sure Marlon and RoDa will give her exclusive interviews." I looked at Marlon. "Right?"

"You bet," he said.

"I think you'll want to pick up the senator and Lamar Bilbo," I told Nelson. "I have all the evidence you need to lock them up for a long time. And by the way, RoDa really is at the hospital this time, along with Ana McCants, who will soon be inhabiting a jail cell."

After I'd answered more questions, I pulled Sheriff Nelson aside. "Just one quick question. Will you charge RoDa with shooting Ana? He saved my life. And Marlon's, too. She was going to kill us."

"It sounds like he was working within the law. I suspect he'll be fine."

"Thanks. He's a good guy who was only trying to help his friend. Shot twice. I think that's enough punishment."

Nelson gave me a side glance, then laughed. "Sheriff Peters told me you were pushy."

I smiled. "Yep. And he loves me anyway."

It was a great ending to a long, anxiety-fraught day.

As if nature were cooperating with Marlon, the next three days were filled with wind and rain. Word from Greenville was that the movie was finishing, great guns. Marlon had all of nature's drama working to help him create stunning visuals.

Marlon wrapped the film to cheers from a crowd of locals who gathered to see the final scene shot. That very evening, the cast and crew were at Tinkie's house celebrating.

Tinkie had outdone herself with the decorations for the movie party. Hilltop was lovely. The food, catered from Millie's Café, was incredible, and Oscar was mixing the drinks strong. Coleman and I sipped our Jack and water and held hands as we talked with different groups of the cast and crew. The movie had come in slightly under budget.

Despite her fury at Marlon, Ana had captured some excellent scenes while waiting for Marlon to reappear. It was my personal belief that she'd planned on finishing the movie herself and taking the credit if the senator killed Marlon. RoDa confirmed my beliefs when he told me she'd asked him to double as Marlon in the final swashbuckling rescue segments. Ana had convinced RoDa that she was acting in Marlon's best interest—to finish the film he'd staked everything on.

"Yes, Ana had it plotted out so that she'd finish the film and get the credit," RoDa said. "She made me believe it was all for Marlon. I never suspected her." RoDa had one arm in a sling and a limp that would heal. He was in fine spirits.

Marlon had joined us, and he put his arm around my shoulders. "You didn't stop looking, even when you believed I was dead and had been eaten by a shark."

"You were too handsome to write off as dead," Tinkie said as she came up. "Sarah Booth has exquisite taste in the men she decides to keep alive."

"Very funny." But I was laughing. "Marlon, you promised to premier the movie in Greenville."

"Yes, and I will. Next year, for sure." He looked around the room. "Everyone here played such an important role in making this happen. The film will open in Greenville, you have my word. And you're all invited."

I had a question for Marlon when all the toasts had been completed. I touched his shoulder and moved him to a corner of the foyer where we could talk privately. "Were you really going to expose your ancestors as bank robbers and murderers?"

He thought for a few seconds. "Yes, I was. I felt I had to."

"Why would you do that?"

"The truth is necessary to really move forward. I love Mississippi. We must learn how to do better."

It was a noble sentiment, but it had almost cost him his life. And Jules Valiant was dead because of it. RoDa had been shot—twice. Truth came at a high price.

"What's going to happen to Ana?" I asked him.

"She shot and killed Jules. That's murder. She'll be staying in Mississippi a lot longer than she intended. It's so very strange, Sarah Booth. I thought I loved her. I did want her to see the real Brandon family and then make her choice. But now, after all of this betrayal, I feel more relief than heartbreak."

Ana had confessed to being in the woods and shooting RoDa, too. She'd also been the person who flattened the tires on my car. She had numerous charges pending. Greed and ambition had ruined her life.

"And the senator?"

Marlon frowned. "He's in this up to his eyebrows, but I'm sure he's arranged everything where a scapegoat will take the blame. Likely Lamar Bilbo."

"I don't think Sheriff Nelson will allow him to get away with that."

"I hope you're right."

"I know I am, Marlon. Trust me."

He grinned wide. "Now that's an invitation to danger."

Award talk buzzed around Hilltop as platters of food and trays full of drinks were offered to guests. Millie had finally hired a catering crew so she could keep an eye on things and enjoy. Cece was snapping photos of the celebration. I noticed a corner in the front parlor where Jane Bernardo, the movie's insurance executive, was talking with Jennifer Williamson, Jules Valiant's girlfriend. Jules's family was there, and they had dropped their threats of a lawsuit when they understood Jules had been murdered and hadn't died from carelessness on the set.

James the butler and Bianca the waitress were having a fine old time with Orie Ruth and Nancy Aldren. Even Larry, the little boy who'd disappeared, was there with his mother. He had cake icing smeared all over him and a wide grin on his face, as did RoDa. The two were playing with Tonka trucks on the foyer tile.

All the people who'd helped or tried to help the movie were there, including the entire Washington County sheriff's department and search and rescue. The lawmen were out on the patio, enjoying the crisp spring evening, drinking bourbon and sharing war stories.

Maylin was dressed in the christening gown I'd given her—she'd been stellar in her movie role. Cece had also taken part in the movie as Maylin's mother. Along with a walk-on part, Cece had gotten terrific photos and interviews for the paper.

Everyone was so excited and happy that the film had wrapped after so many crazy hurdles. And the film was good. Tinkie and I had seen the daily rushes. It was going to be perfect.

Saturday, Marlon and his crew, along with Delilah, the Mississippi Film Commission member, were hopping on the raft and heading downriver to make the documentary. When they launched the raft, they would not return to Greenville. They would dock at Vicksburg and rent a car to get to New Orleans. He had a flight booked to Los Angeles.

Life in Greenville and all down the river would soon settle back into a normal rhythm.

Looking at the smiling faces and listening to the laughter and chatter, I caught sight of Mary Dayle. The shark had been saved. As far as I knew, it was swimming free. I wasn't going to ask. I didn't want to know otherwise, and Mary Dayle looked so happy I took it as an omen.

I took a tray of plates and glasses to the kitchen for the catering crew to wash in case they needed more. When I peeked out the kitchen window, I saw Poe the raven sitting on the branch of a tree. He was staring right at me. He hopped to another limb, as if inviting me outside for a visit. I obliged, ready for some peace and quiet for a moment or two. My body was still in shock from the close encounter with the shark and running around in the woods. While my heart would recover, I wasn't sure my gluteus maximus would ever work properly again.

As I inched toward the door, Coleman slipped up behind me. I could see Harold in the corner, grinning. "You look like you've been rode hard and put away wet," Coleman said about my peculiar walk.

"Yep. I'm in need of a good massage."

"That could be arranged," he whispered. "Where are you going?"

"Out to take some crackers to Poe. He loves those Triscuit things." He did. I'd taught him to perform tricks for a cracker.

"Hurry back inside. I think Marlon is planning a toast for you and Tinkie and all of your helper friends."

"Ten minutes." I kissed him and slipped out the side door. Poe had chosen a perch away from the noise of the party, and I stepped into the shade of a big poplar tree, glad for a chance to just inhale and relax. Poe flew onto my shoulder, then took off for a tree farther in the woods. Because I was eager to hear the birds and rustling of wild creatures, I followed him.

"Nevermore!" he called to me, then squawked like crazy. I looked back to see Sweetie Pie, Pluto, and Chablis following me. They loved a good party, but they loved a visit in the woods more.

It was a perfect evening—still light enough for me to see, but the lavender edges of dusk were coming down hard. I couldn't linger. Poe, though, had other ideas. He flew deeper into the woods, and out of curiosity I went along with him.

When we came to a series of natural springs that had formed a pool of crystal clear water, I had to laugh. It was such an idyllic setting—fairies, wood nymphs, Pan, all types of wondrous creatures could be there. But I needed to get back to the party.

I whistled up the dogs, but Poe flew in a circle about my head. "Nevermore," he said in his croaky voice.

"Right. We can 'nevermore' tomorrow. Now it's time to help Tinkie."

Poe flew to the edge of the pool, his reflection so striking against the clear water that I bent closer to look at it. A giant shark rose out of the pool and snapped, missing my head by inches.

I fell backward onto the ground, scooting on my butt, scrabbling like a fool. I knew it was impossible. That pool wasn't big enough for a koi, much less a shark. But it hovered in an upright position. "I can't sleep worth a damn," it said. "You know if I sleep, I'll die."

"Jitty! Who the hell are you supposed to be now?" I was really outdone.

"I am Lamia. In ancient Greek mythology, I stole Poseidon's affection from his wife. She was so furious, she killed all of my children."

"Homewrecking is a dangerous activity." I was too annoyed with her scaring me to be compassionate about her loss. She was one big ugly shark.

"It's okay, Big Daddy Poseidon turned me into a shark so I could eat other people's children! You know, soften the blow."

"That is awful." The Greeks and Romans had been a bloodthirsty lot with their gods and goddesses. Jitty was far too pleased with herself.

"The downside is I haven't had a good night's sleep since that happened. But Poseidon gave me eyes that I can close while I swim. It's better than nothing, but it isn't a good rest. I think if I could really sleep, I would stop eating children."

She was yanking my chain, and I wasn't going to show it. Poe settled on a branch near her sharky head and gave a triumphant caw. When Jitty the shark looked up at him, I said, "Don't you dare. Poe is my pet."

The rustle of branches alerted me to the fact that someone was coming. I glared at Jitty, who melted back into the clear pool. The pool vanished. There was no evidence she'd ever been there.

Poe flew to my shoulder. He weighed a ton, but I was glad to have him so I could get out of the woods and back to the party.

Tinkie stepped into the clearing. "What are you doing here?"

"Poe." I pointed to the bird.

"Who were you talking to?" she asked.

"Poe." I pointed to the bird again.

"I don't believe that for a second, but I'll let it pass. Hurry up, Marlon wants to make a toast." Even as she was herding me out of the woods, she was looking around to see if anyone else was there.

Side by side we headed back to the lights of Hilltop. The night was coming down fast, the winking starlight growing more powerful. I was so lucky to be with all the critters and the best partner anyone could ask for. I would deal with Jitty at another time.

We stepped in the door and the party surged around us as Marlon made his toast to the Delaney Detective Agency—and to the fact that the senator, Bilbo, and Ana were all in jail.

It was the perfect conclusion to the case.

Acknowledgments

Many thanks to my agent, Marian Young, and to the entire team at St. Martin's Press. Hannah O'Grady is a fabulous editor to work with, as is Kim Davis. The art department, publicity, all are terrific.

I also want to thank my niece, Jennifer Welch, who keeps me straight on timelines while I'm writing. Math has never been one of my talents.

Thanks are also due to booksellers, librarians, and readers who talk up my books and keep the series going. It's been so much fun working with all of you.

About the Author

Hope Harrington Oakes

Carolyn Haines is the author of the Sarah Booth Delaney Mysteries. She is the recipient of both the Harper Lee Distinguished Writer Award and the Richard Wright Award for Literary Excellence. Born and raised in Mississippi, she now lives in Semmes, Alabama, on a farm with more dogs, cats, and horses than she can possibly keep track of.